Innocent

Book 3 of
the Maiden Series

By

Aishling Morgan

Try the rest of the Maiden Series:

Maiden: Book One
Captive: Book Two
Princess: Book Four

Published by Xcite Books – 2013
ISBN 9781909840317

Chapter One

'He has her now, surely.'

Cianna's hand tightened on her necklace at the words, her excitement rising steeply. In front of her, one of the two men who had been fighting for some half-an-hour had the other on the ground, pinning him face down. Beyond them, a red haired girl stood on a dais, clutching nervously at her dress.

The man beneath made one last effort to rise, then slumped down, defeated. Cianna clapped as the victor rose, unsteadily, and raised his hands to the crowd. The girl on the dais hung her head, watching from beneath half lowered eyelids as the victor walked towards her. He was massively built, powerful, with a great mane of copper red hair and huge hands. As he approached, the girl braced herself, then kicked out at him, only to have her leg caught one handed. The man pulled, setting her down on her bottom with a thump and drawing laughter from the audience. Catching the girl up from the dais, he slung her across his shoulder, to carry her kicking to where the defeated man lay.

Cianna found herself smiling as the girl was thrown down across the man on the ground and her skirts tossed up to reveal a full white bottom. Putting his hand to his codpiece, the victor pulled it aside, exposing heavy genitals in a nest of coarse red hair. He began to masturbate, tugging at his cock with his eyes fixed on the naked bottom in front of him. After a while he stopped, to reach down and tear the girl's bodice wide, spilling out heavy pink breasts, which he fondled as he sank to his knees, his cock now erect in his hand. The girl was mounted, from the rear, her bottom humped up over the defeated man's hip.

The girl began to pant as she was fucked, her buttocks bouncing to the man's thrusts, her big breasts swinging and slapping beneath her chest. With her eyes glued to the sight, Cianna pressed her skirts to her sex, suddenly uncomfortable, then glanced back to see if her action had been noticed. It had not, the whole audience as rapt as she. There was her mistress, Sulitea, large eyes moist as she twisted a pale curl around a finger. There was the Princess Talithea, struggling to appear poised but with both shock and excitement showing in her face. There was Prince Kavisterion himself, openly pleased. There was the Reeveling Aeisla, taller than any other woman there, making no effort to conceal her delight in the girl's ravishment. Others stretched away on both sides, people unknown to Cianna.

The man was getting urgent, his face red, his fingers dug deep into the soft flesh of the girl's hips, his front slamming again and again against the plump meat of her bottom. Her control had gone, squealing and moaning as she was fucked, with her fat breasts in her hands and her bottom pushed high to meet his thrusts. Again Cianna sneaked a hand to her crotch, wondering if she dared rub herself through her skirt, to bring herself to the orgasm she so badly needed. It would have taken moments, and she was going to do it, only for the man to grunt, whip his penis from the girl's sex and spray sperm across her buttocks and back. Immediately clapping rose on all sides, along with the thumping of tankards on the wooden benching and calls of congratulation.

'A fine ravishment!' the Prince declared. 'Ho, Rath, here's another five thalar piece for the purse, and Groy, a single. Well fought!'

The victor caught the coin as it was thrown to him, the defeated man pulling himself painfully to his elbow to take his own. The girl had risen, and was straightening her skirts, red faced with embarrassment but smiling, only for the look to turn to annoyance as she discovered that her bodice was ruined, the material torn clean across. The Prince laughed, tossing out another coin.

'And another for a new dress, Sian, if you'll leave those fine titties out for now.'

Immediately the girl's face lit up again. Catching the coin, she curtsied to the Prince, then walked back to the stands, still with her breasts bare.

'Absolutely barbaric!' Talithea remarked.

'Nonsense, she is only a peasant girl,' the Prince answered. 'So, what now?'

'A recitation of the saga of Thane Etharion,' Talithea said.

'Excellent!' he declared. 'Boy, more mead, and fill my Princess' goblet, the others also.'

'I do think she might have put up a little more fight,' Aeisla remarked. 'A few feeble kicks hardly make for a spectacle.'

'Undignified, also,' Sulitea agreed, 'even for a peasant. Prince Kavisterion, put Aeisla up on the dais, with a purse of a hundred thalars. See how your men do then!'

'A fine spectacle, no doubt,' the Prince answered, 'yet she is a Reeveling, above such public exposure. Now be quiet, here is the minstrel.'

A lank, fox-faced man with golden red hair cut short had stepped to the dais and was unrolling a scroll of charta. Silence fell on the audience as he cleared his throat, then began to read, a tale of heroics that Cianna had heard many times before. Her attention quickly wandered, across the valley from where a field had been prepared for the festivities, to the dark bulk of Ateron keep on its conical hill, with the houses of the town below and the grey sea beyond.

The keep was larger than any she had seen, a cluster of high towers set behind crenellated walls, all in black stone. No less impressive was the town, with rank upon rank of houses rising up the hillside, many of them larger than the Thane's hall in her village. Yet both were familiar enough, if grander than she was used to, and it was to the sea that her eyes were drawn, a great sheet of rippling grey, with waves breaking on a distant headland to the east. The lakes of her homeland in central Aegmund were tiny by comparison, and to the north and west it seemed to stretch forever, fading into grey where a bank of heavy clouds marked the horizon.

For a space she watched the waves break, awed by the sheer scale of what she could see. To the north and east she knew there was a long rugged coast and finally a great sheet of ice. East, she could see the Spine Mountains, beyond which she knew was the kingdom of Mund, from which Talithea came. That had always seemed a place of fable and riches, with odd customs and peculiar sensibilities. Yet Talithea, Sulitea and Aeisla also had been further still, beyond the sea that separated Kora from the southern continents, to places stranger yet, a fact which invested all three of them with an air of mystery and glamour.

Turning, she stole a glance at Aeisla, so tall, copper haired, heavy chested, lean, her body sleek yet muscular, listening to the minstrel with a faraway look in her eyes. Beside Aeisla, Sulitea looked small and ordinary, save for the pale blonde hair so typical of the high-born. Yet as a witch it was Sulitea who drew the cautious, respectful looks, a fact which made Cianna swell with pride to be her maid.

The minstrel finished the saga, leading to a fresh round of applause and crashing of tankards on wood. Sulitea reached down, to tousle Cianna's hair, then moved her legs. Cianna adjusted herself, leaning into Sulitea's skirts.

'Is there any gossip?' Sulitea asked. 'We hear nothing in Boreal.'

'Why you insist in living there is beyond me,' Talithea replied. 'You could hardly be more remote if you had gone to the edge of the ice cap.'

'This is simple. In Boreal I have respect, both as a witch and as a High-Demoiselle. Few know of my disgrace, and in any case it carries little sting. Even here in Ateron there are strange glances and whispering; there, none. The people are savage, superstitious also. Look at little Cianna here, who is as faithful as a puppy, and a deal more obedient, for all that she files her fangs and wears a necklace of her ancestor's teeth.'

Again Sulitea reached down to tousle Cianna's hair. Cianna looked up with a smile. Talithea shrugged and turned to allow her goblet to be filled with mead before speaking again.

'There is news of interest, as it is, from Thieron itself. In the autumn my brother came up to hunt. Do you recall the magic powder used in bombards?'

'Yes.'

'Well it seems that the Glass Coast has gained the secret of its making. Long boats seeking to raid up the Rai estuary were met with great iron balls, hurled across the sea. Now nothing will do for Father than we have the secret ourselves.'

'Indeed?'

'Yes. Father planned an expedition, wonderfully bold. The men of three long boats came in to a lonely beach at night and overran a small fortress from the landward, taking both powder and bombards. Sadly the effort was wasted.'

'How so?' Aeisla asked.

'We have the powder, but we do not know what it is. Nor did the men in the fort. It seems the secret is known only to a handful.'

'And none were able to fathom it?'

'None.'

'Men! Idiots!' Sulitea broke in sharply.

'Not so!' Talithea replied. 'It was a brave move, and all they could do. Have more respect for my father, who is still your King, for all you plant yourself in the wilds of Aegmund.'

'An idiot,' Sulitea insisted, 'and do not forget that he is my uncle as well as you father. He is brave yes, but like all men he blusters and shouts, swinging his axe and cursing his enemies, only to fail when anything arises which requires so much as a moment of thought.'

'And you could do better, I presume?' Talithea retorted hotly.

'Certainly,' Sulitea answered her. 'It is a simple matter of process. Utharion is going about it quite the wrong way. The men of the Glass Coast have only just gained the secret, and furthermore, they face us across the sea. Naturally they will take every precaution to stop us gaining it in turn. Better to go further afield, where the knowledge is more commonplace and our enmity is of no consequence.'

'Raid a thousand leagues or more to the south?' Talithea snapped. 'Now who is the idiot?'

'You think like your father,' Sulitea answered. 'Violence is not always the answer. What I would do is simply to arrive at some suitable place and find a man with the appropriate knowledge. I would flatter him, praising his skill and valour, bed him perhaps, and in due course ask in an awed little voice how the black powder is made. Eager to boast, he would answer me, and the precious secret would come tumbling out. Simple.'

'Mere talk,' Talithea replied, 'and you are a dishonourable slut besides. Bedding men to gain their secrets! I am ashamed to call you cousin!'

'It is not mere talk!' Sulitea snapped. 'I could do it.'

'Mere talk,' Talithea sniffed.

'I shall do it,' Sulitea answered, 'and with ease. Indeed, it will be little more than a pleasure jaunt.'

Cianna watched as Sulitea spread a map out on the table, weighting each corner of the charta with a piece of raw crystal. Unable to read, and understanding only vaguely that the lines in some way indicated the boundaries between land and sea, she could only look on in awe as her mistress and Aeisla bent to study it, both clearly with full understanding.

Having said she intended to discover the secret of the black powder, not only to her cousin, but in front of the Prince, Sulitea had been unable to back down. Instead she had attacked the project with enthusiasm, behaving as if she was doing her kin a minor favour. Privately, she had put a great deal of time and effort into persuading Aeisla to accompany her, eventually succeeding. For Cianna, as Sulitea's maid, there had been no question of not accompanying them, a prospect which she found both exciting and terrifying.

They had travelled back to Boreal together, south through the steep hill country inland of Ateron, through groves of oak and coffinwood, then to higher land of lakes and dark forests. At last they had reached Boreal, at the very centre of Aegmund, Cianna's own land. There, she had ordered provisions and briefly visited her parents, who had accepted the news of her coming journey with a mixture of concern and pride. On her return to the spire Sulitea had established on a high meadow, she had found the two girls already well into their preparations.

'We need a people who have little or no knowledge of Kora,' Sulitea was saying. 'The Glass Coast is impractical, also the Dwarven Kingdoms, and the Aprinia States too. Vendjome must tempt…'

'We would be taken as slaves,' Aeisla pointed out. 'Auctioned on a block, naked. Besides, even now I may still be wanted as a runaway. Not Vendjome.'

'Where then?' Sulitea demanded. 'It must be well south. What of this great island, here? Makea it is called.'

'Irqual the pirate was a Makean,' Aeisla replied. 'They had bombards.'

'What of his character?'

'He was certainly boastful,' Aeisla said dubiously. 'He was also vicious, cruel, cunning and dishonourable.'

'He was a pirate,' Sulitea answered. 'What do you expect? The ordinary folk of Makea are doubtless more reasonable. What do we know of them?'

'Little or nothing,' Aeisla admitted. 'They may well take slaves.'

'Or they may not. The point is moot. Indeed, what could be more harmless than a girl slave? They will tell the secret without the slightest concern.'

'To be a slave! Sulitea!'

'You will not be a slave, silly. They will merely think you one. It is not the same, as you should know. As we need them to think that we are in awe of their knowledge, so we need them to think us under their command.'

Aeisla answered with a sceptical grunt. Cianna, who had been listening to the conversation with growing alarm, clutched at her necklace for strength.

'Come,' Sulitea went on, 'do not be timid. Is this the girl who has been raiding alongside men, who has an escutcheon to put all to shame? Where is your spirit, Aeisla?'

Aeisla shrugged, her face colouring.

'Besides,' Sulitea continued, 'it is no great task, for me. Each detail will be planned, and you need merely follow my lead. For instance, we will come in at night, when there is cloud or the moons show little light, low over the sea, to land on a remote beach.'

'Your confidence is extraordinary,' Aeisla said, 'but then it always was.'

'As I say, it is no great task,' Sulitea answered. 'A simple matter of process and organisation. Cianna, our provisions are due to come?'

'They will be delivered shortly, Mistress,' Cianna answered.

'Excellent,' Sulitea replied, 'then we leave as it grows dark. There is no sense in unduly alarming the peasants. Now, there is the matter of service. Cianna, you will maid for Aeisla as you do for me, and I will have no reticence to create poor feeling. You had best get used to it, so kiss her tuppenny, now.'

'Mistress?' Cianna queried, glancing doubtfully at Aeisla, who returned the uncertain look.

'Kiss her,' Sulitea repeated. 'Look, Cianna, do you suppose that I will forego the pleasure of your agile little tongue because Aeisla is with us? She and I were lovers before. You both enjoy such pleasures, so to feign modesty is merely foolish. Come, Aeisla, up with your skirts, let her kiss you, or better yet, lick you.'

'I think, perhaps…' Aeisla began.

'Then I will do it first, if you must be so coy,' Sulitea broke in. 'Here, Cianna.'

Sulitea sat at a bench, pulling up her skirts and petticoats even as she did so. Beneath she wore drawers, of richly embroidered wool, which she pulled open, exposing the lace ruffles of her pantalettes, which in turn came open. Cianna swallowed as the plump, golden haired mound of her mistress' sex came on show. She could feel the blood rising in her cheeks, and cast another uncertain glance at Aeisla.

'You do this all the time?' Aeisla asked.

Cianna nodded, unable to find words, burning with embarrassment that what she had always held as the most intimate secret between her mistress and herself should be so casually revealed.

'She always was a slut,' Aeisla remarked to Cianna. 'Lick her then, and when you are done I would be flattered for you to give me the same favour.'

Again Cianna nodded, her face colouring rapidly as she dropped to her knees in front of Sulitea, shut her eyes, and buried her face in warm, soft flesh. Sulitea sighed as Cianna's tongue found her clitoris, lapping at the little bud, with her own heat rising quickly at the sheer impropriety of what she was doing. It was common enough in the village, between sisters or the closest of friends, but always taboo. Never was it mentioned openly.

Sulitea let herself slide forward on the bench, pushing her sex into Cianna's face. In response Cianna began to lick lower, at the trim lips of her mistress' sex, then in moist hole. With a yet sharper pang of shame, she went lower still, dabbing at Sulitea's anus with her tongue tip.

'Good girl,' Sulitea sighed. 'She is licking my bottom ring, Aeisla. Delicious, Cianna, little pet, now in, clean in the hole. Yes, perfect.'

Cianna let her tongue tip burrow into the tight hole of Sulitea's anus, her face burning hotter than ever. She could taste her mistress' bottom, an acrid, earthy tang, not unfamiliar to her, but another intimate secret, now exposed to Aeisla. She did it anyway, probing and licking at the little hole until it was pink and shiny, before once more moving higher. Sulitea gave a contented purr as Cianna's tongue once more found her clitoris, reaching down to stroke the maid's hair. The gesture was immediately soothing, and Cianna licked more firmly, her feelings of admiration and love finally overcoming her shame. Again Sulitea sighed, her thighs tensing against Cianna's face, and she was coming, crying out in pleasure as Cianna's lapping reached a crescendo.

'Glorious, beautiful,' Sulitea declared as Cianna finished with a kiss to her clitoris. 'Now the same for Aeisla, little one. Why not kneel, Aeisla, let me admire your lovely bottom while she licks you.'

'You always were imperious, Sulitea,' Aeisla answered. 'Maybe I am not ready to be licked in so rude a position.'

'Then get ready,' Sulitea said. 'Spank her bottom if it pleases you, bare, by hand, for her shame. You always did enjoy reddening other women's bottoms.'

'True,' Aeisla admitted, and rose.

Cianna looked up in fear and shame, her mouth open. Aeisla was too tall, too powerful to resist, even without her status. Facing the humiliating prospect of having her bare bottom spanked, she cast a last pleading look at her mistress. Sulitea merely smiled. Aeisla stretched, also smiling, casually confident in her strength, taking two long paces to where Cianna cowered by her mistress's legs, seating herself on the bench, grabbing Sulitea by the scruff of her neck and hurling her down across her lap.

The movement had been too fast to follow, and Cianna could only squeak in shock and scramble hastily back out of the way of her mistress's frantically kicking legs. Sulitea fought, screaming and scratching and threatening and begging, none of which made the least difference. Aeisla held her down easily, one handed, as her skirts and petticoats where lifted, her drawers and pantalettes pulled open, to expose her meaty white bottom. At that Sulitea went wild, thrashing crazily, but to no avail as Aisla cocked a knee up between her victim's thighs, spreading the ample white buttocks to display both tuppenny and bottom ring, still wet with Cianna's spittle.

'Shall I... shall I fetch an implement?' Cianna enquired, certain that Aeisla could not be about to inflict the ultimate indignity of a bare bottomed hand spanking.

'No,' Aeisla answered coolly. 'I often used to spank her by hand before, and I shall do so now.'

'No, Aeisla, this is unreasonable!' Sulitea blustered. 'Not in front of my maid, Aeisla! I mean it! No!'

The last word trailed off in despair as Aeisla's hand smacked firmly down on Sulitea's naked bottom. The spanking began, firm and steady, Aeisla's palm applied hard to Sulitea's quivering cheeks. Cianna could only watch, mouth open in shock, trying to hide her delight at seeing her mistress spanked, and in such an ignominious way. Sulitea cheeks were well flared, showing everything, sex agape, bumhole winking in her pain, the chubby buttocks wobbling and bouncing, their milk-white skin turning rapidly pink.

Nor did Sulitea take it well, wriggling and squealing with no more dignity than any spanked peasant girl. She complained though, bitterly, in between her squeals of pain, alternately begging Aeisla to stop and threatening revenge. Aeisla took no notice, spanking merrily away until at last Sulitea's cries turned to sobs. At that Aeisla laughed, cocked her knee higher still to further spread her victim's thighs and casually pushed two fingers into Sulitea's sex. Sulitea groaned miserably, but she had stopped fighting.

Aeisla began to masturbate her victim, using her fingers to rub at Sulitea's clitoris and all the while pushing her thumb in and out of the wet vagina. In no time Sulitea's disconsolate little sobs had changed to sighs of pleasure, ending in a long, ecstatic scream as she was once more brought to orgasm. She was dropped immediately, to sit down on her hot bottom with a bump. Aeisla was grinning, indifferent to the look of angry reproach on Sulitea's face.

'Now, Cianna,' Aeisla said, 'if you wish, you may lick my tuppenny, but not as a servant, as a friend.'

'I can never be anything more than a servant,' Cianna answered. 'Not to you.'

'I was a maid all my life,' Aeisla replied, 'to the Demoiselle Elethrine Korismund. Surely Sulitea has told you this?'

'Yes,' Cianna admitted.

'Then why so timid?' Aeisla demanded, starting to pull up her skirts.

Cianna shrugged, pulling herself around and crawling closer as Aeisla spilt her drawers to reveal a rich tangle of deep red curls with the moist pink flesh of her sex clearly visible at the centre. Cianna could smell the rich, feminine scent, and found herself wanting to do it, both for pleasure and to abase herself before the woman who had dared to spank her mistress. Yet still she glanced at Sulitea.

'Do it,' Sulitea ordered. 'Why not? Now you have seen me thoroughly humiliated. Aeisla, now that you are a Reeveling you must seek to maintain respect for your rank among the low-born, mine also.'

Aeisla merely laughed, and reached out to take Cianna gently by the hair. Cianna went with the pressure, allowing her head to be pulled in to Aeisla's sex, rubbing her face in the wet folds before starting to lick. Aeisla's sex was neat, but her clitoris big, like the tip of finger, and upright, in the manner of a tiny, erect cock. Cianna kissed it, and sucked it in between her lips, making Aeisla gasp.

'Beautiful, she is good,' Aeisla said. 'Come, Sulitea, pull up her skirts, lick her bottom for her while she does me.'

'I will do no such thing!' Sulitea snapped.

'She is haughty isn't she,' Aeisla addressed Cianna, 'and powerful too, but at heart she is gentle and a slut as well. Yes, like that. Now lower.'

Guessing what was wanted, Cianna dipped her tongue, dabbing at the tightly knotted flesh of Aeisla's bottom hole. She began to clean the little ring, with her gratitude and loyalty rising all the while, glad to be performing such an intimate service, proud that she should be permitted to do it.

'There, Sulitea,' Aeisla said, 'she is cleaning my bottom ring, as she did yours. You are a good girl, Cianna. Now higher again, make me come.'

Cianna obeyed immediately, lapping firmly at Aeisla's clitoris, to elicit a gasp, then a long, low moan of pleasure. Aeisla came, full in Cianna's face, calling out in her ecstasy with her eyes closed. The orgasm faded only slowly, Cianna still licking until at last Aeisla pushed her head gently away.

'There,' Aeisla remarked, 'now we should all get on perfectly.'

As dusk began to fall, Cianna found herself growing rapidly more frightened. If Sulitea had seemed less than awe inspiring bent red-bottomed across Aeisla's lap, Cianna's respect had quickly returned. Working casually, with no more concern that Cianna had shown in making the evening meal, Sulitea had summoned a colossal winged demon, a hideous, neckless thing with vast, leathery wings, which now crouched on the meadow. Unable to meet its malevolent red eyes, Cianna had stayed in the spire, pretending to go over the provisions which had been brought up from the village. Even Aeisla was clearly scared, feigning nonchalance, but staying well clear of the demon as she assembled a broad wooden cage to Sulitea's instructions.

Finally, Cianna was forced to approach the hideous being, to help lift the cage into place on its broad back and secure it with broad leather straps. Twice she touched its flesh, finding it cold and dry, quite unlike any ordinary creature. All the while it watched her, brilliant red eyes the size of her fists following her every move, so that when the time finally came to climb aboard she found her fear tempered by relief at being able to avoid its gaze.

Sat in the cage, she gripped the bars, Aeisla also, Sulitea standing at the front whispering to the demon, and using a long stick to tickle the it behind the ears. The cage shuddered, Cianna clutching her necklace as the demon pulled itself to its feet, its vast leathery wings unfolding to either side. She began to mumble prayers, her fingers flicking the little tooth cages along their thong. Sulitea called out and the demon began to walk, slow, long steps, each of which sent a shudder through the cage.

It turned, its back to Sulitea's spire, the meadow in front, a long line of grey-green with the darker woods to either side, ending in nothing where the ground fell away towards the village. Beyond was air, with distant mountains lit red as the setting sun caught their snow capped peaks, Cianna's last sight as she shut her eyes tight.

Sulitea called out, the demon once more began to walk, faster, breaking into a lumbering trot, a run, as fast as a man, as fast as a horse, impossibly fast with the air ripping at Cianna's clothes and hair. She clutched at the cage, screaming her fear into the wind as the demon hurled itself into the air, screaming again as the whole world tilted to one side. Her bladder burst in her terror, to spray piddle out between her thighs as the great demon turned on the air, swinging slowly towards the south.

All night Cianna rode the demon, gripping the bars of the ride cage in stark fear. No disaster overtook them, and in the face of Sulitea's open amusement she gradually relaxed. By dawn she had managed to gain enough control of herself to change her soiled dress and prepare breakfast, but with her eyes half-lidded to prevent herself from seeing outside the cage.

Aeisla had recovered more quickly, peering down from the edge of the cage with interest and occasionally exclaiming at some feature visible far below. At last Cianna's curiosity overcame her fear, and she crawled to the edge, peering down only to jerk sharply back at the sight of blue sea and jagged grey peaks an impossible distance below her.

Over the next two days her confidence rose slowly. The demon flew in long glides, broken by periods of climbing at places were warm air rose from the land below. Its broad back was stable, and still, save for the rare times when it was obliged to flex its wings. Even the rushing wind became familiar, and by the evening of the second day, while kneeling between Sulitea's spread thighs and busy with her tongue, she even managed to briefly forget where she was.

Sea passed beneath them, changing in tone from grey to green to blue, and land, jagged mountains, red desert. At one point two great volcanos were seen, on either side of a narrow strait, with smoke issuing from craters at their summits. On another an island appeared, with a round bay, in which rode ships seemingly no larger than toys. At noon on the third day they found themselves above a low green coast, which Sulitea declared to be the continent of Cypraea.

Choosing an island with no evidence of human habitation, Sulitea brought the demon down in a great spiral, Cianna keeping her eyes tight shut until at last the motion ceased. She opened them to find the demon squatting on a beach of fine golden sand, with blue sea to one side and tall trees each bearing a cluster of spiky fronds to the other. Sulitea was whispering to the demon, Aeisla fanning herself with a hand against the sudden heat.

'He is stable,' Sulitea declared, swinging open the door of the cage. 'Come down.'

She jumped to the sand, paused to scratch the demon behind an ear and strolled up the beach, Aeisla and Cianna following.

'Food first,' Sulitea said, 'and perhaps a wash in the sea… but what extraordinary fruit! Look, Aeisla, like a parade of yellow cocks, each prouder than the last!'

'They are called bananas,' Aeisla replied. 'I saw them in Apraya. It is the fruit from which Babalyn N'Jukolana made that fiery spirit. They are good to eat also.'

Cianna looked up at the bananas, some four times her own height above her head. Sulitea whistled, made a complex gesture with her hands, and one great wing unfurled from the demon's side, rising, to hook a clawed tip around the stem of the banana bunch, which landed with a thump in the sand. Sulitea took one, bit it and made a face.

'You remove the skin first,' Aeisla explained.

'I see,' Sulitea answered as Aeisla demonstrated. 'Even more like a cock. Hmm, a better taste though. Delicious in fact. Now, by my reckoning Makea is some four to five hundreds of leagues to the south and west. This means, that should we rise aloft at dusk, eight to ten hours of flight will bring us to the Makean coast in the dead hours of night, with only two moons in the sky, one gibbous but both low. Thus we keep the risk of observation to a minimum.'

Aeisla shrugged in response.

'Once there,' Sulitea went on. 'I will banish the demon and in the morning we will claim to be the victims of a shipwreck. None will have reason to disbelieve us. After all, how else would we be there, three women alone on a strange shore?'

'Might they not guess?' Aeisla queried.

'Unlikely,' Sulitea answered. 'It is the habit to men to assume inferior intelligence in others, women especially. Besides, we must be meek, submissive, feigning awe. Obviously we say nothing of our true intentions, to anyone. Praise them, flirt with them, take them to bed, but choose carefully. You will wish to court savants, or high warriors perhaps, maybe skilled artisans, those likely to have the knowledge we need.'

'And if they simply take us as slaves?' Aeisla demanded.

'Why you should assume them to be slavers I do not know,' Sulitea said, 'but if they are, what matter? Those rich enough to purchase us are likely to know the secret. If not, behave badly. Dissatisfied, they will pass us on.'

'Doubtless after a good whipped,' Aeisla responded. 'You make it sound so simple, as if we were on a hunting expedition! What if we become separated? What if we are put in a seraglio, like the one at Vendjome, with only girls bred for pleasure as company?'

'Naturally we must accommodate ourselves to circumstances. Rely on me. In the case of extremity I will merely scry for you, summon, collect you both and we try our luck elsewhere.'

Aeisla sighed and shook her head.

'Explain to me, please Mistresses,' Cianna asked. 'What is this slavery we risk?'

'It is an abomination!' Aeisla answered immediately. 'A vile foreign habit! Men and women are sold, for money, as if they were cattle! It is hideous, unthinkable! In…'

'All this is true,' Sulitea broke in, 'but it misses the point. To be a slave is a thing of the mind, a concept valid only if the person enslaved believes it so. To be sold as a slave does not make you a slave, as Aeisla well knows, from experience. So long as you are free in your mind you are free, no matter how many chains weigh you down.'

Cianna stared blankly, understanding nothing of Sulitea's explanation, as was so often the case.

'Let me explain,' Aeisla. 'You have given your oath of fealty to Sulitea, yes?'

'Yes,' Cianna agreed.

'Yet if some Thane or Reeve where to mistake you for another girl, a vassal of their own, it would not make you so, would it?'

'No.'

'Then there we are. You know you are Sulitea's vassal. Just so, as you would know you are Sulitea's maid, if taken in slavery, you would know you are free, whatever others may think. '

Cianna nodded doubtfully.

'In truth,' Sulitea went on, 'it occurs to me that the distinction between our system of fealty and slavery is more limited than we care to believe. The primary distinction is that the exchange of oaths replaces the giving of money...'

'An oath given freely!' Aeisla broke in. 'To one deserving of loyalty! The difference is absolute!'

'It is conceptual, no more,' Sulitea insisted. 'In practise, the relationship is the same, an obligation to obedience within a system of law crafted by those in authority...'

Cianna picked up a banana and began to peel it, feeling both awed and confused. Sulitea and Aeisla continued to talk, in an increasingly heated argument which Cianna was unable to follow. Soon she had stopped even trying, instead looking out across the blue sea to where some huge fish or even a monster had briefly broken surface.

She lay back, resting her head on her arm, thinking of how awed her friends and family would be when she returned to Boreal. Her eldest brother had been to Aegerion, where the High-Prince of Aegmund held court, a journey of some three hundred leagues. Sulitea had said they were some three thousand leagues to the south, ten times as far, and in a land almost totally unknown. Better still, she would be able to say she had ridden a demon, without having to reveal how terrified she had been.

With the sun striking long shadows from the banana palms, they once more took to the air. The demon ran into the evening breeze, out along a spit of sand exposed by the tide, then over water, tearing up spray with its great claws until it finally managed to wrench itself into the air. Flapping ponderously, with the girls clinging against the heave and twitch of the great muscles which controlled the upstroke of the wings, it rose above the island in a great spiral, using what little heat was still rising from the land to gain altitude. Throughout, Sulitea whispered to it, urging it to greater effort, until at last she stood back, the demon banking to the west before settling into a glide.

'When we leave Makea,' she stated, 'remind me to summon on a hillside. Now, supper, a little play, then rest. Cianna, fetch out the last of the mead.'

Cianna hastened to obey, going about her tasks kneeling, with her legs well splayed, for balance. Making up plates of dried meat garnished with a pickle of fruit and vegetables, she served both girls then herself, while the flask of mead was passed between Sulitea and Aeisla.

The meal was finished with the sun its own breadth above the western horizon and the land in the east no more than a dim line of dull grey-green. Licking the last of the pickle from her fingers, Cianna knelt back, waiting to see what was expected of her. Sulitea licked her lips and gave a quick glance to the west before speaking.

'This evening, Cianna,' she declared, 'you shall provide us with a little show, masturbating with the bananas. We will watch, until we are ready, when you may lick us both.'

'Yes, Mistress,' Cianna answered, blushing.

'Come then, up with your dress and in with a banana!'

Cianna responded hesitantly, lifting her knees to get her dress high enough, then peeling a banana from the bunch. Sulitea was watching, smiling openly, Aeisla too. Trying to push her sense of duty over her embarrassment, Cianna pulled up her dress, exposing her sex. Pressing the banana to her tuppenny, she began to rub, sliding the smooth, firm skin up between her lips and over her clitoris.

'Put it in yourself, I said,' Sulitea ordered.

Shutting her eyes, Cianna knelt right back, sticking out her sex towards the watching girls. With the banana in her hand, she felt for the hole of her vagina. She was moist, and the tip slid in easily, followed by the thick yellow shaft as she pushed it up, her flesh opening to accept it. She sighed, imagining it as the feel of a cock, or one of the carved dildos Sulitea occasionally fucked her with.

'Now on your knees,' Sulitea said. 'Come, little one, bottom up. Aeisla help me.'

Cianna opening her eyes to find Sulitea sat cross legged with her skirts rucked up to her waist and her drawers and pantalettes split wide to expose the plump, yellow furred mound of her sex. Aeisla was beside

Sulitea, a hand on her friend's belly, then burrowing down. Cianna turned over, lifting her bottom as she caught the wet sound of Aeisla masturbating Sulitea and a little cry of pleasure.

On her knees, Cianna reached back, feeding the banana in and out of her open tuppenny. Her embarrassment was still there, but fading behind the need to please her Mistress and to come herself. Pausing, with the banana held firmly in her sex, she made quick work of unlacing her bodice, letting her breasts tumble free.

'Wonderful!' Sulitea crowed. 'That's right, titties too. You do look comic, Cianna! Put another one in, up your bottom!'

'My bottom?' Cianna answered.

'Why not?' Sulitea giggled. 'Come, I want to see how absurd you look, with a fat yellow fruit in each hole!'

Despite a fresh, sharper pang of shame, Cianna reached out to twist a new fruit from the bunch. Realising that what she was being made to do was likely to get messy, she tugged off her dress, tossing it to one side. Now nude but for her short boots and necklace, she knelt once more, with her bottom stuck well up. Placing the banana on the leathery surface between her knees, she reached back behind herself with both hands, pulling the cheeks of her bottom wide to put her ring on full show. Using her longest finger, she touched her anus, feeling the tight little muscle twitch in anticipation of what was coming. Her face was burning with blushes, and she could her the slapping sound of Aeisla masturbating Sulitea.

Still with one hand stretching her bottom wide, she put the other in her mouth, all four fingers, to collect as much saliva as she could, slapping it between her buttocks and onto her anus. Letting her ring relax, she touched it again, finding the flesh wet with spittle. Her finger went in, probing the tight, hot hole, and Sulitea sighed with pleasure, then giggled.

For a moment Cianna fingered her bottom, pushing deep into the slimy cavity of her rectum, to lubricate her ring properly, until the flesh was puffy and soft, the hole slack enough to take the thick banana. She had been buggered, caught in the woods by three of the boys from the village and made to take one in each of her holes. Despite the breach of a strong taboo, she had been pleading for it deeper and harder by the time the one up her bottom had come, yet the use of her anus still filled her with shame. Now she had been told to do it, which made it so much easier as she took the firm, cock-like fruit and pressed the tip to her slimy bumhole.

For a moment it hurt, as her ring stretched, and then it was in, sliding up her, to fill her rectum as her vagina was filled, leaving her feeling gloriously bloated sexually, as well as lewd. Sticking her bottom high, she wiggled it, showing off what she had done to herself.

'Oh but doesn't she look funny?' Sulitea laughed. 'Come, Aeisla, up with your dress. I want to touch you too. Cianna, masturbate, but you are not to come until I say.'

'Yes, Mistress,' Cianna managed.

There was the rustle of cloth behind her as Cianna began to show off, probing her holes with the bananas and rubbing at her sex and breasts, to keep herself on heat but short of orgasm. Behind her, peering back between her dangling breasts and spread thighs, she could see Sulitea and Aeisla, kissing, their fingers busy between each other's thighs. Both had their breasts out, plump and pale in the light of the dying sun, the nipples straining out in their arousal. Despite their passion, both had their eyes open, fixed on the rude display Cianna was making of her rear view.

Knowing it would not be long before she was permitted to come, she began to rub her nipples against the leathery skin beneath her. She had a thumb to her clitoris, teasing the little bud as she pushed the bananas in and out of her gaping holes. Fluid was trickling down over her sex, leaking from both vagina and anus as she probed herself. She rubbed it in, over her clitoris, bringing her right to the edge of orgasm, even as she saw Sulitea's thighs lock on Aeisla's hand.

Cianna rubbed harder, shutting her eyes, feeling her sex and anus squeeze on the intruding bananas. She was coming, in blinding ecstasy, rubbing frantically, with one banana pushed deep up, in her bumhole, as her contractions squeezed the other slowly from her sex, a glorious rude feeling as she called out her Mistress' name in wanton bliss.

When she at last opened her eyes, it was to find Sulitea knelt between Aeisla's legs, licking busily, with her broad white bottom lifted high and bare. Aeisla was smiling, and stroking Sulitea's blonde curls, and as she saw Cianna, she beckoned. Cianna came close without hesitation, to take one heavy breast and start to suckle, kissing and mouthing at Aeisla's erect nipple.

The light was fading fast, and as the sun finally sank into the sea, Cianna caught the outline of a great double mountain against the red orb, a plume of smoke rising from one peak, for a second, before her sight was blotted out by plump breast flesh. Sulitea's hand found her bottom, touching the banana stem which was all that protruded from Cianna's anus.

They tumbled together, licking and groping, their fingers and tongues probing at wet holes, lips kissing other lips, nipples and wet, open sexes. Aeisla came, her sex pushed in Sulitea's face, Cianna's head pressed between her breasts. With that they came apart, to finish the flask of mead together in the darkness, before once more coming together. They quickly became passionate again, giggling with drink, Sulitea and Aeisla bottom up as Cianna licked their holes. Cianna was buggered, held by Aeisla as if by man, the fat yellow fruit fed in and out of her rectum until she was panting out her lust into Sulitea's breasts. With her bottom thoroughly used, she was allowed to pull out the banana, and made to suck it, to the sound of giggles of disgust and delight in equal measures.

From then, the sex became ever more lewd and uninhibited. For the first time, Sulitea kissed Cianna's sex, sucking at her clitoris to bring on a second orgasm. Cianna responded in kind, while to her delight Aeisla licked the sloppy orifice of her bottom ring, tongue burrowed deep up, to provide the most exquisite feelings as Sulitea came in her face.

Again and again they came together, in combinations ever more lewd and intimate, indifferent to status or taboos, all three nude but for boots. Drunk and dirty, slimy with each other's juices and their own, they were lost to everything except the pleasure of each other's bodies. Cianna had even mounted Aeisla's face, eyes shut in bliss as her tuppenny and bottom ring where licked, when the demon lurched, banking steeply, to send them sprawling across the cage.

Cianna screamed in shock. as her shoulder hit the edge of the cage. Wood snapped. She clutched at a spar, almost upside down, hearing Sulitea's scream of command, jolted, screaming again as the spar snapped in her hand, falling, striking the leathery surface of the demon's wing, which rose, squirming beneath her and she was rolling, clutching at the wing, then at nothing, screaming, tumbling through air, jolted hard, and still, in blackness.

She lay dazed, too shocked to moved, vaguely aware of the cries of Sulitea and Aeisla, then the thunderous crash of the demon's wingbeat, once, twice and no more. Only slowly did awareness of her surroundings penetrate. The darkness, not absolute, but with the pale crescent of a small moon showing above her, and clouds scudding across a starlit sky. She was on hard earth, in long grass, which a fresh wind whipped against her bare skin. There was scent too, grass seed, animal dung, and something else, something as familiar as it was horrifying. The musk of goblins.

It was gone as soon as it had come, snatched away on the wind. Still it was enough to drag her from her shock, her mind full of awful images of what would happen if she was caught. Images of being dragged down and ravished where she lay, with their grotesque cocks in every hole, to be left sperm sodden and in all likelihood pregnant. With her fear rising quickly, she scrambled through the grass, feeling before her in the hope of shelter, near to panic, only to stop, realising the futility of her actions. Forcing herself to calm, she took a firm grip on her necklace

For a moment she considered calling for Sulitea and Aeisla, only to decide that her voice would either be lost on the wind, that or summon the goblins or some yet worse beasts. Besides, the demon had flown on, she was sure of it, and equally sure that they would search for her in the morning. Deciding to stay still, she curled her body into a tight ball, praying to her ancestors that she could come through the night unharmed.

Chapter Two

As dawn came up Cianna found herself in a world of grass and rock and air, a wide open hillside, with the sighing wind whipping at her skirts and sending broken cloud scudding across the sky. To all sides was a sea of long yellow-green grass, stretching to the haze of horizon, broken only by jagged pinnacles of grey rock and the vast double peak in the distance, with its ragged plume of smoke. Of the demon, Sulitea and Aeisla there was no sign, save an area of flattened grass, and at one place twin gouges in the black earth of the hill. No trace of human habitation was visible, not so much as a hut or a track

Her first thought was to wait, convinced that they would return for her, but as the sun rose into the sky she became ever less hopeful. Of Sulitea's faith she had no doubt, but other thoughts began to intrude, of disaster, with the demon dissipating a thousand feet above the ground, or of capture, with the girls stunned from their rough landing, and taken, gagged and bound before they could resist. The first did not bear thinking about, the second suggested that she herself should seek out people and hope to be brought together again. The more likely choice, that they had simply lost her in the darkness and confusion, suggested she look for a village or at least a house.

Finally deciding that it was pointless to sit waiting in the grass any longer, she got up, brushed herself down and set off, walking down the slope. As she entered a sheltered dip she once more caught the scent of goblins. Quickly fighting down the immediate pang of lust the scent brought her, she left it for more open ground where she would be able to run before the smell of their musk overcame her. With her need for shelter growing ever more urgent, she began to hurry, yet when the irregular shape of a horse and rider finally appeared far out across the grass, she felt as much fear as relief.

The fear grew as the rider changed direction, clearly having seen her. She stopped, waiting, one hand over her sex in an instinctive gesture of protection and concealment, the other working at her necklace. He came closer, and she realised that his face and hands were dark, and grey-black, the colour of charcoal. She almost ran, only to remember that Sulitea had said the people of the south were dark skinned and hold herself. He also seemed small, and was certainly thin, as if poorly fed.

Pulling the horse to a stop a good hundred paces from Cianna, the man dismounted. She watched, cautiously, as he dug in his saddle bag. Pulling out what appeared to be a leaf, he unrolled it, revealing a dark shape. He approached, holding out the brown lump, his face set in a crafty leer. Cianna caught a scent on the breeze, sweet and rich, like honey. Instinctively she licked her lips and the man's grin grew broader.

'Here, my pretty,' he said. 'I have toffee, fine sweet toffee, for you.'

'Food?' Cianna answered. 'Thank you, you are kind.'

'You speak?' the man said, his expression immediately changing to surprise, mingled with disappointment.

'I speak,' Cianna confirmed, struggling to comprehend his accent but catching the meaning easily enough.

'You are no nymph then. A half-breed? An albino?'

'None of these. I am Cianna, a human girl, shipwrecked on your coast.'

'Shipwrecked? We are fifty leagues from the sea!'

Cianna shrugged, not knowing what to say.

'You are no Makean, that is plain,' he went on. 'Nor from any land I know. How is it that your skin is white and your hair red?'

'How is it that you skin is the colour of burnt wood and your hair black as coal?' Cianna responded.

The man looked puzzled, then laughed, holding out the toffee once more.

'You are human, that is plain,' he said. 'You may as well have this anyway.'

'Anyway?' Cianna asked, taking it cautiously and sniffing at it.

'It's not poisoned,' the man said. 'It was to stop your teeth while I fucked you.'

'You mean to fuck me?'

'I did, naturally. What else would I do with some strange nymph hybrid? I think I might anyway.'

'You might?' Cianna responded. 'You want to ravish me?'

'What's to stop me?'

'You are small, and seem undernourished. Are you sure you could achieve me?'

'Not for certain, no. What say we fuck anyway? It has been a month since I have seen a woman.'

'Why would I wish to fuck with you?'

'You might not, granted, so let me express myself another way. I have shelter, and there are goblins hereabouts, living in crevices beneath the tors. You have smelt them perhaps?'

Cianna nodded.

'And you know what goblins do to girls like you, don't you?'

Again Cianna nodded.

'Just so. And if in the day you can escape them, they'll get you tonight. They can smell human cunt just as you can smell their musk. Once they catch you, you won't be able to resist for a moment, will you? No, you'll be sucking and jerking at them like a greedy little slut, and flaunting yourself for their attention. Think, fat green cocks well up your cunt, your arsehole too, until every one has had his fill. Then they'll drag you down underground for further use, fucked and buggered in some dank earth lined chamber, fed on worms and goblin sperm…'

'Very well, you may have me in return for shelter,' Cianna babbled quickly.

'A wise choice,' he answered, dropping the toffee down on a rock, 'and if we are to enjoy each other's bodies, we should know each other's names. I am Gaidrhed, a goatherd, admittedly of no great consequence.'

'Cianna,' she replied, 'a lady's maid.'

'And well trained in the art of licking cunt, no doubt,' he said. 'A good thick cock will make a change, I'm sure. Now down on all fours with you, I like my mates that way.'

Cianna went down, reluctantly, kneeling among the long grass. Gaidrhed wasted no time on preliminaries, simply lifting his smock and pulling open the flap of his crude leather trousers to flop out his cock and balls. She opened her mouth, expecting to be made to suck him hard, but he ignored the offer, stepping up to her and pushing down on the small of her back to make her flaunt her bottom.

'Well, you have the shape of a girl, and the smell of a girl,' he said as he sank to his knees behind her. 'But your skin, so pale! Even the hair of your cunt is red! Strange indeed, not that it will stop you from getting your fucking. Now, hold still, and a touch lower. Your legs are inconveniently long.'

Resignedly, Cianna spread her knees, opening and lowering her sex. He hawked and spat, his phlegm catching her full on her sex, between the folds of her tuppenny. A moment later his cock touched her, rubbing the spittle between her lips and over her hole. He was jerking at it too, his knuckles brushing at her inner thighs and catching her clitoris to draw an involuntary moan from between her lips.

'That's better, is it not?' he said. 'There is nothing quite to equal a stiff cock in the right place now, is there?'

As he spoke he prodded his near erect cock to her hole, pushing it in. Cianna sighed as she felt herself fill, then braced herself as his hands closed in the soft flesh of her hips. He began to fuck her, using long, slow strokes, his thin body slapping against her buttocks. She looked back, finding his eyes glued to her bottom, watching his cock move in her hole. It was getting faster as he quickly became more urgent, the pushes jammed her forward into the grass and making her pant and sigh.

'Not in me, please,' she said.

He made a wry face, and went on fucking her, faster, harder, only to suddenly jerk his cock from her body. Tugging at it hard, he sent a spurt of come across her bottom and the small of her back. Cianna reached behind herself, using her thumb to wipe the mess off her skin and flicking it away into the grass. Gaidrhed was already on his feet, squeezing his cock back into his trousers.

'So,' he said, 'you have earned your shelter. My hut is nearby.'

'Thank you,' she said, grudgingly, as she got to her feet. 'Might I have something to cover myself? Also some of your confection?'

'Do. There is a blanket on the horse. So, what land are you from, and how did you come to Makea.'

'On a ship, as I said,' Cianna answered, frantically trying to decide on her story and remember what Sulitea had told her. 'A Cypraean longship.'

'I have seen ships, once,' he answered. 'When I travelled to Kefra, on the coast. I would not wish to set a foot on one. Here, among the high grassland is my place. The open sky, the wide plain, the call of my goats. Here are things I understand.'

He went on, Cianna glad of his garrulity and seldom replying. With her wrapped in a coarse blanket and mounted behind him on the horse, they rode west. Cianna ate toffee and listened to him casually describing how he had intended to catch a wild nymph and fuck her while her teeth were sticky with the toffee. He laughed as he talked, apparently assuming her approval of an act which if done in Boreal would have been thought highly perverse.

For over an hour they rode, across the open grassland, then down, into a shallow valley in which grew a straggle of trees unfamiliar to Cianna. Gaidrhed turned the horse, towards a hut not unlike the longhouses of her own village, built of stone and thatched with grass. Two goats peered from the doorway.

'My hut,' he declared. 'So, this evening you may cook for me, and I will fuck you once more, perhaps twice. Then I will decide what to do with you.'

'I have friends,' Cianna answered cautiously. 'Somewhere.'

'Citizens?'

'No. Others from the ship.'

'They are not here. I am.'

He pulled the horse to a stop and jumped down, helping Cianna with a hand beneath the meat of her bottom. She made no objection, but allowed him to fondle her briefly before she was sent into the house with a smack to one buttock while he went to tend to the horse. Inside it was much as she had expected, a long room, the lower part of which served as shippen, the other for Gaidrhed's storage and work. A crude ladder led up to a square opening in the plank ceiling, which she climbed, finding a long room, sparsely furnished, with a single window looking out over the hills. There was a pallet on the floor, made of tied bundles of grass and spread with goat skins, which she sat down on, hunched into the blanket, feeling worried and very alone.

Eventually Gaidrhed returned, as talkative as ever. Cianna listened half-heartedly, all the while trying to decide what she should do. When he once more demanded that she get down on her knees she obeyed without hesitation, letting him fuck her from behind. Food followed, course bread and a pungent soup, which she heated over a peat fire. Having finished, he produced a bottle of arrack. Once he had become thoroughly drunk he fucked her again, and a last time as they lay together on the pallet, with the scent of goats and the drink strong in Cianna's nostrils.

Cianna awoke to the unfamiliar smell and the feel of the coarse hair of Gaidrhed's skins. For a moment there was confusion, to be replaced by a deep sense of loneliness as full awareness sank in. Gaidrhed was gone, but she could hear movement in the room below. Rolling onto her back, she lay staring at the crude beams above her, their surfaces glistening black with age in the brilliant sunlight.

Her situation seemed entirely hopeless. She was lost in a strange land, friendless, save for those who wanted to amuse themselves with her body, and without protection. There was still faith in Sulitea, who she knew would expect her to continue as they had planned, alone or not. Yet Gaidrhed seemed unlikely to know any deep secrets, or indeed anything beyond the running of his tiny farmstead, which was all he had spoken of. It was easier to wait, and hope Sulitea and Aeisla came to find her.

She was still undecided when Gaidrhed's head appeared in the hatch leading from the lower room. He climbed up, a bucket in his hand, which he held out. Cianna saw that it was half full of goat's milk, and took a grateful swallow, until he pulled it back.

'There,' he declared, setting down the bucket, 'that is the important work done. Now, you may see to my morning erection.'

As he spoke he had pulled up his smock, exposing a half stiff cock. The garment came off, over his head, and he was nude, save for his boots, which he left on as he climbed aboard the pallet. With a sigh of resignation Cianna spread her thighs.

'Over,' he demanded, 'arse up.'

Cianna gave another, deeper sigh, but rolled onto her front, lifting her bottom for penetration. He mounted her immediately, and began to rub, squirming his cock against her sex lips. In no time he was fully hard, and he popped it inside her, fucking at a steady pace and pawing her bottom. She made herself comfortable, parting her thighs to let him have the best angle and supporting herself on her elbows to let her breasts hang. He took a brief grope, then went back to fondling her bottom.

'A rare treat,' he grunted, 'soft and full and fat, breasts and bottom too, if a trifle loose in the cunt.'

'My tuppenny is not loose!' Cianna protested.

'By what I am used to your are loose,' he insisted. 'Now quite, and let me get the scent of you.'

He moved his hands, spreading her buttocks with his thumbs and drawing in his breath happily. She caught her own scent, rich and female, bringing back the taste and smell of her mistress' sex to her, and Aeisla's too. The thought brought a fresh pang of loneliness, and worry, making it impossible to enjoy the fucking. If Gaidrhed noticed he gave no sign, poking merrily away at her hole until at last he gasped, pulled out his cock and sprayed come across her upturned buttocks.

'That I enjoyed,' he stated, as he climbed from the pallet. 'You are less tight than a goat, perhaps, but you smell better, look better and you struggle less.'

'A goat!?' Cianna demanded.

'I am a goatherd, as you know,' Gaidrhed replied mildly. 'Now, today we visit the town of Ketawa, and Ikail's slave market.'

'Slave market?'

'I cannot afford to keep you,' he answered with a shrug. 'Certainly I would like to, but with the money you will fetch I might buy perhaps three or even four fine longhair goats, or a billy of good pedigree.'

'You plan to sell me? To make me a slave!'

'Of course. What else would you be?'

'Why must I be a slave? What right have you!?'

Gaidrhed merely laughed. Cianna clutched for her necklace, feeling her anger rise. The teeth in her grip seemed to twitch, yet beyond him she could see out of a window, the empty land of green grass and grey rock, a strange, hostile land, a land where there seemed to be no difference in men's attitude to women and to beasts. For a moment her anger warred with her fear and loneliness, only to die in the certain knowledge that she had little choice but to be compliant.

'Keep me here and I will provide you with every comfort,' she said. 'You may use my body as you wish, while I have some skill in the husbanding of animals, in other matters too. Only say that I am not a slave.'

'I am tempted,' he admitted, 'but as I say, I cannot afford to keep you. Besides, when the taxers come up from Kea they would take you anyway, as too fine for a mere goatherd. Best to sell you now.'

'And if I run?'

'Where to? I am amazed you came this far from the sea without capture. True, you might live wild, raiding for what food you need, if you have such skills. Why trouble? There are the goblins, trolls also, beasts aplenty. Better surely to live as the pet of some wealthy merchant or noble, pampering yourself all day and fucked regularly at night. Would that I had such an easy lot.'

Cianna made to answer, but stopped, remembering Aeisla's words on the state of slavery. In her mind she would still be free, and when Sulitea came for her she would be free in practise as well. Sulitea would come, she had no doubt, and Gaidrhed was right. It was better to wait in comfort than not, while if she was to be fucked regularly, better by some wealthy man of status than a minor who barely preferred her over his goats, let alone by goblins.

'I will come,' she said reluctantly.

'A wise choice,' he replied, 'and an attitude which will save you much pain. You are a strange one, unlike any woman I have ever known. Here in Makea, the women are wise, accepting their status as the lesser sex. Are the men feeble then, in your land?'

'No,' Cianna answered, 'but we have more pride, men and women both. Nor do we fuck goats.'

'No? More strangeness! Now come, we must leave if we are to reach Ketawa before the best of the livestock is sold.'

He returned to the lower level, preparing the horse as she dressed herself in a wrap of dirty cloth, all that she could find. She was feeling confused and praying that Sulitea would come for her before too long. When she was ready she climbed down, to find Gaidrhed with the horse saddled. As before, she climbed on behind him, and they set off, following the narrow stream that ran down from the heights.

For hours they rode, through grassland set with rocks and straggling trees, passing the occasional longhouse of a design similar to Gaidrhed's, and once the ruins of a keep. At noon they paused for lunch, and sex, Gaidrhed making Cianna kneel in the lee of a rock to mount her from behind, once more comparing the feeling of her tuppenny to that of a nanny goat's.

Shortly afterwards, the track dropped into the head of a larger valley, in which the landscape changed abruptly, lush leaved trees and dense shrubs replacing the grass and rock. There were more buildings as well, clusters of longhouses and others, some of two or even three stories. These became more frequent as they descended the valley, until both sides of what was now a broad road where lined with houses and she realised they had come to the town. At an open square Gaidrhed tethered the horse, continuing on foot. The street became narrower, the air closer and hotter, leaving Cianna uncomfortable, her skin prickling with sweat.

Despite her feelings it was impossible not to be fascinated. Before they had walked a hundred paces they passed more goods than would be seen in her village in a lifetime, both mundane and beyond her comprehension. Great open pots held grain and dried beans, while vegetables and fruit hung in clumps from hooks or lay in trays. Other shops sold meat and fish, or pottery and ironware, also glass and silver finer than any she had seen. One held books, to an astonishing number, another brightly painted mannequins which she guessed to be children's toys, a third harness and riding gear, a fourth strange metal machines.

There were people too, hundreds of them, thronging the streets. Most had the same grey-black skin as Gaidrhed, these in gay clothing, wraps of brilliantly coloured cloth, gold and green and scarlet, with elaborate patterns of blue and black and brown, worn loose by the men, belted at the waist by the women.

Others, with skin tanned or a rich dark brown, were clearly slaves, of both sexes. The men were in loin cloths, the women stark naked, most with either a tattoo at the centre of their chests or with a slim metal collar around their necks. Not that they seemed cowed, or even especially servile, often talking together or pausing to admire the displays in the windows of the shops. Cianna looked on in shock, amazed by how anybody could accept so degrading a status, and at how the women could tolerate nudity with no show of shame.

Gaidrhed walked on, apparently oblivious to the sights and sounds around him, save to occasionally turn his head for a second glance at a particularly fine bottom or pair of breasts. Cianna watched everything, so awe-struck that her own situation was driven from her mind until they reached a tall gate, beside which a green robed clerk sat at a table, writing figures in a ledger.

'Ikail's market,' Gaidrhed announced, then rapped on the clerk's table.

'Yes?' the clerk answered, looking up with obvious disdain. 'You wish to buy, here?'

'I wish to sell,' Gaidrhed announced.

'You are in the wrong place,' the clerk said, glancing at Cianna. 'You want the beast market, a street further and some four hundred paces east. Here we buy only human slaves.'

'She is human,' Gaidrhed stated, 'despite her strange colouring. Or as least so she assures me.'

'She is?' the clerk queried.

'I am,' Cianna said.

'Are you certain?' the clerk insisted, peering up at her. 'She looks more like some sort of hybrid. Red Ape and nymph perhaps.'

'I am human,' Cianna answered him, 'also my mother, father and their ancestors before them.'

'You see,' Gaidrhed said. 'Human, and with the pride and spirit of a man. She should fetch a good price.'

'Hmm, maybe,' the clerk said doubtfully. 'There is not much call for exotics these days. Still, if she is yours to sell?'

'She is free of tattoos and no others claim her. She says her ship was wrecked on the northern coast, and I caught her wandering the heights.'

The clerk grunted and jerked his thumb to the gate, immediately returning his attention to his work. Gaidrhed pushed through, drawing Cianna behind him, into an empty yard, dry and dusty in the hot sun. Across it was a building, into which they stepped, finding another clerk seated within. Beyond, a high door stood a fraction ajar, and Cianna peered within as Gaidrhed spoke to the clerk. The room was brightly lit, and she could see girls within, dark skinned beauties, stark naked, many with collars around their necks. She found herself swallowing and took hold of her necklace, less certain than ever.

'Well girl,' the clerk addressed her suddenly, 'let us assess your worth. Strip.'

Cianna hesitated, angry at the tone of the clerk's voice but mindful of Sulitea's instructions to be meek and compliant.

'Strip,' he repeated, making a mark on the piece of charta in front of him. 'Hmm, obedience poor, and not instinctive.'

Gaidrhed pulled irritably at Cianna's wrap, jerking it off her body. She barred her teeth at him, briefly, but held herself, shyly covering her sex and breasts.

'Coy also,' the clerk said, 'not good, not good. Place you hands on your head, girl, and turn slowly around.'

Again Cianna hesitated, but obeyed, her face and chest flushing as she displayed herself.

'Bizarre,' the clerk said. 'never have I seen hair of such a peculiar colour, like copper, and on her cunt too. Are you dyed, girl?'

'Dyed?' Cianna queried.

'Is that your natural hair colour?' he asked.

'Yes,' she answered. 'What else might it be?'

For a moment the clerk looked at her, then laughed.

'A mere savage,' he said. 'Where is your homeland, girl?'

'Aegmund, north of here,' she answered.

'Never heard of it,' he said. 'No matter. You seem healthy, and agile, with plenty of muscle to your legs and buttocks. A trifle slim hipped, perhaps, but with good sized breasts, and firm by the look of things. Bend forward.'

Cianna obeyed, letting her breasts swing beneath her. The clerk reached out, taking a handful and squeezing gently, then flicking one nipple with a finger. It popped out, Cianna once more baring her teeth, which the clerk failed to notice.

'A good sexual response,' he said. 'Do you juice well?'

'My... my tuppenny? Does my tuppenny make juice well?' Cianna demanded in shock.

'Does you cunt juice easily, yes?'

'Well enough.'

'Turn, bend.'

With her shame and anger rising quickly, Cianna turned and put her hands on her knees with her feet well apart, sticking out her bottom. The clerk's finger touched her skin, tracing a line down across one buttock to her sex, then poking at the hole and tickling with his fingernail.

'No virgin, I see,' he said.

'I am low-born,' Cianna answered with a sob

'I didn't ask for your status. Are you a virgin?'

'I am low-born, I may fuck as I please.'

'I'll put no then. You have a weird one here. She juices well, yes, but she will not fetch much, I fear. Too strange.'

He had continued to tickle Cianna's sex as he spoke, and for all her shame she could feel herself responding, growing warm and open. Suddenly the finger went higher, tickling her bottom ring, and she squeaked in surprise and shock, jumping up.

'An anal virgin?' the clerk demanded. 'Do the boys not use girls' bottom holes where you come from?'

'No!' Cianna responded angrily, lying.

'Now there we might have a selling point,' he said. 'A bottom like that, and unpopped! It looks tight too.'

Cianna said nothing, blushing furiously and thinking of the banana and other things that had been pushed into her bottom ring.

'So,' the clerk added, once again addressing Gaidrhed, 'I can offer you twelve standard now, or you may take a risk and have half of whatever she fetches when she is sold.'

'Twelve standard?' Gaidrhed replied. 'Surely not? Look at her. Have you ever seen a girl so tall? Or of such strange colouring? She is unique!'

'She is strange,' the clerk answered, 'also surly, slow to obey and somewhat savage. Twelve standard, unless you would rather take ten. Or as I say, you can return for the half. Who knows, Jelkrael the Impresario has been bargaining for a new fighting girl. He might take her, for as much as forty standard perhaps, or not. Sometimes a girl goes unsold for a month.'

Gaidrhed grunted and held out his hand. The clerk gave a knowing chuckle and ducked down beneath his desk. Twelve silver coins were counted out. Gaidrhed took them and left, with hardly a backward glance for Cianna.

'So,' the clerk said, rising, 'I will show you to the hall. Our rules are simple. Make no disturbance and do as you are told. Fail once and you go without food for a day, twice and you are on dung duty, thrice and you will be whipped. Do you understand?'

Cianna nodded, following him as he walked to the door, pushing it open. Beyond was the hall she had glimpsed before, a space twice as long as wide, with a high ceiling and a balcony some twice her height above the floor. A roof of glass panes in an ironwork grid admitted the brilliant sunlight, a feature she stared at in amazement for some while before looking down once more. Broad benches lined much of all four of the walls, with a second door opposite her. In an alcove there was a cluster of buckets, while at the centre a long bench stood in a depressed area. Perhaps three dozen girls crowded the room, with skin in varying shades from the rich brown of old oak, through red-brown and the charcoal of the Makeans to jet black. Many had turned as the door opened, and were watching her, their surprise evident in their expressions. A whisper went through the room, and Cianna gave a nervous smile in response.

'Find a place on the bench,' the clerk was saying. 'Potential buyers walk the balcony, there. Drink at the left spigot, wash at the further, evacuate in a pail. This is all you need to know.'

He left, closing the door behind him. Cianna stood fidgeting with her necklace, uncertain what to do, only to see that she was being approached, by a voluptuous girl with near black skin and twists of silver wire in her nipples, belly button and sex. Their eyes met, and Cianna was surprised to see a look of recognition, only for it to fade.

'You are of Kora, in the north?' the girl asked

Cianna nodded.

'I am Babalyn N'Jukolana, of Blue Zoria, in the Aprina States,' the girl went on.

'You thought you knew me?' Cianna asked.

'I knew a Koran girl, named Aisla,' Babalyn responded, 'with copper hair, like you, but she was taller, and her face more lean.'

'I know your name,' Cianna responded. 'My Mistress, Sulitea, met you in the Red Parch desert, with Aeisla too. They are here, somewhere in Makea…'

She hesitated, wondering if she should have admitted what she had, but Babalyn was smiling, friendly and open, the first person in Makea who had shown any desire other than simple carnality.

'They are slaves too?' Babalyn was demanding. 'They were taken, in Cypraea?'

'No,' Cianna answered, hesitantly, 'that is… there was a shipwreck. On the northern coast.'

'And you were taken! Are not these Makeans unspeakable? Helpless girls cast up on their coast, and what do they do? They take you as slaves! Never in Aprinia would be behave with such barbarism! It was the same with me, although we were not wrecked. I was on a ship of my father's, trading into Rojome, when we were becalmed. A Makean warship came up with us. We were outgunned, and could do nothing, for all their primitive cannonry. We were taken, all of us, and made slaves. Can you believe it?'

'Very well,' Cianna answered, somewhat taken aback by the stream of words.

'That was nearly a year ago,' Babalyn went on. 'Come, let us fetch our portions, the meal is served. Since I was taken I have changed hands nine times! Nine! The last was some old fool who thinks himself a philosopher, and had come out to the mountains for the air. Always he said that I spoke too much, and then, when he was in conversation with some other ancient, equally foolish, and I pointed out the idiocy of some cherished theorem, he sold me, for twenty standard! Two weeks I have been here, two weeks! Still I am unsold.'

'Why?' Cianna asked, following Babalyn towards where a couple of older women were handing out folded pieces of a flat, pale bread from a great basket. 'You are beautiful. Is this not what men want in Makea?'

'They prefer the little Vendjomois girls,' Babalyn answered, 'who think it a privilege to serve. See how they chatter and simper together. They are little better than nymphs!'

Babalyn had pointed to a group of brown skinned girls, small but curvaceous, naked, and apparently quite happy with their condition. Some munched on bread, others patiently waited their turn, chattering together in high pitched voices. Cianna pushed into the crowd of girls behind Babalyn, who reached out and plucked a handful from the basket. Cianna took the offering, looking at it dubiously.

'Apatta,' Babalyn explained, 'spiced vegetables cooked in ghee and rolled in bread. It is filling, if hardly refined. At least as a slave you may be assured of adequate food. Too skinny and our price drops.'

'How are we sold?' Cianna queried. 'The clerk said the buyers come to the balcony.'

'They do,' Babalyn answered, pointing. 'There are couches up there, see, where they may sit and be served wine. You can be called up, tested...'

'Tested?' Cianna queried, seating herself at a bench.

'You know,' Babalyn went on, 'made to serve, to suck their cocks, whatever amuses them.'

'And we must do as we are told?'

'Naturally, unless you wish to be punished. I have already missed a day's food for refusing to allow myself to be sodomised by some great oaf. His cock would have looked too large on a donkey! He would have split me, but my explanation found no favours. The next time I am on dung duty, collecting the nightsoil pails and spreading the dirt out on the drying pans, and making the patties also. It must be a filthy job.'

'They collect our dung? What do you do with it? Put it on the fields?'

'No. It goes to make powder.'

'Powder!? As high-born ladies use to dry their bodies?'

'No, silly! Gunpowder, for their cannon!'

'Cannon?'

'Cannon. Like large rifles. Bombards, I think Aisla called them.'

'Bombards, yes, which hurl great balls of iron by magic.'

Babalyn burst out laughing, slapping her thigh.

'What is funny?' Cianna demanded.

'Nothing, I am sorry,' Babalyn answered. 'It is not magic. The powder turns to gas when lit, creating an explosion. That is what propels the ball.'

'Magic, as I said,' Cianna repeated. 'So the powder, it is made from dung?'

'No, well, not entirely,' Babalyn said. 'In Blue Zoria, each week the dunny cart comes to collect our nightsoil, which is then taken to the mill. There it is prepared in some way to make nitre. The nitre is an ingredient for gunpowder.'

'With what besides?'

'How would I know? I am the daughter of the leading citizen of Blue Zoria, not an alchemist. No, I was. Now I am just one more Makean slave girl. Do you know, when I was free, I used to masturbate as I thought of how it would feel to be a slave, to have my body used as and when men wished? How foolish I was!'

' "So long as you are free in your mind you are free, no matter how many chains weigh you down," ' Cianna recited. 'This is what Sulitea says.'

'Try telling that to the clerks here,' Babalyn responded.

'I did not understand it either,' Cianna admitted.

'A slave is a slave,' Babalyn said, 'and I suspect you will prove no more popular than I, with that attitude. Even the Makean girls are more compliant. They are in demand, actually, especially those sold from once high families who have fallen into debt. Less so those sold by poor families to make ends meet, speaking of which, Yuilla is coming this way, with her friends. Do as she says and all will be well.'

Cianna looked to where four Makean girls were walking towards them, the one in front taller and more solidly built than the others, her black hair shaved close to her scalp, her mouth set in a confident, aggressive sneer.

'Give me your bread,' Yuilla demanded.

'Why?' Cianna asked.

'Because I want it,' Yuilla answered, to the sound of laughter from her friends, 'and also because if you do not I will push your head into my soil bucket and make you eat what is in it.'

'Give it to her,' Babalyn said. 'There will be more in the morning.'

Cianna lifted the bread to her mouth and tore off a bite. Immediately Babalyn took a step to the side, while Yuilla's eyes set in hard anger. Cianna chewed and swallowed her mouthful, then stood, finding herself looking down onto the top of Yuilla's head. Yuilla took a step back, looking into Cianna's face. Cianna barred her teeth, flicking her tongue over one sharpened fang. Yuilla hesitated, then stepped away, laughing and making a remark about not wishing to eat food Cianna had touched.

'Wonderful!' Babalyn exclaimed. 'She was terrified! What did you do?'

'Nothing,' Cianna answered. 'Only showed willing to fight.'

'She would never risk anything other than an easy victory, or course. Still, be cautious of her. She was a wrestler, I am told, for one of the shows that travel the country. Barbarian louts!'

'I too can wrestle. I have three brothers older than me. All used to use me to practise their holds and moves.'

'Still, watch out. For one thing she will covet that necklace you wear. What are these things, ivory beads? And the mesh, some exotic alloy?'

Babalyn had reached out, turning one of the objects threaded onto Cianna's necklace in her hand.

'They are teeth,' Cianna replied. 'Here, to the left, are those of my maternal grandfather. To the right are those of my father's father, and…'

'I do not wish to know!' Babalyn cut in, dropping the necklace. 'How awful! Why wear such a ghastly thing?'

'They hold a portion of the spirits of each man,' Cianna explained. 'To hold them gives me courage, and wisdom also.'

Babalyn shuddered, only to look up as a peel of masculine laughter rang out from the gallery above them. Cianna looked up, to see a group of five young men leaning over the iron balustrade. They were richly dressed, in robes of brightly coloured silk, each with an elaborate golden bangle hanging from one ear. They were looking at her and Babalyn, and as she met their eyes one blew a kiss, causing a ripple of laughter among his comrades.

'They come to buy us?' Cianna asked nervously.

'No,' Babalyn answered. 'They're just the sons of wealthy townsmen. Ikail tolerates them because they may one day be good customers.'

'They come to see the naked girls?'

'They see plenty of naked girls in the street. They come to get their cocks sucked. If they ask, do it, or you get a punishment.'

'And if I still refuse?'

'They will hold you down and fuck you, then complain to the clerks.'

'I will suck, I suppose. They are high-born, it would seem, at the least.'

'Certainly in their own eyes. Proud too, look up.'

Cianna did, finding to her surprise a thick black cock sticking out through the ironwork of the balustrade above her head, with the owner's face grinning down above. The others were also looking, and laughing as the expression on her face. Several other girls had noticed as well, the Vendjomois giggling, the Makeans giving sidelong glances and smiles, the Cypraeans casual.

'See, she has never seen one so big!' the youth laughed.

'Often enough,' Cianna answered, 'on donkeys, and a troll once, too, but yours is uglier.'

The other youths burst into laughter, to the discomfort of the one showing his cock, who withdrew it, vanishing from sight.

'Now you've had it!' Babalyn hissed. 'He is sure to ask for you.'

Cianna shrugged.

'I warn you, they have no compunction about how they use girls,' Babalyn went on, 'and I wouldn't stand there if I were you, they have been known to piss on girls who answer their taunts.'

Moving quickly away from the balcony, Cianna looked up again, to find the youth who had taunted her talking to a clerk. The clerk nodded, looked round and beckoned to her, pointing to the door.

'There we are,' Babalyn said. 'I did say. You'd better go, the way you came in, and up the stairs. I hope you've had it up the bottom before.'

'Up my bottom,' Cianna answered, in sudden shock. 'They are sodomites, the Makeans?'

'At every chance!' Babalyn answered. 'Oh you poor thing! Here, stay still.'

Quickly Babalyn squeezed the remains of her Apatta over the palm of her hand, producing a trickle of thick, orange gee.

'What are you doing?' Cianna demanded, glancing up to where the clerk had now come to the balustrade and was gesturing impatiently.

'Turn around,' Babalyn ordered, 'stick out your bum. I'm going to grease your ring.'

'My ring? I…' Cianna stammered, but Babalyn had already taken her by the arm and was pulling her around.

She went, blushing as Babalyn's fingers sank into the cleft of her bottom, wiping the gee over her anus. The youths had seen, and where laughing and pointing, while there was a great deal of giggling among the girls. Cianna made to protest, then squeaked as Babalyn's finger pushed into her anus, probing.

'Ow! That stings!' Cianna complained. 'Ow!'

That's just the spice in the gee, and it stings a lot less than taking a cock without being properly greased,' Babalyn answered. 'Now hurry, or you'll earn yourself a punishment too.'

Cianna hurried, scampering across the room, her face red with blushes, to the sound of girlish laughter. In the hallway the clerk merely pointed to a flight of stairs, which she ran up, finding herself on the balcony. Everybody seemed to be looking at her, naked girls, green robed clerks, the rich youths and two other clients, more elderly. One of the youths was talking to a clerk, and handing over coins, then turning to grin at Cianna.

'Be fast when you are wanted,' the clerk snapped, then turned to the youth who had shown Cianna his cock. 'I apologise, Elite, she is some sort of savage, and knew in this afternoon.'

The clerk took Cianna by the arm, pulling her towards the door of a room. She followed, allowing herself to be pushed inside. The youths followed, arranging them selves on couches upholstered in the same rich green as the clerk's uniforms. She stood uncertainly in the middle.

'Come then,' the one she had insulted said. 'If my cock is so ugly, let's see how it looks in your face. On your knees.'

He leant back as he spoke, splaying his legs as he lifted his robe, to expose his cock once more, the thick shaft lying against one thigh. Cianna hesitated, but got down, blushing furiously as she knelt in between his legs. She could smell his cock, urgent and male, with the fat head already half out of the thick prepuce. He took it, holding it out and beckoning her to come closer.

She obeyed, her mouth coming open, telling herself it was what Sulitea would have expected of her as she gulped in the thick, meaty penis. The youth chuckled as she started to suck, taking her firmly by the hair.

'Stick your arse out,' he ordered. 'Let them see the little hole your friend so kindly greased.'

Cianna obeyed, lifting her bottom to make a show of her sex and bottom hole. His cock was stiffening in her mouth, and from the corner of her eye she could see two of the others, both with their robes lifted, stroking at big, dark cocks in readiness for her body. Despite the shame in her head, she could feel herself coming on heat, and the loose, greasy feel where Babalyn had lubricated her anus.

She began to stroke the first man's balls, feeling the coarse hair and wrinkled skin. He was hard in her mouth, his scrotum tight, the big testicles moving sluggishly under her fingers. She sucked more firmly, hoping to make him come in her mouth and avoid having her anus invaded. He sighed happily, moving a little way down the couch.

'Bitch on heat, just like the rest,' he said. 'Do it then, Claides.'

It was all the warning Cianna got, and then something firm and fleshy had been pushed to her anus, even as the youth's grip tightened in her hair. Her eyes went round in shock as her greasy bumhole stretched wide, and then she was gasping on her mouthful, with a great, fat cock head wedged up her bumhole. She was panting immediately, trying to lift her head off the cock in her mouth as the man behind forced her passage, shoving inch after inch of hard shaft into her rectum to the tune of her muffled squeals and the laughter of the others. It went up, all of it, packed into her reluctant bottom until his thighs met the meat of her buttocks and his balls squashed out against her empty sex. The others burst into applause to see her properly sodomised, clapping and cheering their companion.

Cianna could do nothing, only clutch onto the legs of the man in her mouth as her body quivered and shook in reaction to the buggery. She was unable to speak, hardly able to breath, her breasts swinging and slapping to the motion of the cock in her rectum, her head dizzy with shock. The awful, desperate feeling in her bowels was worse by far than the effect of anything Sulitea had put up her, worse than she had ever imagined, dirty and helpless and out of control, but far, far too good to make her want to stop.

She fought for control, struggling to take it, all the while to the sound of their laughter and calls for Claides to bugger her harder and to come in her rectum. The other man still had her by the hair, his cock wedged deep into her throat, wanking into her mouth as his friend buggered her. Another had come close, and eager hands took her breasts, fondling and bouncing them, commenting on how fat and heavy they were, then twisting her nipples cruelly in their fingers. She tried to scream, only to gag on the fat penis head in her throat. The youth grunted, called out, jerked hard at his shaft, and suddenly her throat was full of thick, slimy male come, and she was choking, gagging on his erection and fighting for breath, all the while with the cock in her bottom slamming harder and harder into her body.

Wrenching herself back, she jerked her head off the man's cock. Coughing and spluttering, with sperm bubbling from her nose in a thick froth, she clung on to him, her body jerking against his. Claides too cried out in ecstasy and she knew that he had given her the final humiliation and come in her rectum. Not that they stopped, the man who had been fondling her breasts grabbing her by the hair even as the first moved to one side. His cock was shoved rudely into her mouth, and she began to suck, with streamers of saliva and the first man's sperm hanging from her chin to catch in his pubic hair.

Even as she sucked, Claides' cock was pulled slowly from her burning anus, only for hard hands to lock immediately in the soft flesh of her hips. A cock head found her bottom hole, pushing in easily past the gaping, sperm sodden ring, and up, jammed into her rectum with three hard pushes that left her struggling for breath around the penis in her mouth. Fresh hands closed on her breasts, one on each, and a third, between her thighs, cupping her sex, the palm pressing to her clitoris. Immediately she was in ecstasy, unable to resist her feelings as whoever it was started to masturbate her. The man up her bottom gave a crow of delight as her anus contracted on his invading cock, and she was coming, gulping and slavering over the cock in her mouth, bucking her hips against the one up her bottom, wriggling and squirming in their hands, totally wanton, with all pretence of modesty or restraint completely gone.

The man in her bottom groaned loudly, coming deep up her rectum as her ring clamped over and over on his penis. Another cock was against her face, rubbing in her hair. A man grunted and she felt the wet of his come splash out aver her face a moment before her head was wrenched from one cock and stuck onto another. She sucked, draining his sperm down her throat as her own orgasm slowly faded. The last man came, full in her face and over her hair, even as her anus closed with a long fart as the cock in it was withdrawn.

They let go, and she collapsed, exhausted, eyes closed, down into the puddle of come and sweat beneath her. They were still laughing, and boasting, about the wanton state they had driven her into, their voices fading as they left. Cianna lay still, no longer caring, and when she at last looked up, it was in response to a gentle prod at her leg. A woman stood above her, one of the older slaves, holding out a bucket and a mop.

Chapter Three

Cianna spent the night beside Babalyn on one of the benches in the slave hall. They cuddled together, not for sex but for comfort. After her sex with the youths, Cianna had been quite pleased with herself, until she had discovered that the man Claides had bought her supposed anal virginity, and for more than the clerks had given Gaidrhed for her. The act she had enjoyed, and they had been no rougher than many of the boys who enjoyed her in Boreal. Yet the suddenness of it, and the casual way it had been done made it so hard to accept, and had brought home to her what it really meant to be a slave. She had still been shivering with the humiliation of it when the light had faded from the great skylight, despite Babalyn's best efforts to comfort her.

Now she lay in hot darkness, with the sticky touch of Babalyn's skin beside her on the bench, the warm smell of bodies, some sighs and sobs, the occasional muted cry of ecstasy. One hand was clutched tight to her necklace, and she was praying quietly, asking her ancestors for the strength to cope with the Makeans, for the sort of courage Aeisla displayed, or better still, Sulitea's extraordinary insouciance.

Finally she slept, to wake to bright light and cool air. From the angle at which the sun struck through the skylight she knew it was early, but there was already activity. Yuilla and her friends were gathered at the washing trough, with others waiting at a respectful distance. Two of the older women, who seemed to belong to the house itself, were standing by a great sack, handing what seemed to be some sort of cake to a queue of girls. Beside her Babalyn was stirring.

'I was at home,' Babalyn said suddenly, 'in my dreams, in Blue Zoria, on a soft bed, with two of my favourite admirers.'

She looked near to tears, so Cianna reached out to take her hand, drawing comfort as well as giving it. Babalyn responded with a weak smile, and sat up.

'The nights are always worst,' she said. 'In the day I can forget, but at night it comes back. Who I really am. Who I was. Come on, let's wash, and eat. Who knows, maybe today a shipmaster will be up from the coast, to buy me and eventually I will be wrecked on the Cypraean coast.'

'Sulitea will come for me soon,' Cianna answered, 'and when she does, you may come too. We will set you down in Blue Zoria.'

'What could Sulitea do?' Babalyn asked.

'Summon a demon,' Cianna answered, 'to break the walls and bring us free, as easily as you or I would comb our hair.'

Babalyn laughed, 'your dreams are wilder than mine! But keep them, all the same.'

'She will come,' Cianna said confidently, rising to follow Babalyn towards the washing trough.

As they approached, Yuilla was coming away, and sneered as Cianna and Babalyn passed, making a remark to her friends which caused a ripple of laughter.

'Does she seek to make me fight?' Cianna asked.

'Not really,' Babalyn answered, 'the clerks would not allow anything that might mark us. She seeks to cow you, really, because if you are seen not to be obedient to her it will weaken her authority over the others. Still, she might risk catching you at night, me also, as your friend. She can be cruel without leaving evidence for the clerks to see.'

'You are afraid of her?'

'Of course! She is a vicious, barbarian jungle cat! I am gently bred, Cianna. In Aprinia women do not fight together. It is uncivilised! The Makeans are nothing but brigands, slave takers, savages... Always here I am bullied! Look, Cianna, it is not wise to make friends here, when we are likely to be sold apart, but would you agree, to try and be sold with me?'

'Gladly,' Cianna replied.

Babalyn kissed her, suddenly happy.

'You will be my charm,' she said cheerfully, 'my defender, and in return I will teach you how this rotten country works.'

They washed and ate, returning to their places on the bench. At mid morning the first of Ikail's clients began to drift in. Most were simply looking, browsers, as Babalyn called them, or seeking bargains. Babalyn had seen most before, and made comments on each to Cianna, until a short, balding man in robes of rich green silk appeared on the balcony.

'That is Ikail himself,' Babalyn whispered. 'There must be an important client. See.'

Another man had appeared beside Ikail, tall, lean, with a great hook nose, his hair a pale ash grey against the charcoal of his skin. He wore a robe of the deepest blue, elaborately embroidered in gold, with a number of heavy golden chains around his neck, each displaying a symbol.

'Military, I would guess,' Babalyn whispered. 'A retired general perhaps? A good prospect. Straighten up, boobs out, stroke my hair, and chatter playfully. They love the appearance of mindless vanity.'

'He is somewhat old,' Cianna said doubtfully.

'Old and wealthy, perfect,' Babalyn answered. 'We will have nothing to do all day but lounge around and look pretty.'

'Should we flirt?' Cianna asked. 'To show interest.'

'It is not necessary,' Babalyn said. 'There is no creature more vain than the Makean male. Each thinks himself irresistible to women, no matter that he is ancient, stunted, deformed even. He will take your attraction to him for granted. Merely pose, and if we are called up, be meek, simper a little, and recite your skills in the erotic and culinary arts.'

Ikail and the client were walking slowly around the balcony, looking down at the slave girls. Occasionally one or the other would pass a comment, while one of the other clerks explained the characteristics of particular girls. As the little group reached the place opposite where Cianna sat, she looked up, smiling, then went back to admiring Babalyn's crinkly black hair. The men passed on, but a moment later the clerk signalled to them.

'We must stress our virtues as a pair,' Babalyn said as they hurried up the stairs. 'We are lovers, right, as when we are made to perform together, real passion is always popular. Say you trained as a concubine as well...'

'A what?' Cianna demanded.

'A concubine, a girl trained to give men pleasure.'

'We do not do this, in Aegmund. It is…'

'Never mind, just say your are a trained pleasure slave.'

'I…' Cianna began, but they had reached the balcony, and the tall man was looking at them.

Babalyn smiled sweetly, taking Cianna's hand and walking forward with her hips swinging. Cianna tried to imitate her, acutely conscious of her naked body, as both Ikail and the tall man watched her as if her nakedness were of no consequence whatever.

'Here, Elite, ' the clerk spoke, indicating them, 'an odd pair, who seem to have taken to one another. The dark girl was of high status in her homeland, one of the Aprina states, and she has all the haughteur of her kind. It would perhaps amuse you to break her? The pale is an oddity, indeed, I at first thought her a hybrid. You two, why are you not kneeling before the Elite Admiral Assivetes?'

Babalyn knelt immediately, pulling Cianna down with her.

'Peculiar,' the one addressed as Assivetes said. 'The pale one is a northland savage, I think. She might do, but I want no arrogant Aprinian girl.'

'I am not arrogant,' Babalyn said sweetly. 'I have learnt my place in life, and the worth of Makean men. I am skilled also, in all the erotic arts of Opina. Please take me, great Elite.'

The man grunted.

'She is well broken in,' Ikail remarked. 'She has been some time in Makea and has been taught much. And look at her body. Such breasts are rare, and above a waist so slim, with hips in perfect proportion. Her bottom is no less magnificent. Turn, girl.'

Babalyn scrambled around immediately, pushing her bottom out for the man's inspection. Cianna caught her friend's scent, and found herself blushing at the rudeness of the pose.

'Cunt jewellery, I see,' Assivetes remarked. 'Fat lips, and a big clitoris, which always implies passion, big cheeks too, and firm.'

He had reached down to fondle Babalyn's bottom, squeezing one cheek, then the other, and giving each a gentle slap. Cianna stayed still, wondering if she was going to see Babalyn fucked, even buggered, in front of her, or if she might get the same herself.

'A pretty anus too,' Assivetes went on, 'and perhaps not too loose. So girl, what do you do, other than fuck.'

'I am widely trained,' Babalyn said, making no move to get up from her exposed position. 'I can dance, and recite, and serve in all ways.'

'Fair,' Assivetes said. 'I am tempted. What of the other one?'

'I am a maid,' Cianna answered promptly. 'I cook well, and I sew, while I have some knowledge of animal husbandry…'

'I am no farmer,' Assivetes laughed. 'What of erotic arts?'

'Yes,' Cianna answered uncertainly.

'She is not virgin,' Ikail supplied, 'but she is somewhat innocent. How old are you, girl?'

'I have seen seventeen winters,' Cianna answered.

'And when were you first fucked?'

'Last summer.'

'Barely broken,' Assivetes said. 'Let us see her.'

'Legs wide,' Ikail ordered, 'show the Elite your cunt, and hold up your breasts.'

Cianna obeyed, blushing furiously, spreading her knees and taking one breast in each hand.

'Good breasts,' Assivetes remarked, 'firm and heavy, if not so lush as her Aprinian friend's. A fine cunt too, and so pale.'

'Never have I seen hair of such a colour,' Ikail put in, and on her cunt too. 'is she not fine?'

'Fine, if a little simple,' Assivetes replied. 'I don't know…'

'Her bottom is a joy also,' Ikail said quickly. 'Get over, girl.'

Cianna went, reluctantly adopting the same pose as Babalyn, with her head down and her bottom stuck out and up, showing every rude detail between her cheeks. From behind her Assivetes gave a grunt of appreciation.

'Even her anus is pale,' Assivetes remarked. 'Has she been buggered?'

'Last evening, by Claides, the son of the Exquisite Elandor,' Ikail said. 'He was most satisfied.'

'No doubt,' Assivetes replied. 'Here also I am tempted. She amuses me. She is naïve, a savage, really. Yet the Aprinian has a fatter bottom and is perhaps the better trained.

'Take us both, Elite!' Babalyn said suddenly. 'Please! We are lovers. We will perform together for you, with true passion, in any manner that pleases you!'

'We will,' Cianna agreed. 'Anything.'

'Silence!' Ikail ordered. 'Yet it true what they say, Elite. Would they not make a fine show together? How your guests would envy you!'

'Both?' Assivetes said. 'Maybe. The price?'

'A mere two hundred standard,' Ikail said quickly, 'for the pair, a price which reflects both your standing as a valued customer and…'

'No,' Assivetes cut in. 'It is too much. I value the Aprinian at sixty standard, the savage at forty. Eighty should be a fair price for the pair.'

'Eighty standard?' Ikail answered. 'But Elite, as a pair they have more value than separately. They are lovers. Think of the pleasure to be gained in making them whip one another and suchlike sport!'

Assivetes gave an amused grunt.

'Imagine,' Ikail went on. 'You might have one make the other her toilet, or devise a cunning game, so that they are obliged to betray each other into some debased and painful fate. The possibilities are endless!'

'True,' Assivetes admitted. 'Very well, a hundred for the pair, which is my last offer.'

'One hundred?' Ikail said. 'Ah, so slim a margin, but for you, a customer of long standing, taken.'

Cianna walked beside Babalyn, through the hot, dusty streets of Ketawa. A collar had been fixed around her neck, Babalyn's also, and from each a lead led forward, to the hand of fat man in blue robes who had been sent to fetch them from the slave market. He was several paces in front, and ignored them so long as they kept up, which his slow, waddling pace made easy.

'Why is there no guard?' Cianna whispered after a while. 'We could jerk the leashes from his hand, then run.'

'You stand out from a thousand paces,' Babalyn answered. 'Anyway, slave girls do not do such things, or if they do, they are caught and punished. They have some nasty habits, the Makeans, so believe me, it is best to remain obedient. Besides, where would you run to?'

Cianna shrugged, realising the sense of what Babalyn was saying, but wanting to do something to reassert her pride. Yet Sulitea had told her to be meek, and it was to Sulitea she owed her loyalty, regardless of circumstance.

The fat man walked on, through a jumble of street and little squares, to stop at last beside a door set in a high wall. Opening it, he gestured Cianna and Babalyn through, following and locking it behind them. Within was a garden, green and very still after the bustle of the streets. Fruits trees and low palms were spaced out on a lawn, and in a raised pond great golden yellow fish lazed in the shade of water lily leaves. Beyond was the house, of white washed stone and marble, an elegant, airy structure finer than anything she had seen.

'Remain here, kneeling,' the fat servant ordered, dropping their leads.

Babalyn obeyed, Cianna still standing as she looked about at the unfamiliar surroundings. The servant disappeared into the house.

'Kneel, Cianna,' Babalyn insisted. 'Do you want to be whipped?'

'No,' Cianna admitted, sinking to her knees, 'but it is undignified to kneel, save before the high-born to who I owe fealty.'

'You are his slave!' Babalyn hissed, then went quiet as Assivetes himself stepped from the house.

He walked over to them, a tiny cup in one hand, from which rose a wisp of steam and a scent unfamiliar to Cianna. As he walked around them, inspecting their bodies, he was smiling.

'A fair bargain,' he finally said, 'if you are capable of all you claim. I am a mild enough man, and demand little. Primarily obedience, prompt and without question, to all my commands. For erotic indulgence, I detest both reluctance and modesty. You will enjoy serving my body, and show it.'

'Yes, Elite Master,' Babalyn answered quickly.

'Yes,' Cianna agreed.

'You have much to learn,' he went on, giving Cianna's bottom a gentle prod with his foot. 'My title for one thing, which is Elite, and to you, Elite Master. Perhaps you are not fully aware of who I am?'

'No,' Cianna admitted.

'Very well, so that you may be properly in awe of me, you should know. I am the Admiral Assivetes, who commanded the vanguard of that fleet which drove the Vendjomois back off Cape Jendrine, eighteen years ago now. I have commanded in a dozen other engagements, and served for forty years before returning here, to my estates.'

Cianna struck her fist on the ground in the traditional Aeg gesture.

'Do you mock me?' Assivetes demanded.

'No,' she answered. 'I am greatly awed, although in Aegmund it is considered beneath a man to boast of his own achievements.'

For a moment his face clouded with anger, then he laughed, and continued.

'Well, pretty barbarian, you are no longer in Aegmund, wherever that may be. You are in Makea, and my property, so you must learn correct behaviour and proper respect. Where you a slave in this Aegmund?'

'There are no slaves in Aegmund,' she said.

'No slaves?' he demanded. 'How is anything done? No, don't answer that. I know enough of the Aprinians, with their insufferable superiority. Speaking of Aprinians, I am glad you've lost your arrogance,

Babalyn. Still, be warned, I will suffer no airs. Now, tonight I entertain. You will assist in waiting on my guests and myself, and afterwards you will perform. I wish passion, but I wish structure as well, so you are to decide upon an arrangement, something on the lines Ikail suggested. Fail to satisfy and you will both be whipped.'

He turned on his heel without further comment, disappearing inside the house. Cianna got up, Babalyn following suit more cautiously. Nobody was visible, only the fat orange fish and a bird with striking green plumage, perched in one of the trees.

'What are we to do?' Cianna asked.

'Something cruel, it must be,' Babalyn answered. 'Cruel yet subtle…'

'I mean now,' Cianna broke in.

'Now? Nothing, just sit in the garden and look pretty. This is the way with pleasure slaves. He has not bought us to wear ourselves out scrubbing and polishing. That will come when we are older.'

'We just sit here? All day?'

'No, silly, there will be a courtyard inside, and in the monsoon we are doubtless allowed under cover. You must remember that we are here not only to provide pleasure, but to allow him to display his wealth. To have slaves only for pleasure is a mark of some rank. Doubtless there are others, so remember, we may excite jealousy, especially if we have replaced some older pleasure slave who has now been assigned to the kitchen. Still, what comes will come. For now we must work out this entertainment.'

'We are supposed to play together, sexually?'

'Naturally.'

'I would be pleased to touch you, Babalyn, in any way you desire, as I do for Sulitea. Yet to perform nude, for men?'

'Women also, but please, Cianna, do not make it hard on us. I cannot bear to be whipped, I am simply too sensitive. I know your people are shy of your bodies, but we must do this, and well.'

'I will do it then, for your sake. What should we do?'

'Ikail suggested a game in which one of us is forced to betray the other, so sparing herself some indignity. They like to do that, especially to girls who are lovers, it affords them no end of amusement, the pigs! It could be simple, like tying us head to toe, side by side, and telling us the first to pee in the other's face will be let off, the other to be sodomised by all the male guests in turn.'

'That is cruel.'

'They think it funny, and place bets on who will break first.'

'You can spank me, if you wish, even by hand. Seeing me so humiliated should provide enough to slake their lust.'

'No, in Makea a spanked slave girl is too ordinary to arouse more than casual interest. Anyway, I suspect they would rather see me, the Aprinian who was a lady, spanked by you, the barbarian girl, without meaning offence. In any case, it is the idea of being forced to betray our love that really amuses them. Makean stories are full of the theme of betrayed loyalty. Fortunately we are not really lovers... not that I do not like you, but...'

'I understand. There is no formal bond of loyalty. I owe you no fealty.'

'No, so it should be easier than they imagine. Speaking of which, be affectionate, stroke my hair or skin occasionally. I have no wish to be sent back to Ikail's. Not that it is likely, but still.'

Cianna nodded and reached out to trace a slow line down the curve of one of Babalyn's big breasts, ending just short of the nipple. Babalyn gave a little shiver and glanced up to the house.

'Careful,' she said, 'or you will make it real. Now, as to our show. Assivetes wants passion and betrayal. There are sure to be women there, and for some reason they love to break slave girls' affection for one another. What of this? During the meal, I will feign a fancy for one or another of the women. You grow angry, and punish me, a spanking will do, after which you make me lick you. I then ask the woman to have you spanked in turn. Can you manage that?'

'Yes, although I would rather not be spanked by hand if it is avoidable.'

'Good, I'll suggest a cane or quirt. That they will enjoy, and while we have to tell Assivetes and the others of his household, the guests can think it is all genuine, which they will enjoy all the more. We will do well here, you'll see.'

Cianna bent, pouring the rich red drink, wine, into the goblet held out by Admiral Assivetes. As before, she was naked, but she and Babalyn had been washed and scented before the meal, by other, older female slaves. As Babalyn had predicted, there had been a touch of jealousy, but the women had seemed wary of her as well. Once fully clean, her hair had been combed out and tied up with a cloth in the gold and dark blue of the

Admiral's household. Slippers had also been provided, again in blue and gold, but nothing more.

Since then, she and Babalyn had been serving, pouring wine and offering sweetmeats to guests, running minor errands, such as fetching cushions, and bringing fresh supplies from the kitchens. There was also a great deal of fondling, with both the men and the women quite casually stroking the girls' bodies, also commenting on them, especially Cianna's skin. It was done in the same casual way she might have petted and praised a dog, making Cianna blush, until she had followed Babalyn's advice and simply blocked it from her mind.

Assivetes had approved their plan for the entertainment, and Babalyn had chosen who to flirt with. This was a woman of late middle age, dressed in flowing gown of gold cloth set with jewels. From the first she had seemed interested in Babalyn, tickling her under the chin and making her hold up her breasts for inspection. Babalyn had begun to flirt in response, mildly at first, then more openly, attending to the woman in preference to the others, and kneeling beside her chair to wait for instructions.

That left Cianna with most of the work, making it easier to cast jealous glances in Babalyn's direction. Cianna waited her moment, until she was in the little room from which they were serving the drink at the same time as Babalyn. Catching Babalyn's eye, she nodded, getting a wry smile in return.

'It is enough!' Cianna spat. 'I'll teach you to shirk!'

She stepped forward, grabbing Babalyn by the ear. Babalyn squeaked, in genuine pain, then again and she was pulled roughly down across Cianna's lap. They went down on a bench by the door, Babalyn's plush bottom stuck up in full view of the main room. A man saw, grinning as Cianna twisted Babalyn's arm tight up. Babalyn squealed, kicking her legs apart to give them a fine view of plump brown sex, and Cianna had started to spank, smacking the fleshy cheeks hard.

Babalyn was squealing immediately, for real, her chubby brown bottom dancing and wobbling under the punishment. Cianna kept on as the guests came to gather at the door, watching Babalyn punished with open delight, laughing and calling encouragement to Cianna. Soon Babalyn had lost all control, kicking and bucking her bottom up to show off her anus as well as her sex, to the yet greater amusement of the onlookers. The big buttocks began to take on a purple flush, goose pimples rising all over the well smacked surfaces, while Cianna could feel Babalyn's body shaking. Deciding that the punishment was sufficiently convincing, she delivered a last hard slap to the crest of each cheek, Cianna stopped, rolling Babalyn off her lap to sit down hard on the floor.

Her mouth wide, and with the first hint of tears in her eyes, Babalyn rose, rubbing at her sore bottom. Throwing Cianna a quick look of genuine admonishment, she scampered over to the woman she had been flirting with, falling to her knees. The woman looked down, smiling.

'Have her beaten, Elite Mistress!' Babalyn squeaked. 'Not for what she did to me, but for presumption.'

'Presumption, child?' the woman laughed. 'It what way is it presumptuous to spank a slave girl?'

'I mean her presumption in punishing me for showing favour to you, Elite Mistress,' Babalyn went on.

'Showing favour? To me?' the woman laughed. 'Oh you funny little thing! You do as I please, girl, do not forget that, you do not show favour. Assivetes, dearest, I fear you have an arrogant one here.'

'Aprinian,' Assivetes answered. 'Much of it has already been beaten out of her, but clearly not all.'

The woman nodded, then reached down, placing a finger under Babalyn's chin to tilt it up.

'How many times have you been sold, child?' she asked.

'Ten,' Babalyn admitted.

'Ten?' the woman answered. 'Then you are lucky still be in a worthy household. Let me explain to you what happens to girls who fail to learn proper respect, and perhaps you will be less conceited in future. They are sold, from place to place, and after a while they gain a reputation. At length it becomes clear that they are of no use whatever to anybody of taste and intelligence, and they start to be sold more cheaply, to lesser establishments. You wouldn't be lolling in a garden all day in that sort of household, let me assure you. No, you would be hard at work, scrubbing the floor with your ridiculous fat bottom wobbling behind you. Do you understand?'

'Yes, Elite Mistress,' Babalyn answered.

'And then,' the woman continued, 'if you still failed to please, you would be sold down, always for less, ever lower, and do you know where you will end up?'

Babalyn nodded her head, her eyes wide with fright.

'You will end up in the powdermills,' the woman went on, 'up to your knees in other peoples excrement by day, and what do you think the male slaves there will do to you? I'll tell you. They'll fuck you, they'll use your mouth, your fat tits, your bottom, all night, every night, at the bottom of a dark, stinking hole. Now are you going to behave?'

Babalyn nodded frantically.

'Good girl,' the woman said, straightening up. 'She is beginning to understand, Assivetes, dearest. I have a special touch with these things. Now the other. I think she should be punished. Why not, after all?'

'Indeed,' Assivetes agreed. 'In fact I think the pair of them need a lesson in obedience. Both of you, in here.'

Cianna went, into the main room where they been serving. A group of men had gathered around the central table. One beckoned to her, grinning and patting the table. She stepped forward and strong hands took her, spreading her out on the table top, legs and arms wide. She was held, hard, as cords were twisted around her wrists and ankles, then tied to the table legs, leaving her spread-eagled, helpless. Looking back, she could see them, grinning and making comments as they inspected her naked sex. She was blushing, and she could feel her tuppenny twitching in anticipation, her bottom hole too. A man noticed, and laughed, pointing. At that the woman Babalyn had been flirting with gave a lewd chuckle and stepped back, pulling a stubby candle from its holder.

'Hold her wide,' she said, 'this should do her some good.'

Cianna could do nothing as they laid hold of her bottom, pulling her cheeks wide to stretch out her anus. A man spat on her, full between her cheeks, and put a finger to her bottom ring, rubbing the spittle in before penetrating her. She gasped as she felt the finger slide up her bottom, then again as it was pulled out, to be replaced by the base of the candle, hurting as it went up, to wedge in her anus. She shut her eyes, her body trembling, waiting for the pain of the wax. It came, a sharp sting on the sensitive flesh of her straining bottom ring, making her cry out. They laughed at her response, and somebody slapped her bottom, sending fresh wax spraying across her cheeks and over her sex. She cried out again, drawing fresh laughter, and more slaps on her bottom and legs.

'Get the fat bottomed Aprinian slut up on this one's back,' somebody called.

'Fine,' another answered, 'and with a candle in her arsehole too. Let's see who begs for mercy first!'

'And whip them while the candles burn,' a third suggested. 'Hoy, you, fetch quirts'

Cianna saw the girl he had addressed run from the room, then turned her head at a touch, to find Babalyn crawling up onto the table, assisted by eager hands. Babalyn was laid down across Cianna, who felt the sweat on her friend's skin and the shivering of her flesh. Babalyn was lashed in place, whimpering as her hands and feet were tied down, then crying out as a thick candle was pushed up her bottom hole. The slave had returned, handing out quirts, and immediately they began to beat Cianna, Babalyn also, calling out their bets as they struck. The cuts stung, a sharp, biting pain, delivered across her bottom and thighs, as often as not sending a splash of hot wax onto her tortured skin. She held back, her teeth gritted, trying to ignore the pain and also the rising, shameful heat in her sex.

In no time Babalyn was crying for mercy, begging for them to stop as her flesh twitched and shivered against Cianna's. Their tormentors took no notice, save for those who had hoped Babalyn would hold out longer to curse and apply fresh, harder blows to the black girl's quivering buttocks. Still Cianna held herself, shaking her head in her pain, writhing in her bonds, with the burning pain of the wax and agonising snaps of the whip coming again and again.

Her defiance only drove them to beat her harder, three of them lashing at her bottom and legs. Others took new candles, dripping the hot wax over her buttocks and legs, Babalyn's too, until both where squirming their sweaty bodies on the table, screaming and gasping. Somebody began to whip Cianna's sex, smacking the tip of the quirt down, over and over, full onto her clitoris. She screamed, cursing them, but unable to hold herself back, and she was coming, sticking her bottom high in tortured ecstasy.

'Oh do look!' a woman called. 'She's had a climax, how funny!'

'A typical slut!'

'Make the other one come too! Oh they are amusing!'

Cianna heard Babalyn's grunt of pain and frustration as the attention was turned to her. She was near exhaustion, her skin wet with sweat, every welt a line of fire on her skin, but all that she could think of was that she'd never begged for mercy, even when they'd whipped her tuppenny. Squeezing her anus, she pushed out the candle, which was quickly snatched away by one of the older slave girls.

Babalyn had started to come, whimpering and mewling, her flesh squirming on Cianna's as she was masturbated and whipped at the same time. She had been begging for mercy, pleading with them to stop, only to suddenly cry out in helpless ecstasy as her sex responded, and Cianna knew she too had been brought to climax.

'I shall have the pale one lick me, I think,' a fat woman in a brilliant green robe announced. 'If I might, Assivetes darling?'

'Naturally, my dear,' the Admiral, 'everybody must enjoy them just as they please. That is, after all, what they're for.'

There was a burst of laughter and hands began to pull at Cianna's bonds, Babalyn's also. She was dragged from the table, down onto the floor. Immediately she was mounted, some man holding her up under her bottom as he pushed the full length of his erection into her sex. She saw Babalyn fucked, rolled up on her back and held by the ankles, with the man watching as his penis filled her hole. Then the scene had been blotted beneath the fat woman's robes as a plump thigh was swung over her body. For a moment she saw a huge bottom poised over her head, green within the emerald robe, and then it was in her face, the big, soft buttocks spread wide, the sex on her mouth, her nose up the anus. Helpless, she began to lick.

They took turns with her, one by one, using her without the slightest thought for her needs. She was fucked repeatedly, in a dozen different positions, buggered again and again, and more than once made to suck cocks that had been up her bottom. They made her drink wine, and some stinging spirit, twice pouring it up her sex before plunging a fat cock into her wet hole. She was made to lick Babalyn, anally, with the onlookers clapping in delight as they watched her tongue wriggle into the fleshy, brown bottom hole.

Not long after that, Babalyn simply collapsed, with a cock up her bottom and another in her mouth at the time. Both men finished off in her unconcious body, and Cianna was made to lick up the sperm that bubbled and spurted from her friend's anus, before two of the older slave girls helped her away. From then the orgy began to calm down, until Cianna at last found herself unattended, lying over a stupefied man's lap with his fingers still up her sex.

She freed herself, rising unsteadily to her feet. Her head was swimming with drink, and she was sore all over, with sperm coating her face and breasts and dribbling from her tuppenny and bottom ring. Nobody was paying attention to her, the guests spent. Assivetes was still awake, boasting drunkenly of his exploits to the fat woman who had sat on Cianna's face. The woman who Babalyn had chosen was not, but lay sprawled on a couch, face down, a goblet still clutched in her nerveless fingers. Cianna risked a gentle kick at one slim buttock, just enough to bruise.

Exhausted, Cianna let herself be led back to part of the house where the slaves slept. It was a single room, illuminated with one smoking candle. She was shown a threadbare blanket, and collapsed onto it immediately, face down for the comfort of her sore bottom. The candle was extinguished and she was left in darkness. They had punished her, and tortured her for their sexual amusement. She had submitted to it, and even come, an act of shameful wantonness, yet it was impossible not to feel some restoration of her hurt pride. She had taken it, all of it, never once begging for mercy, unlike Babalyn.

To have been defeated by a dozen men and nearly as many women was no disgrace. What mattered was that she was unbroken, not snivelling and whimpering on the floor. It felt good, and she wondered if that was what Sulitea had meant about chains not being important.

Thinking of Sulitea reminded her of how the woman had threatened Babalyn, with being sent to somewhere called the powdermills. From what Babalyn had said before, it seemed likely to be where the black powder was made. It also seemed to be where the worst girls were sent, the ones who never learnt, the ones who, ultimately, could never be slaves in their own minds. To try and be sent there was what Sulitea would have expected of her, and it also let her keep her pride. She nodded to herself in the darkness, smiling.

Unfortunately Assivetes proved an indulgent master, content as long as she did more or less what she was told. His own preference lay in watching her, generally tied up, as the fat steward or one of the two male Makean slaves fucked her. When they were done, and she was lying trussed and helpless with sperm dribbling out of one orifice or another, he would put the tip of his erect cock in her mouth, vagina or bottom hole, to finish himself off by hand. It was a technique that gave her little scope for disobedience.

It was also difficult to know what to do about Babalyn. The two of them had become closer and closer, until they were sleeping together and having sex by choice as often as to entertain guests. This seemed to be taken for granted, and Cianna quickly found herself getting over her embarrassment at public sex, as she had over public nudity. Nor where Babalyn's fears of jealousy realised, with the other three female slaves all quite happy to go about their domestic chores and with no urge to try and enforce their seniority.

There was also the possibility of getting the knowledge she wanted directly from Assivetes. Asking him directly was certain to seem strange, yet when there were no guests he was more than happy to boast of his achievements as she and Babalyn knelt at his feet after the evening meal. Most of these involved battle, and the interminable conflict that existed between the Makeans and the Vendjomois on the mainland of Apraya. Eventually she was sure she would find an opening so that she could ask how the black powder was made. Her chance came on the evening of the tenth day, as she listened to his account of the defence of a coastal fort.

'We were nearly out of powder,' he was saying, 'ball also, with three of their ships lying off, each with some two hundred men. We might have sunk one as they came in, perhaps, two, but never all three, when I lit on the idea of heating our ball to incandescence…'

'Could you not have made more powder?' Cianna asked. 'And used rocks for ball?'

'No,' Assivetes laughed, 'ball must fit the mouth of the bombard, almost exactly. Rocks would be likely to jam, and kill us all. As to the powder, it is not so easily made.'

'It is made from dung, I thought,' Cianna said, 'by some process.'

'In part,' Assivetes answered, 'but not solely. Yet with the right ingredients it is remarkably simple to make, which is why it is not suitable knowledge for slaves. Not that I think for a moment you would attempt a revolt, little Cianna, yet knowledge spreads. Even at the powdermills each component is kept strictly separate, with the slaves never meeting. The actual mixing is done by citizens. But as I was saying…'

He went on, describing how he had forced the Vendjomois to retreat with their sails blazing. Cianna had begun to play with her necklace, feeling frustrated, but sure that it would be unwise to press the point. Babalyn returned, with the flagon of wine she had been sent for, the fat steward immediately behind her, bowing unctuously to Assivetes before speaking.

'The Elite Lady Lai-Kasae is here, Elite,' he announced.

'Indeed? Show her in then,' Assivetes answered immediately.

Even as he spoke a woman appeared in the doorway, the one Babalyn had chosen to flirt with. She was in a robe of gold and scarlet, her hair set with jewels, and clearly drunk, resting on the arm of a muscular male slave.

'Lai-Kasae, my dear,' Assivetes greeted her. 'What brings you here? Do sit. Babalyn, a fresh goblet, wine for the Elite.'

Babalyn hurried to obey, Lai-Kasae allowing the male slave to help her down onto a couch.

'I came for a favour,' she asked, 'just a little thing, which I'm sure you won't deny me, dearest.'

'As you know, I can never refuse you,' Assivetes answered.

'I had hoped you would let me play with your pretty new slaves,' she went on. 'We had such fun the other night, and my own girls seem so dull. They have no spirit, and I do so want to hear that fat bottomed Aprinian slut howl again. The pale savage too. I want to break her. Just let me have them for the night, and I'll send over three of my little nut coloured Vendjomois bitches to keep you amused.'

'They are yours,' Assivetes answered casually, gesturing to Cianna. 'I ask only that they are sent back with their skin intact.'

'Oh I shan't hurt them, dearest,' Lai-Kasae went on. 'No more than a little, anyway. I don't suppose their bottoms are even healed yet, after all.'

'Not entirely,' Assivetes admitted, reaching down to smack at Cianna's thigh.

Cianna moved, showing her bottom, and the back of her thighs, which were still welted, with fading bruising covering much of her skin.

'It does show up on such pale flesh,' Lai-Kasae remarked. 'No matter, she can take a little more I dare say, and her breasts are quite fresh.'

Babalyn came back, to pour wine, which Lai-Kasae swallowed at a gulp, holding out her goblet for more.

'You're coming home with me,' Lai-Kasae announced. 'Your savage friend too. Aren't you lucky little things?'

'Yes, Elite Mistress,' Babalyn answered, failing to hide the tremor in her voice.

'She is already scared,' Lai-Kasae laughed. 'How wonderful! Does anyone train a slave girl quite like me, Assivetes dearest?'

'You have a knack, certainly,' Assivetes admitted.

'I do,' Lai-Kasae admitted, then gestured to her male slave. 'Now, this big ox here will help me home, and come back with my girls. He can fuck them for you too. I know you like that, don't you, dearest?'

Assivetes nodded as Lai-Kasae made to rise, leaning heavily on her slave. Cianna exchanged a look with Babalyn, who seemed to be on the verge of tears, but followed obediently as the woman they had been given to for the night lurched from the room.

Walking behind Lai-Kasae, they left the house, making their way through the warm, sticky Makean night, to a door in a wall, much like the one which led into the garden of Assivetes. Inside was a small courtyard, with twin cressets throwing black shadow and red light from trees and bushes. Cianna took Babalyn's hand, finding it trembling and wet with sweat.

Three of the small brown skinned Vendjomois girls sat on the grass beneath the cresset. At the approach of their mistress they put their faces to the ground, to be dismissed at a word, following the Makean from the courtyard. Cianna and Babalyn followed Lai-Kasae into the house, which was oddly silent. They climbed the stairs, into a wide chamber illuminated by a dozen candles, with the arches that normally gave onto the outside hidden behind drapes.

'We are alone,' Lai-Kasae stated, 'and we shall remain alone until the morning. Pour wine.'

Babalyn moved to where a tray stood on a table, with a jug and three goblets. Pouring one, she brought it to Lai-Kasae.

'You also,' Lai-Kasae said. 'Both of you.'

Babalyn obeyed, pouring a second goblet with a shaking hand, then a third. Cianna took hers, sipping at the rich red wine.

'Have you tasted such wine before?' Lai-Kasae asked.

Cianna shook her head.

'Yes, Elite Lady,' Babalyn answered quietly.

'When you were free, I suspect you often drank vintages as fine,' Lai-Kasae went on.

Babalyn nodded.

'You were as high, perhaps, as I,' Lai-Kasae said. 'How does it feel, to have been made a slave?'

Babalyn cast Cianna a worried look, mumbling something incoherent.

'You need not be afraid, little one,' Lai-Kasae went on. 'Answer me.'

'Terrible,' Babalyn answered quietly.

'Still unbroken then,' Lai-Kasae said thoughtfully. 'My little Vendjomois girls welcome their role. They understand that it is their nature. Some of us are free, little Babalyn, some slave. You, I think, are truly slave. You, Cianna, I am less certain of. Perhaps we shall discover? Now, we shall play dice, and on each throw, she who looses will be punished. First then, for a breast whipping. Kneel on the floor.'

As Cianna and Babalyn knelt, Lai-Kasae walked quickly to a trunk, opening it to extract a horn cup and three six sided dice. Cianna took another swallow of her wine, her determination not to be broken rising inside her. Dipping further into the trunk, Lai-Kasae pulled out a short quirt, then a hank of red silk cord, the sight drawing a little whimpering noise from Babalyn.

'To add spice,' Lai-Kasae said as she returned to them, 'I must exceed your score if I am to punish you. Now, Babalyn, throw.'

Babalyn took the cup, her hand trembling, and threw the dice out onto the rug. A total of fourteen spots showed, and Babalyn's lips moved in what might have been a prayer. Lai-Kasae took the dice, shaking them in the cup and throwing them out. Only seven spots showed, and to Cianna's surprise she gave a little drunken giggle. Cianna exchanged a look with Babalyn, but said nothing, taking the cup herself. She rolled, her heart sinking to see only five spots showing.

'Quirt her, Babalyn,' Lai-Kasae ordered. 'Six cuts. Stick out your breasts, Cianna.'

'I should whip her?' Babalyn queried.

'Do as you are told,' Lai-Kasae answered.

'Yes, Elite Mistress,' Babalyn answered, picking up the quirt.

Cianna had placed her hands behind her head, thrusting out her bare breasts towards Babalyn. The quirt came up, and down, a light blow, barely stinging.

'Harder,' Lai-Kasae ordered. 'Make her cry out.'

Babalyn nodded, again bringing down the quirt across Cianna's breasts, now harder, making them quiver and leaving a pale red line across the milky white surfaces.

'Harder, I said, much harder,' Lai-Kasae demanded. 'Come, I want passion. I want pain.'

The quirt smacked down again, and Cianna gasped, the leather tip catching one nipple. Both were erect, sticking proudly up from the crests of her breasts, one now marked with an angry red line.

'Better,' Lai-Kasae said, 'now underneath. Make them jump.'

Babalyn obeyed, planting a firm cut on the undersides of Cianna's breasts to make them bounce and wobble. Cianna gasped at the pain, feeling the tears start in her eyes. Again Babalyn cut, higher and harder, and again Cianna squeaked in reaction, then again as the sixth cut fell, full across her nipples.

'Enough,' Lai-Kasae stated.

Cianna sat back, hugging her whipped breasts. Her breathing was fast, and ragged, her sex warm, and she knew that even if she was broken, she was likely to reach a climax first.

'Again,' Lai-Kasae said. 'Twelve cuts this time. Cianna, throw.'

Cianna took the cup and threw, her mouth coming open in horror and all three dice settled to show a single spot. Babalyn giggled, Lai-Kasae giving a faint click of her tongue. Taking up the cup, Lai-Kasae threw, scoring twelve, then Babalyn, with eight. Cianna already had her breasts pushed out as Lai-Kasae reached for the quirt.

She was trembling, her breasts quivering as Lai-Kasae bent the shaft of the quirt back, eyes glittering with pleasure. It snapped in, hard across Cianna's breasts, drawing out a cry of pain. Lai-Kasae laughed, again drawing the shaft back, and again letting go. Cianna was watching, and saw the quirt smack into the flesh of her breasts, high up, making them quiver and bounce as she gasped in response.

A third cut was laid in, and a fourth, until Cianna was trembling hard and mumbling prayers, struggling to keep her chest pushed out and not to beg. Lai-Kasae kept on, stroke after cruel stroke, until Cianna's breast flesh bore a mess of scarlet welts, wet with sweat, the nipples straining to attention. Yet she held herself, until it was over, taking a hurried swallow of wine. Lai-Kasae was plainly excited, her eyes bright and her mouth slightly open, her full lips quivering slightly as she once more picked up the cup.

'A cunt whipping,' she said softly. 'Six strokes.'

Cianna swallowed hard, watching as the dice rolled out, to show six spots. Lai-Kasae gave a little sob, to Cianna's surprise, and passed Babalyn the cup. Babalyn rolled, scoring ten, then Cianna, with a full fifteen, looking up to find Lai-Kasae wide eyed and trembling.

Without a word, Lai-Kasae turned, pushing out her bottom. Cianna and Babalyn exchanged looks of surprise, but Lai-Kasae was already pulling up her gorgeous robe, exposing a slim, naked bottom, the dark cheeks spread wide.

'Am I to beat you?' Cianna queried.

Lai-Kasae nodded. Her eyes were closed, her lower lip trembling hard, but her bottom was flaunted, lifted high enough to show the pouting lips of her sex, with white fluid glistening at the mouth of her vagina. Cianna glanced at Babalyn again, who shrugged and passed her the quirt.

Cianna took it, bending the shaft back as she moved it close to Lai-Kasae's trim sex lips and letting go to smack the tip down onto the soft flesh. Lai-Kasae screamed, then sank face down onto the rug, sobbing, but still with her bottom lifted. Cianna smacked her again, on the mound of her sex, wringing fresh cries, to leave Lai-Kasae shaking and panting on the floor. Again Cianna applied the quirt, and again, leaving the dark flesh of Lai-Kasae's sex criss-crossed with purple lines. She was clutching at the rug, and making little snivelling noises, but she stayed still, for Cianna to finish off the whipping, with two firms cuts, full between the lips of her sex.

Lai-Kasae sank face down, in tears, her swollen, puffy sex pushed out towards the girls. Cianna reversed the quirt, and slid the handle into the wet hole of Lai-Kasae's sex, provoking only a low moan. Slowly, Cianna began to fuck her, moving the quirt handle in and out. When Lai-Kasae made no protest, Cianna became bolder, reaching under Lai-Kasae's sex to stroke the welts and rub the big, glossy clitoris that was poking out from between her sex lips.

Babalyn moved closer, reaching out to stroke Lai-Kasae's bottom, then to plant a timid, experimental smack on one trim cheek. In response Lai-Kasae gave a tiny, broken sob and lifted her bottom. Babalyn smacked again, more firmly, making Lai-Kasae's bottom quiver. Again Lai-Kasae gave a muted cry, unmistakably of pleasure. Gaining confidence, Babalyn began to spank, slapping Lai-Kasae's bottom with firm, open handed swats. Lai-Kasae moaned, pushing her bottom right up, and she was coming, under Cianna's fingers, her sex contracting on the quirt, her anus winking, calling out in ecstasy.

'Tie me. Use me,' she sighed as she rolled over onto the floor. 'Debase me, anything.'

Cianna took the cord, still uncertain, but Lai-Kasae said nothing, only lifting her arms as Babalyn reached out to pull off the robe. Nude, Lai-Kasae seemed younger, and smaller, her pert body no different from that of any other girl, slave or not. Her chest was heaving, her eyes glazed, and as Cianna began to tie her ankles together she merely sighed. Babalyn joined in, pulling Lai-Kasae's arms down to her ankles, to allow Cianna to tie them off. More bonds followed, in a pattern Cianna had herself been put in more than once, knees tucked up to her chest, wrists bound to ankles, thighs tied to the upper body, helpless, with her sex vulnerable, also her bottom.

'Now use me,' Lai-Kasae sighed as Cianna tied off the last knot. 'Make me learn how it feels to be a slave. Punish me, debase me, make me lick you both.'

'She is like me,' Babalyn said, 'before I was taken. I used to come over how it would feel. Not now. Her need is genuine though, use her.'

'I'm going to sit on her head then!' Cianna declared gleefully. 'To make her lick my tuppenny, and to put her tongue well up my bottom, as that fat woman made me the other night.'

Babalyn clapped in delight as Cianna rolled Lai-Kasae onto her back, face up, eyes wide, full mouth a little open. Giggling, Cianna took a draught of her wine, then cocked a leg across Lai-Kasae's prone body, settling her bottom down onto the bound woman's face.

'Lick me!' Cianna ordered, rubbing her sex in Lai-Kasae's face. 'Tuppenny first.'

Lai-Kasae obeyed immediately, probing Cianna's sex with her tongue, in the hole, then onto the clitoris.

'She's doing it!' Cianna sighed. 'Oh lovely! Yes, like that. Fuck her, Babalyn. She's sure to have a dildo for her slaves!'

Babalyn went to the chest, laughing, rummaging briefly before pulling out a great wooden phallus with a system of straps attached to it. As Cianna rode Lai-Kasae's face, Babalyn fitted the dildo, fumbling the straps in her haste. Cianna turned, eager to watch, settling her bottom on Lai-Kasae's face once more, only now with her anus against the woman's nose. As Babalyn squatted down, Cianna wriggled her bottom, squirming her bottom ring against Lai-Kasae's snub nose so that the tip went up. Babalyn took the phallus, pushing the head to Lai-Kasae's sex, and up, laughing as their erstwhile Mistress' vagina filled. Lai-Kasae was shivering, her whole body tense, moving on the fat dildo inside her and licking at Cianna's sex.

For a moment Cianna moved forward, pressing her bumhole to Lai-Kasae's mouth and laughing aloud as a little sharp tongue poked up her bottom ring, licking the hot, wet hole.

'She's tonguing me, Babalyn!' Cianna called. 'Right up my bottom ring! Right in the hole!'

Babalyn laughed in response, and leant forward, taking Cianna in her arms. They kissed, mouths open, tongues entwined. Cianna put her hands on Babalyn's breasts, feeling the meaty globes and stroking the big nipples, each with its twist of wire. Babalyn was squirming, rubbing her sex on the base of the dildo, and all the while fucking Lai-Kasae. Cianna moved once more, pressing Lai-Kasae's nose back up her bottom. Once more her clitoris was being licked, urgently, and she was starting to come, holding on tight to Babalyn, kissing hard, wiggling her bottom into Lai-Kasae's face, her whole body going taught as the climax hit her. Babalyn was still trying to get there, and Cianna held on, cuddling her friend and stroking her breasts, until with a gasp she too came.

They climbed off, giggling. Lai-Kasae lay still, breathing deeply. Her face was a mess, smeared with Cianna's juices, her sex open, gaping for entry. She said nothing, but as Cianna put the goblet to her lips she swallowed, spilling some wine to add to the white fluid around her mouth.

'Do we untie her?' Cianna asked.

'Only if she orders it,' Babalyn answered. 'Meanwhile, she said she wanted to be used, and I need to pee.'

'To pee?' Cianna demanded.

'Why not?' Babalyn answered. 'She made me drink hers the other night, from a goblet, with everyone watching, including the other slaves. It's probably her favourite thing to be made to do it herself.'

Cianna shrugged, but Lai-Kasae made no move to resist as Babalyn squatted over her, plump, dark sex directly above Lai-Kasae's face.

'Here?'

Babalyn merely shrugged and let go, sending a spray of urine out into the woman's face. Immediately Lai-Kasae's mouth came open, taking the pee in and struggling to swallow, but failing, leaving it bubbling out at the sides of her mouth. Babalyn laughed, and squatted lower, directing the full force of her stream in Lai-Kasae's open mouth. Cianna put her hand to her mouth, giggling to see the woman who had always been cruel to them drinking her friend's piddle in obvious pleasure.

'Do it up her tuppenny!' Cianna laughed, and Babalyn responded, rising, with pee still spurting from her sex.

For a moment the thick stream of yellow fluid was splashing over Lai-Kasae's bound legs, then onto her sex, filling the open hole to gush out and run down between her buttocks. Cianna laughed aloud, wondering what further indignities they could inflict before the game came to a halt. Lai-Kasae was drunk, very drunk, and it seemed likely that in the end both Babalyn and Cianna would suffer, but for the moment they had their victim helpless and highly aroused. It was too good to hold back.

Taking the quirt, Cianna began to flick as Lai-Kasae's sex, sending Babalyn's pee spraying in every direction. Babalyn giggled and squatted lower, pissing directly onto Lai-Kasae's clitoris as Cianna flicked at the little bud with the quirt. At that Lai-Kasae called out, in ecstasy, coming a second time.

'Oh do look!' Cianna called, in mocking imitation of Lai-Kasae's voice. 'She's had a climax, how funny!'

Babalyn giggled again, standing to empty the last of her pee into Lai-Kasae's face. Wiggling her bottom to shake free the last few drops, Babalyn climbed off Lai-Kasae, and jumped onto the bed, beckoning Cianna to follow. They came together, kissing and stroking, laughing as they petted each other, with the woman they had used so well looking on meekly from the floor. Before long they were head to tail, faces sunk in each other's tuppennies, licking and stroking. Cianna was going to come, lost in the pleasure of her friend's body, her face buried in the plump black sex lips, when she heard the thump of a closing door. She was coming, holding tight to Babalyn and licking desperately, telling herself it was the wind, only to see new light flare, flickering on the ceiling.

A voice sounded, male, calling Lai-Kasae's name. Babalyn jumped up, Cianna too, making for the doorway in desperate hope of putting the newcomer off, but too late. He was already on the landing, a young man in the fine robes of a Makean Elite, looking into the room with his mouth open in amazement.

'Help me,' Lai-Kasai quavered, 'they've violated me.'

Chapter Four

Cianna lay huddled in the bottom of the cart, sore, miserable and furious. Her buttocks and thighs were sore from the vicious whipping she and Babalyn had been given for the supposed ravishing of Lai-Kasai. It had been done with them strung up by their hands, face to face, in the courtyard of the house. Their pleas and protests had gone for nothing, Lai-Kasae's word accepted without question, theirs dissmissed, only earning them slaps and curses.

Once thoroughly beaten, the girls had been tied hand and foot, gagged and thrown into a cellar. All night they had lain there, terrified, until in the morning the fat steward who worked for Assivetes had arrived, with two male slaves. Without a word, their questions ignored, the girls had been bundled into the back of a cart. Old blankets had been thrown over them and they had left Lai-Kasai's house, and Ketawa itself, until as the dawn light penetrated the thin weave over her head, Cianna found that she could glimpse trees to either side of them.

She stretched, trying to free her head. A voice warned her to stay down and a whip cracked against her leg. She lay still, confused, wondering where she was going, wanting to struggle and try to spit the foul tasting gag from her mouth, but knowing it would only earn her further blows of the whip.

The cart moved on, bumping along an uneven road. Three times it turned, before it finally stopped and Cianna heard the creak of a gate being opened. Her interest rose, her fear too, as the cart moved in under an arch, then out of the sunlight. She heard the driver dismount, and a moment later the blanket was pulled from her head. A man was standing over her, hugely fat, in leather trousers like the ones Gaidrhed had worn, but dyed a brilliant scarlet and held up by a thick black belt.

He was grinning, with no anger or malice in his face, just satisfaction, and Cianna felt an immediate wave of relief. Looking down on then, he reached into a pocket, extracting a long tube that appeared to be made of leaves. In shape it looked uncomfortably as if it might be made to go up girl's tuppennies. Cianna felt her apprehension rising again. Digging in his pocked once more, he produced a small stick with a yellow tip, which he struck smartly on the wall, causing a puff of flame and an odd smell. Cianna's apprehension turned to fear as he lit the end of the roll of leaves, only to fade as he stuck the other end into his mouth and took a long suck on it, blowing smoke out through his nose. Stepping closer, he tweaked the gag from Cianna's mouth, then Babalyn's.

'Twenty standard the pair!' he said with immense pleasure as his eyes wandered down their naked bodies. 'Now that is a bargain! Well, I'd better untie you then, if you're going to behave?'

'I will, Master,' Babalyn said immediately, Cianna nodding agreement.

'You will indeed,' he said, ducking down to start on Cianna's bonds.

He hummed to himself as he untied them, happily, then helped them from the cart. They were in a high room, open to the air at one side, through which a courtyard could be seen, with a wall beyond, trees and distant hills beyond that. The man attended to the cattle which had pulled the cart as Cianna and Babalyn rubbed the circulation back into the limbs. Finished, he came to lean on a squat wooden frame, on top of which had been fixed a broad leather saddle. Cianna glanced at it with new apprehension.

'A horse and saddle,' he said, gesturing with the roll of leaves, 'both for the sake of discipline and my entertainment.'

'Have mercy,' Babalyn answered. 'We've been whipped, terribly!'

'Oh I've no mind to whip you, he answered, just to introduce myself, to your cunts. Up on the saddle, both of you.'

'Both?' Cianna asked, looking doubtfully at the thing.

'Just do as he says,' Babalyn said quickly. 'You first.'

Puzzled, Cianna climbed onto the saddled, parting her legs around the broad seat to leave her thighs well spread and her bottom pushed up, the highest part of her body. The man watched, puffing smoke and grinning as Babalyn climbed on in turn, mounting Cianna and pushing her down onto the soft leather. The man laughed at the sight and put his hand to his belt, pulling it free. Cianna winced, expecting her thighs beaten again, only to have him wrap it around the horse, herself and Babalyn, buckling it to fix them firmly in place.

'That's to make sure you stay were you're put,' he said. 'Now, some cock for you to share. Get me hard.'

His trousers had fallen, and he kicked them off, lifting his smock to expose a huge, hairy belly and an ample set of genitals. Stepping to near their heads, he pushed his cock at Babalyn's face. She took it, sucking as Cianna reluctantly began to kiss his balls, then to lick at them as he grew in Babalyn's mouth. As they sucked he fondled as much of their breasts as he could get at, and also Babalyn's bottom. In no time he was hard, and after making perfunctory use of Cianna's mouth with his cock, he stepped behind them.

'What a sight!' he crowed. 'Two fat cunts, one above the other. Arseholes too, and all with a fat cigar! I don't know where to put it first.'

Babalyn gave a little gasp and the man chuckled. A moment later Cianna felt something firm press to her sex and up, oddly warm, until she realised that he had put the unlit end of the cigar in her tuppenny. The smoke was filling her sex, hot enough to have her gasping until he took the cigar out and substituted the head of his cock. She sighed despite herself, but the attention was immediately transferred to Babalyn.

In no hurry, he amused himself with them, rubbing his cock against their sexes. Again and again the head of his cock was popped into one hole or the other, smacked in the wet flesh of their vulvas, or pressed to their bottom rings to taunt them with sodomy. He used the cigar as well, poking it into all four holes, ever deeper as they became more slimy. After each instertion he took a puff, enjoying the taste of the their vaginas and bottom holes. As he did it he masturbated, tugging at his big cock left handed.

At last, when Cianna was wondering if she was actually going to get fucked at all, he had put the cigar down and put his cock in properly. It was big, stretching her tuppenny, and she sighed despite herself, taking a firm grip on the horse as he began to fuck her.

Her welts smarted, but her pleasure was rising, the pain growing dim with the feel of the cock inside her. Again she sighed, relaxing, only to have it pulled out and put up Babalyn instead, fucking her, with his balls now slapping on Cianna's flesh.

He began to grunt, then to gasp, slamming into them, his fat stomach squashing over and over against their flesh. His cock went up Cianna again, hard, unexpectedly, but was pulled out after only a few thrusts. An instant later wet, hot sperm splashed across her buttocks, and between them, on Babalyn too, to drip down and pool in Cianna's anus.

'Fine,' he grunted, 'fuck them well on the first day and they'll eat out of your hand, that's my way.'

He undid the belt, allowing the girls to climb off. Feeling stiff and sore, Cianna went to sit on a pile of sacks, to which the man made no objection. Leaning on the cart, he waited until both of them were ready, then spoke.

'I am Jelkrael, your new owner. By profession I am an impresario, of a specialist nature. I run fighting girls for pits both public and private, a sport you may know something of?'

'A little,' Babalyn admitted carefully.

'It is not important,' he continued. 'What is important is that both of you are now part of my stable, and will shortly be taking part in a tour. Cianna, you are to be a fighting girl...'

'Who do I fight?' Cianna asked. 'And what with?'

'Other girls, nude, with nothing but your bare hands, this is entertainment, not some barbarian brawl,' he answered. 'Babalyn, you will announce the rounds and assist me with the books. You can do math, I trust?

Good. All will go well, I am sure, but above all things I require the loyalty of my staff and girls. Is this clear?'

'Naturally,' Babalyn said, 'we are your property. Yours to command as you please.'

'Exactly,' Jelkrael replied, 'but in case of doubt, note that the horse and saddle over which you have just been fucked can work equally well when girls need to be whipped. The rules are these. Obey me, and the staff also. Speak to nobody outside the camp, ever, and if somebody should attempt to speak to you, report it immediately. Dalliances with outsiders are forbidden, absolutely. I and the staff will fuck you as we please, but if you want sex at other times, amuse each other. Now come, I wish to introduce you to your stablemates.'

They followed as he made for a low door, into the interior of the building, a structure much like the house of Assivetes but plainer. Passing along a short passage, he pushed his way through a beaded curtain to where three people sat on mats around a low dais.

'Here,' Jelkrael said, indicating a thin young man, 'is the crafty Yufal, adept in all matters pertaining to the placing of bets. And here, Klia, my seasoned warrior, and here, my last acquisition, who I intend to make a champion.'

Cianna turned to the last person indicated, finding herself staring at Yuilla.

For two days Cianna remained in Jelkrael's house, never once stepping outside. Jelkrael himself had gone, to arrange a contest, leaving the house to be managed by Yufal, the two males slaves he kept as guards and the girls. Of these, Klia was friendly, Yuilla cold, issuing orders as if she herself were free until she became put off by Cianna's failure to respond. Sexually, they were left largely unmolested, Yufal generally preferring Klia and Yuilla apparently determined to keep both the male slaves permanently satisfied. Glad of the respite, both Cianna and Babalyn spent much of their time on their pallets, allowing their bruises to heal.

On the third day the girls found themselves growing bored, and determined to explore. It had been made clear that they should not leave the compound, and Babalyn had managed to convince Cianna that escape was pointless, but there was a substantial garden, which seemed likely to contain fruit trees. Leaving by a side door, they came out into a yard, bathed in bright sunlight, and empty except for a squat kennel, outside which a large black and brown dog lay dozing. Cianna gave a delighted exclamation and walked quickly over. The dog looked up, eyeing her suspiciously, then snuffling at her hand as she bent down beside it.

'Do not touch it!' Babalyn urged. 'It is a horrible thing!'

'No,' Cianna answered, stroking the dog's huge head. 'He is lovely. Aren't you, boy?'

'You do not know what you do!' Babalyn insisted. 'That is a cunt dog, trained to run down girls and mount them! They do it for sport, and to punish runaway slaves. Leave it, Cianna!'

'He wouldn't hurt me,' Cianna answered, tickling the dog behind one ear. 'Look, he's just a big baby!'

The dog had rolled, a huge pink tongue lolling out of its mouth as it showed off its belly. Cianna continued to stroke and tickle, laughing as the pink head of the beast's penis emerged from the hairy sheaf. Babalyn gave a gasp of horror, backing against the wall.

'He'll fuck you, Cianna!' she gabbled. 'One chance and he'll fuck you! Quick, come inside!'

'No he won't!' Cianna replied, rubbing the dog's belly, which made its cock extend yet further from the prepuce. 'Well, perhaps he would, but it would be no worse than old Assivetes.'

'Cianna!'

Cianna laughed, and continued to tickle the dog, only to rise as the compound gate swung open. Jelkrael appeared, smoking a cigar and grinning more broadly than ever as he waved them over.

'I see you've met Glaucum,' he said, 'who is trained to provide naughty slave girls with a punishment I find more effective than even the saddle and whip. Run, and he will track you down, should you flee to Kea itself. And when he does... But we need not talk of such things, need we? No, you are loyal slaves, both, and you at least, Cianna, are to play an important part in my coming venture. Inside, and gather the others, I intend to explain.'

They went, calling out for Yufal and the other slaves, who quickly gathered in the main chamber. Presently Jelkrael entered, rubbing his hands in satisfaction.

'Attend carefully,' he began. 'I have arranged bouts in Port Utis and in Ioto. The first will introduce Cianna, who will win against Klia, thus sparking her reputation. The second will be for Cianna to be beaten in turn by Yuilla, whose victory will then seem all the more spectacular. From there, I intend to build her reputation as we travel around the coast towards Kea, with a series of victories over ever more redoubtable opposition from other stables, bought, naturally. Presently, the bookmakers will realise that she is being built up to challenge Moloa, the champion in Kea itself. They will know the matches are being thrown, although the majority of the public will not. Odds on Yuilla will become prohibitive, those on her opponents increasingly long. Now, and here is the clever part. Instead of building her up to a challenge with Moloa, and taking a sixth share of a good gate, I will allow another impresario to buy the last match before we challenge Moloa, probably in Kea itself. Thus I will recoup my expenses in providing Yuilla with her opponents and make a true fortune by the judicious placing of bets. For now, she needs an initial and spectacular victory to set matters afoot. Cianna, is this clear?'

'Yes,' Cianna answered, quickly snatching her attention back from where she had been watching clouds drift past the high windows. 'I am to fight Klia, then Yuilla.'

'And you will lose,' Jelkrael went on. 'You should know, as well, that each fighter has a trademark humiliation to inflict on her victims, a signature. Moloa, for instance, shaves their cunts, lights a splint on the rough bristles and smokes a cigar while sat on their heads, which is effective but somewhat slow. Yuilla, I have decided, will pull her victims up by the hair and urinate in their mouths, then make them lick her to show that they are truly conquered.'

'I thank you for warning me of this,' Cianna replied.

'It is best to be prepared, for the sake of the spectacle,' Jelkrael answer. 'So, we will need to provide you some colour, a name for one thing. You are from the northlands, yes?'

'From Boreal, in Aegmund, on the continent Kora,' Cianna replied.

'Few have even heard of Kora,' Jelkrael answered. 'Still, let me, see... the Snow Demon, no... Cianna, the Barbarian Princess...'

'I am not a Princess.'

'No matter, it is how it sounds that is important. Still, it's no good, too soft. We need something to imply savagery. Show me your teeth again.'

Cianna bared her teeth.

'Impressive, yes, the Ice Cannibal, perfect.'

'I am not a cannibal!'

'Moloa is not a she troll, for all that she resembles one. It is a good name, we'll stick with it. Yuilla is to be Lady Waterfall, on account of her signature. Klia is the Warrior, and cuts a lock from the hair of her victims, each of which is added to her necklace. On which topic, what exactly is your necklace made of?'

'The teeth of my ancestors.'

'Splendid! You'll make the Ladies' blood run cold. We need some savage act as your signature, but nothing too bloody. Humiliation is the key. Hmm, at present nothing comes to mind, but doubtless it will. In any case, get ready, we leave for Port Utis in the morning.'

Cianna sat by the side of the road, Klia beside her, Yuilla a little way to the side. For an hour they had practised, and their bodies glistened with sweat. Behind them was an area of flattened grass, on which Cianna had repeatedly thrown both of the other girls, or held them down, her speed and strength far outweighing either's abilities.

In the afternoon they were due to arrive in Port Utis, where they would wrestle, and Cianna now realised why everyone seemed so certain she would win. Klia was too slow, and reacted poorly to pain, as well as being inclined to elaborate moves and postures. Yuilla was slower still, if more vicious. Cianna had overcome both easily, despite having her mind more on the situation she was in than the wrestling. Being with Jelkrael offered no opportunities for fulfilling her duty to Sulitea, and she had once more begun to consider the option of trying to be sent to the powdermills. Klia was friendly, and talkative, and as a life long slave seemed likely to know what sort of offence would warrant the punishment.

'Tell me,' Cianna asked. 'For what would a girl be sent to the powdermills?'

'Sent to the powdermills!' Klia laughed. 'Has someone been scaring you with tales of what happens there?'

Cianna nodded.

'Jelkrael has never sold a girl to the powdermills,' Klia went on. 'Although he threatened me once or twice, when I was first with him. Not that he would do it. It is just a tale used to scare girls into easy obedience. After all, he would lose money, which he cannot bear to do.'

'It happens though?'

'It happens, yes, I suppose. Not often. Male slaves alone work at the powdermills. Save perhaps for a few girls for the pleasure of the staff. Still, it would be a bad place to be, with much opportunity for cruelty. The mills are remote. Life must be dull, and the torment of female slaves one of the few possible amusements. I have seen the great mills at Julac in the wetlands to the south of Kea, with four great buildings, each surrounded by a wall some five times the height of a grown man. Once inside, a slave never leaves.'

'Why such precautions?' Cianna asked.

'They are remote in case of explosion. As to the walls and restrictions, there was a revolt, years ago, among male fighting slaves. Since then great care has been taken to be sure no male slaves learn fighting skills. That is why only girls now fight.'

'What if I ran?'

'Don't. Glaucum would be set on your trail. He would catch you and hold you by the neck in his jaws as he fucked you, then herd you back to Jelkrael, drag you if you resisted. You would then be whipped, hard, maybe branded. For men, yes, persistent runaways could well end up in the powdermills, or the salt mines, or a dozen other awful places. Not girls, they like to fuck us too much. Besides, you are a good fighter. If you were also a runaway, Jelkrael would only use it to add glamour to your image. In fact, say nothing of this, or he might stage it and you will end up fucked by Glaucum in the dock market at Port Utis.'

'He would do this?'

'He would do anything to gain attention to us, and thus more money. Tonight, before we fight, we will be paraded through the streets. Remember you are supposed to be a savage. Snarl and spit, show your teeth. As Jelkrael says, nine parts in ten of our trade lies in showmanship.'

'I know nothing of this. I know only how to wrestle.'

'So I see. Where did you learn?'

'Playing with my brothers. In Aegmund all low-born men wrestle. It is fine sport, and there is much honour in it. There is a prize, a girl, or a purse of money, both sometimes. The men wrestle, and the victor enjoys the girl or takes the purse. It is also the way when two men seek the same wife. Thus the strongest achieves her. The girl must fight back, to show the man worthy of her. That was my role with my brothers, to pretend to be the prize. Also they would practise their holds and moves on me.'

'You are good, but you remember to display yourself. This is what the people come to see.'

'In Aegmund there is the skill and power of the fight, then the pleasure of seeing the girl taken. It is the better way.'

'You should make it your signature. Fuck me after the match tonight. I will suggest it to Jelkrael and he can buy a dildo when we reach the town.'

'You do not mind?'

'Enjoy me.'

Cianna smiled, and glanced to where Babalyn was preparing their meal. Jelkrael and Yufal sat, deep in conversation, while the two male slaves lounged by the oxen. Breaking off his conversation with a gesture, Jelkrael turned and beckoned to the girls. They ran over, sitting cross-legged in front of him.

'There is a change of plan,' he stated. 'Having watched you three at practise, it is clear that for Cianna to be defeated by either of you others would be an obvious absurdity. She is too quick, too powerful, yet she lacks the skill to make a pretence of her holds. So, tonight Klia and Yuilla will wrestle, with Yuilla the victor, and in Ioto Cianna will defeat Yuilla. Only when we face truly skilled opposition will she lose. Is this understood?'

'Yes, Master,' the two Makean girls responded, Cianna nodding in agreement, and catching a dirty look from Yuilla.

'So we must enhance Cianna's reputation,' Jelkrael went on. 'We still need a good signature, for one thing.'

'We have thought of one, Master,' Klia put in. 'In her homeland, men wrestle with a girl to fuck as the prize. Buy a dildo, and have Cianna fuck her defeated opponents.'

Yuilla's mouth came open, but she said nothing, only throwing another filthy look towards Cianna.

'Yes, why not,' Jelkrael said. 'A good signature. Hmm, what else?'

'I have a thought,' Yuilla put in. 'Cianna's reputation for savagery would be finer still if she was a runaway. Have her run, perhaps after the fight in Ioto, and caught by Glaucum in a public place. The spectacle would be sure to arouse attention, and if she were to repeat the act all would think her savage indeed!'

'True,' Jelkrael answered. 'Yet if she should run after the fight in Port Utis, people might think her a coward. I'll think on the idea.'

'She could be on a chain when we parade,' Yuilla went on.

'Now that is a fine thought,' Jelkrael declared. 'This is what I like to see! All of you, both free and slave, working together as my team.'

Cianna stood, upright in the cart, chained by the neck to a post. Her hands were also chained, behind her back, making it impossible for her even to shield her breasts and sex from the stares of the crowd. Port Utis was larger than Ketawa, a town composed of a swath of docks and warehouse districts running for most of the frontage of an almost circular bay, with the wealthier residential districts in the hills behind. Jelkrael had made sure to tour both, entering the town in a long zigzag that ended at the front. Now, with the crowds thick around them, they had come to a stop before a tall, round building.

Everybody seemed to be staring, and mainly at her, making her feel thoroughly uncomfortable. Not only was she nude, but Jelkrael had insisted on painting her body with a crude pattern of black and red swirls, which he seemed to think added to her image as a savage. That was bad enough, but both Klia and Yuilla were not only loose, but seated comfortably in the forward wagon, waving to the crowds and flaunting their bodies.

'The pit,' Jelkrael said, jerking his thumb at the round building, 'and try and look fierce, will you? That sullen expression just makes you look as if you'd been taken unexpectedly up the bottom.'

'I have been whipped.'

'Yes, the marks add a nice touch, although they would be better fresh.'

He laughed and jumped down from the wagon, her chain in his hands. Cianna was jerked after him, and managed to bare her teeth as she half-jumped, half-fell to the ground. The crowd gave back, and Cianna followed on Jelkrael's heels, occasionally giving a half-hearted snarl if anyone tried to press too close or touch her. Ahead, Klia and Yuilla walked together, both of them were waving happily to either side, and walking proudly naked. Yuilla turned, to throw an amused grin towards Cianna, who answered it by spitting on the ground.

'Better,' Jelkrael said, 'the crowd love to see a fight between girls who hate each other.'

Cianna grunted in response, then kicked out as a pair of intruding fingers took a pinch of her bottom. Her foot met something hard and she turned to see a man clutching his shin before she was pulled into a doorway in the building. Inside it was dark and cool after the heat and brilliant sunshine of the streets. High above them were beams, and what she guessed was the underside of wooden seating, with heavy pillars supporting all. Jelkrael had dropped her chain to fasten the door behind him, leaving her lose for the first time in hours.

She sat down, fidgeting with the chain at her neck. The collar Assivetes had put her in had been removed, which she was glad of, but it had been a great deal more comfortable than the heavy chain. Casting another angry look at Yuilla, she settled down to wait. All around was bustle, with dozens of people hurrying this way and that with no very obvious task. Cianna watched it all, in fascination, until at last the tread of feet on the boards above her head signalled the arrival of the audience.

Yuilla and Klia were talking with Jelkrael, and to Cianna's amazement she realised that they were agreeing on the details of the contest, throws, holds, even what poses the girls should get into. When they finally broke apart, it was for Jelkrael to walk to the narrow wooden corridor that led out to the pit. Both girls followed, Cianna behind them, waiting as Jelkrael made a grand announcement of the contest to come, with Babalyn beside him.

Cianna could see little, only an area of sand, in the middle of which stood Jelkrael and Babalyn, with faces in the stands beyond, mainly male, Makeans in the bright robes and coloured smocks, the richer to the for. The announcement made, Klia ran out, then Yuilla, cartwheeling to the centre of the pit. Both stood, the audience clapping and calling out obscene suggestions, to which the girls responded with equally coarse answers and rude poses. Jelkrael stood back, bowing, then stepped quickly to join Cianna.

'Observe, and learn,' he said. 'Each knows how to excite the audience, and thus to maximise our profit. Some one fifth of our gain comes from thrown coins, a quarter on a good night. Now watch, they begin.'

Klia and Yuilla squared off against each other, squatted down, feet well apart, hands extended. Cianna watched, puzzled, at the girl's movements, which seemed ritualised, almost a dance, and calculated more to show off their bodies than to gain any wrestling advantage. Twice Klia feinted before they came together, twisting around each over, Yuilla falling to sprawl on the sand, legs wide to show every detail of her sex to the crowd. The girls scrambled apart to the sound of laughter, and closed again, this time for Klia to be thrown high, again adopting a lewd and also ridiculous pose before rising to her feet.

Cianna shook her head in disbelief, but the crowd were roaring with delight. A coin fell to the sand, then another, as once more the girls came close, Klia kicking out in an elaborate pirouette. Yuilla caught Klia's foot, twisting, to hurl her to the sand, applying a lock, planting a firm smack on her bottom, only to dance away.

'Why does she lose her advantage?' Cianna whispered.

'For show, naturally,' Jelkrael replied.

Putting her hand to her necklace, Cianna thought how her brothers and father would have laughed at the spectacle, and how outraged they would have been at the suggestion that she behave in the same way. Wrestling was fine, and if it had to be done nude then could console herself that she had little choice. Yet to fail to seek to win was simply absurd.

For five rounds the girls fought, with brief rests between and Babalyn showing placards to announce the start of each. Only as the fight reached its climax did Cianna find her interest renewed. Klia was on her knees, held in a painful grip by Yuilla, and this time they did not break apart. Cianna could see the pain in Klia's face, while the excitement of the crowd was becoming feverish. Finally Klia called out her submission, to be immediately taken by the hair. Yuilla stood, legs braced apart, pulling Klia towards her as the crowd roared approval. Klia's head was pulled to Yuilla's sex, her face screwed up in despair, her mouth coming open, to receive the full stream of urine, directly into it. The crowd was baying wildly as Klia's mouth was pissed in, clapping and roaring approval as the steaming yellow fluid trickled down over the beaten girl's breasts and belly, splashing to the sand. All the while Yuilla grinned, looking down at her victim in delight, until she had emptied the full contents of her bladder into Klia's face. Only then did Yuilla tighten her grip, pulling Klia in, to kiss her sex.

Coins had been raining down as Klia was urinated on, and more followed as she began to lick Yuilla's sex. The act was unhurried, and staged for show, with Yuilla turning to show off, and Klia held so that her tongue was visible as she lapped. The orgasm was real though, when it came, Yuilla's thighs tightening around her victim's head as her eyes closed in bliss, her mouth wide in a silent scream. With that the crowd rose, clapping and showering coins down into the pit, until at length Jelkrael stepped out again, raising his hands for silence as Yuilla strode from the pit, with Klia crawling behind her.

Two days later they reached the town of Ioto. As before, Yufal had gone ahead, to place bets surreptitiously, to spread rumours of Yuilla's prowess and generally whip up interest in the contest. This worked, and they paraded, with Yuilla standing proud in her wagon and Klia bound at her feet, through urgent crowds. Cianna once more stood chained to a post, the subject of even more attention than Yuilla.

The pit proved to be at one side of a great square, in which the wagons were drawn up. Jelkrael was beaming as he jumped down, and giving assurances of a fine display to people in the crowd as he walked down the line of wagons. Yuilla was helped down, dragging Klia behind her, to strut proudly across to the pit. Cianna followed, Glaucum trotting beside her, her chain held in Jelkrael's hand, snarling and spitting at people around her as she had been taught. Within, the pit was identical to the one in Port Utis, with a cool dim space beneath the seating, where Yufal was waiting, along with the pit staff. Cianna sat down, glad to be out of the heat of the Makean day, watching idly as Jelkrael spoke to Yufal and the pit staff. Yufal in particular was animated, making points on his fingers and stabbing the air in emphasis. As Cianna relaxed back against a pile of sandbags, Babalyn came to join her.

'It seems you have created something of a sensation,' Babalyn said.

'Me?' Cianna answered. 'I haven't even fought.'

'No, but Yufal has had plenty to say nonetheless. His rumours have you as a cannibal girl bought from dwarven traders at vast expense. You are supposed to have been trained by the whip, like a beast. The people have never seen anyone from Kora before, and believe everything, which is helped by your teeth and your necklace. Yuilla's signature has also caused some comment, but she is spitting with jealousy, the more so because she is to lose.'

'I have no wish to hurt her. I would rather be friends.'

'Ha! You are to wrestle her to the ground and fuck her in front of maybe a thousand people! She will take it, and doubtless put on a good show, but she would far prefer to be the one to win.'

Cianna shrugged, lying back among the sacks and wondering if she would be able to sleep for a little. Her bruises were fading, but she felt tired after standing chained to the post for over an hour. Closing her eyes, she thought of Sulitea, and her goal, which seemed more distant than ever, then of Boreal, and of cool wind bringing the scent of pines and grass, which had become a dream before she knew it.

She woke to the boom of Jelkrael's voice, finding him standing over her, rubbing his fat hands together in glee.

'This is too good to miss,' he declared. 'We have a full pit, every one laden with coin! Now listen, Cianna, there is a change to the program, from which I hope to profit greatly. You are to fight Klia first, then Yuilla. For the first, use your full strength, hold nothing back. Yufal will watch the odds, and if they swing far in your favour for the second, as I suspect they will, we will reverse the outcome. Babalyn will tell you at a break, but do nothing until the fifth. Is this clear?'

'I...' Cianna began sleepily, only for a pit official to appear.

Jelkrael quickly turned to the newcomer, greeting him warmly.

'You are ready?' the official demanded, with an uncertain glance towards Cianna.

'In all particulars,' Jelkrael replied. 'Cianna, come.'

He stepped to the corridor, Babalyn following as Klia scampered across the join them. Cianna followed, yawning, to the mouth of the corridor. Babalyn stepped out onto the sand, made a pirouette and gestured to Jelkrael as he followed. He raised his hands and silence fell.

'Men of Ioto,' he boomed, 'and Ladies also. It is my pleasure tonight to present not one contest, but two. First, the Warrior, Klia, veteran of over a hundred combats and victor in most, a fighting girl as skilled as she is beautiful...'

He made a sweeping bow, mimicked by Babalyn. Klia stepped forward, bouncing into the pit and waving, then flaunting her bottom for the crowd. Jelkrael waited a moment, then once more raised his hands and spoke.

'...in a combat unique, Klia is pitted against the savage Ice Cannibal, a girl taken by dwarves from her northern wastes and purchased for a most extravagant sum for your entertainment...'

Again he gave his gesture, and Cianna stepped forward, her teeth bared, feeling slightly silly, but with a knot tightening in her stomach. She came out onto the sand, blushing and grinning despite herself, and giving a formal Aeg curtsey, which felt yet sillier without any clothes. The crowd laughed, she caught a dirty look from Jelkrael. Bets began to be called out, largely on Klia.

Jelkrael withdrew, leaving Babalyn to hold up a placard and Klia sunk down into a crouch, her knees well spread and her bottom pushed out to the audience. Cianna followed suit, waiting as Babalyn made her circuit of the sand and disappeared into the corridor. Cianna waited, watching Klia and ignoring the comments on the look of her body, the shape of her bottom, the way her breasts hung or the colour of her pubic hair. Suddenly Klia came forward in an elegant pirouette, one leg extended. Cianna ducked, snatched, caught Klia's ankle and set her down hard on her bottom. The crowd laughed and Cianna danced back. From the mouth of the corridor Jelkrael gave her a pleased nod.

They engaged again, and again Klia was thrown, this time across Cianna's back, briefly spreading her legs to the audience. Bets began to go Cianna's way, cautiously, then more rapidly as for the third time they came together and Klia ended up sprawled in the sand. On the fourth pass Klia managed a hold she had not used in practise, and Cianna was briefly put into a lock, with her body bent back to flaunt her breasts. It was released, and Cianna danced away again, only for Babalyn to signal the end of the round.

The fight continued, Cianna growing more confident and more excited, the shame of her nudity completely vanished beneath the pleasure of showing off her strength. Jelkrael's instructions were forgotten, and if she adopted a lewd or silly pose it was by accident. Klia was also enervated, but clearly tiring by the time Babalyn called out the fifth round.

Jelkrael was making frantic signals from the corridor, to which Cianna nodded. Stepping forward, she wiped a stray piece of sweat soaked hair from her forehead and crouched low. Klia was watching her, breathing slowly and deeply, her mouth slightly open, drips of sweat running down her face and chest. Cianna smiled, darted forward to catch Klia's arm, ducked, rolled, snatched. Klia skipped to the side, only for Cianna's legs to scissor onto her ankle, sending her crashing to the sand.

Even as Klia bounced up Cianna was on top of her, snatching at her wrists. Klia went down, hard, and a moment later both her arms had been twisted hard into the small of her back. She kicked up, catching Cianna with her heel, tried to twist, to buck her body, all of which were ignored.

'I submit,' Klia gasped, and her body went limp, 'fuck me kneeling, Cianna.'

The last had been a whisper, and Cianna was grinning as she rose, showing her teeth as she lifted her hands to take the applause of the audience. A scattering of coins landed on the sand, and Babalyn was coming forward, announcing Cianna as the winner and holding out the dildo and harness.

There was a roar of approval from the crowd at the sight of the thing, and more coins showered down as Cianna strapped it into place. Klia lay face down, looking back with an expression of horror which Cianna would have sworn was real. Stepping forward, Cianna reached down, took Klia by the hair and pulled her up, forcing her to lift her bottom. The move caused fresh cheering from the crowd, along with suggestions that Klia ought to be buggered.

It was tempting, with the dark wrinkle of Klia's bumhole plainly visible and wet with sweat, but Cianna ignored them. Squatting down to ensure that as many of the audience as possible were given a view of Klia's penetration, Cianna spread the soft, dark bottom. Putting the head of the dildo to the mouth of Klia's vagina, she pushed, and watched as it slid inside. Klia moaned in misery and despair as Cianna began to fuck her, with the crowd cheering and calling out in delight.

More coins were raining down around them, on them too. Cianna kept fucking, enjoying the feel of the dildo base on her own sex. Klia's moans began to change tone, leading to yet more catcalling, until she had begun to push back onto the cock inside her. Cianna took mercy, reaching under the beaten girl's belly, to find her sex. A few deft touches to the big clitoris and Klia was there, crying out in orgasm, to the delight of the crowd.

Unsure if she could come herself in front of so many, Cianna let Klia's orgasm signal the end of the ritual humiliation. She pulled out, spun round once to show the juice smeared dildo the to crowd, curtsied and stepped proudly from the pit. Babalyn greet her with a kiss and a pat on her bottom, sending her into the back, where Jelkrael and the others waited.

'Did I do it well?' she asked as rose to kiss her.

'Fine, in its way,' Jelkrael said. 'Certainly a fine fucking. Otherwise, perhaps too fast, if anything. Be wary of disappointing the crowd, always. Also, you made little display. The squat was good, with your full rear view on show, but even then you held yourself like a man. Curve your back, flaunt your buttocks, push out your breasts. Display, Cianna, this is the key!'

He slapped her bottom and strode away to talk to Yuilla and Yufal, leaving Cianna puzzled and slightly put out. Showing off was all very well, but she was already naked, which meant showing everything she had, while it seemed impossible that a race as boastful as the Makeans would expect her to do anything less than her best. She shrugged, putting it aside, and went to get water and a towel. Klia joined her as she washed, hugging her with real passion.

'You did well,' Klia said, 'and thank you for masturbating me. I'd give you a lick if we had the time. Perhaps after you've fought Yuilla?'

'If you like,' Cianna replied, blushing at the compliment. 'So we did well, you think?'

'The crowd liked it, there was plenty of money on the sand.'

'What of my display? Jelkrael says I don't show off enough.'

'You don't really, but then, you have your style. Now be careful, with the next. Yuilla resents you, and though she knows she must lose, she will try and hurt you.'

Cianna nodded, glancing over to where Yuilla was warming up. Above them, the crowd where calling for more, and had begun to stamp, making the decking shiver. Yuilla met Cianna's eyes, and stood, walking forward to near the mouth of the corridor.

'Cianna first, as victor,' Jelkrael said, beckoning. 'Babalyn, go out. Cianna?'

Cianna crossed to him.

'Now remember,' he instructed. 'A spectacle. Plenty of cunt. With Klia you showed too little. Throw if Babalyn instructs.'

'Throw?'

'Yes.'

Cianna nodded as Jelkrael stepped forward down the corridor. Yuilla gave her a hard look, and leant close to her ear, whispering.

'If it goes my way, you slut, you can expect more than just piss in your mouth. I'm going to shit in it. Think on that.'

Cianna made to answer, horrified by the idea and suddenly confused, uncertain if she was still supposed to win or if the fight was now fair. She made to speak, only to hear Jelkrael announcing her. She stepped out and the crowd roared, leaving her smiling and blushing, once more failing to make the display expected of her. Jelkrael gave her an insistent look and she managed to bare her teeth. Jelkrael went on, announcing Yuilla, who stepped out onto the sand, to more stamping and obscene suggestions.

Babalyn raised her placard and Cianna crouched down, pushing her uncertainty from her mind. Yuilla was facing her, her body tense, all that mattered as Cianna dropped lower, watching her opponent's eyes, the crowd now no more than a blur in the background. They circled, warily, moving gradually closer, until Yuilla's right hand came forward, her left back, only to switch, the left darting out at Cianna, to be caught, twisted, and jerked, sending her sprawling into the sand. Yuilla was face up, Cianna remembering what Jelkrael had said and briefly dipping her bottom into her opponent's face. Laughter and cheers rang out from the crowds, along with the hurried calling of bets as Cianna waited for Yuilla to rise.

Yuilla now looked angry, her fists tight as she got up to face Cianna. Poised, Cianna flapped out a hand, swung up a leg in a clumsy pirouette, dropped suddenly as Yuilla snatched for her ankle. Hurling herself forward, she caught Yuilla in the midriff, lifting her, legs splayed, high in the air and over, to crash to the sand. Again she dipped, squatting just low enough to push her bottom into Yuilla's face before the girl could get her breath back, then jumping up to curtsey to the delighted audience. Yuilla cursed, snatching at Cianna's ankle, missing, rolling quickly upright and leaping forward to catch Cianna in the side.

They went down, hard against the wall of the pit, Yuilla clawing for Cianna's face. Cianna lashed out, catching Yuilla's arm to send her spinning back, red faced with fury, spittle running from her mouth. She came in immediately, making no attempt at technique whatever, spitting curses, scratching and kicking. Cianna caught both Yuilla's wrists, holding her back, ignoring one kick, then another, to force Yuilla down by main force. Blind fury showed in the girl's face, but she could do nothing. Cianna felt a wave of elation as she drove Yuilla down into the sand, intent on forcing a submission, first round or not. Twisting suddenly, she forced Yuilla around and into an arm lock, tightening it, only for Babalyn to step out, calling the round.

The crowd were yelling and stamping, calling ever larger bets on Cianna, with the bookmakers calling back, at ever lower odds. Cianna stood back, stretching as Yuilla climbed painfully to her feet. A coin landed at her feet, large and gold, which Babalyn hastily collected, then straightened up to hug Cianna.

'Throw,' Babalyn hissed.

Babalyn broke away with a wink, then ducked again to retrieve another coin. Yuilla had risen and was rubbing at a rising bruise on her thigh, looking absolutely furious. Jelkrael had appeared in the tunnel mouth, and Yuilla glanced at him, her expression changing for a fraction of a second.

Now sure of what she was supposed to do, Cianna braced herself, sinking back into a crouch as Babalyn lifted a new placard. Yuilla was facing her, her fingers twitching, then suddenly rushing forward. Cianna ducked, slamming into Yuilla's legs, to throw her high and send her crashing into the sand. Yuilla stayed down, but Cianna made no move to press her advantage, sure that Jelkrael would expect more of a show. Yuilla got up, slowly, blowing out her breath before once more turning to Cianna. They closed, grappling, their faces briefly together.

'Now, you stupid slut!' Yuilla hissed.

Cianna gave the tiniest of nods, ducked low, slid her hand over the mound of Yuilla's sex, clutched, lifted, held her high and hurled her to the sand. Yuilla stayed down, gasping for breath as Cianna came quickly forward, applying a leg lock.

No!' Yuilla hissed. 'I can't... Let go you stupid slut!'

The crowd were roaring, demanding that Cianna finish Yuilla, hurling coins and baying for the dildo to be brought out. Cianna increased the pressure of the hold, watching as Yuilla's teeth gritted in pain.

'Submit!' Cianna demanded.

'No!' Yuilla hissed and once more Cianna tightened her grip. 'Ow! I submit! I submit, you vicious bitch!'

There was a great yell of joy from the crowd. Cianna released the lock, giving Yuilla's leg a last twist to force her over onto her back, and rose, arms high to the crowd. Yuilla stayed sprawled in the sand, her eyes shut, breathing heavily, her thighs wide, with the centre of her sex pink and glistening. To one side Babalyn appeared, holding up the dildo, the sight of which drew fresh calls from the crowd. It was thrown, and Cianna caught it, strapping it quickly in place to leave herself with a thick, dark phallus sprouting from her crotch. Calls rang out for Cianna to fuck Yuilla, at which point the beaten girl's eyes came open in shock. Staring in horror at the dildo, she began to scramble back over the sand.

Laughter rang out from the crowd. Yuilla was against the wall of the pit, eyes wide in terror, hands crossed over her sex. Suddenly two men in the crowd had reached down, grabbing Yuilla's arms and pulling them up, to hold her, kicking and writhing against the planks. Cianna stepped forward, not sure if she wanted to do it, but telling herself Yuilla's reaction was only show.

Kneeling, she brandished the phallus over the helpless girl's sex. Yuilla gave a cry of despair, but her legs stayed wide. Cianna took one of Yuilla's ankles and held it up, to be grabbed by a willing hand in the crowd. The other followed, leaving Yuilla spread helpless, her sex agape. Cianna lowered the phallus, touching it to the wet opening of Yuilla's hole. It went in, and the crowd roared to see Yuilla penetrated, coins showering down on them and the sand around. Cianna pushed, gently, watching the thick wooden shaft slide up Yuilla's hole, stretching the mouth to a taut pink ring. Slowly she began to fuck, in and out, watching, then taking Yuilla in her arms. The men let go, and Cianna mounted Yuilla as a man would have done, fucking her on the sand. Yuilla's thighs came up and she moaned, drawing delighted laughter from the crowd. Cianna began to fuck faster, pumping madly in Yuilla's body, determined to make herself come against the base of the dildo. It felt good, yet the angle was wrong, the calls of the crowd and the patter of coins on her back and legs distracting. In the end she gave up, deciding to take her pleasure with Babalyn later instead.

Pulling the dildo from Yuilla's sex, Cianna stood, raising her hands to the applause of the crowd and turning once to show off the juice smeared shaft of her toy. Only then did she remember what Babalyn had said. Yuilla lay dazed at Cianna's feet, her nipples stiff, her vagina leaking fluid onto the sand. Ducking low, Cianna took hold of the exhausted girl, lifting her, high, tossing her up onto her arms. The sight was greeted by wild cheering from the crowd. Cianna grinned, showing them her fangs, flexed her muscles and hurled Yuilla out into the midst of them. The response was deafening, roars of delight and encouragement, fresh coins hurled down onto the sand, offers to fuck her, and to buy her, some in the hundreds of standards.

In response she pretended a curtsey, as if she was in a long dress. This drew fresh laughter and calls of encouragement, so she repeated it, then stood tall. Unbuckling the dildo, she let it swing from her hand, striding happily back to the mouth of the corridor. Babalyn was there, looking worried, and immediately put her arms around Cianna, hugging her close.

'A fine fight, was it not?' Cianna asked, suddenly uncertain. 'Jelkrael will be well pleased.'

'Well pleased?' Babalyn responded, her tone utter disbelief.

'Why not?' Cianna asked. 'Did I do something wrong? Should I have waited longer, to provide a better spectacle? The crowd seemed pleased.'

'You were supposed to lose!' Babalyn exclaimed. 'That was the whole idea!'

'How could I lose?' Cianna protested, feeling suddenly hurt. 'She is slow, and weak... You said to throw her, anyway!'

She stopped as Jelkrael himself appeared in the passage, his face crimson with anger. With his mouth set in a tight line, he beckoned her towards him. Cianna went, bemused.

'To the wagons, now,' he snapped.

'The wagons? But…'

'Obey!' he said, through grated teeth, and reached out to take her by the ear.

She was dragged to the door, squealing and protesting, of which Jelkrael took no notice whatever. Outside, the great square was lit with the rich yellow of afternoon sunlight, throwing dark shadows from the wagons. Jelkrael let go of Cianna's ear and took her by the hand, smiling and exchanging pleasantries with the people they passed as he marched her to his own wagon, which had the covers up. Several people were watching, grinning, as she was hustled up onto the rear of the wagon and through the flap, obviously assuming that Jelkrael was about to fuck her. Still confused, she let herself be pushed into the interior. She waited as he sealed the flap, stealing an uneasy glance at the horse and saddle, which had been set up at the end of the wagon. Glaucum lay beside it, one eye open, watching her lazily.

'Get on the saddle!' Jelkrael snapped as he turned back to her.

'You wish to fuck me, now?' Cianna asked.

'I want to beat you, you idiot! Now get on!'

Cianna went, bending over as she had been ordered as much from confusion as obedience. The position left her bottom high and her thighs well parted, a position for whipping girls as well as fucking them, as she knew. The fights had left her aroused, and she could feel the warmth in her sex, so much so that the thought of the coming beating made her giggle. Jelkrael looked at her in angry amazement, his hands already at the buckle of his thick belt.

'This amuses you then?' he demanded. 'That you are to be thrashed for your stupidity?'

'No… Yes…,' Cianna answered in confusion. 'My tuppenny is hot from the fighting. Yet I don't understand. Why so angry? Babalyn says I was supposed to lose…'

'Barbarian idiot!' he shouted suddenly. 'You have cost me thousands!'

'We took plenty of money!' Cianna protested.

'Not on the gate, in bets!' Jelkrael raved. 'The bookmakers were sure you'd win! They were offering ten to one against Yuilla! Ten to one!'

'I don't understand,' Cianna said. 'Is not all well, then?

'Not it is not all well!' Jelkrael yelled. 'Did you not get the signal?'

'Yes. Babalyn said to throw her out of the pit. I did.'

'I said to throw, to throw the match! Stupid savage!'

'I don't understand!' Cianna wailed.

'I will explain,' Jelkrael hissed, suddenly cold, 'so that you understand why you are thrashed so severely. On the gate tonight, and from the pit, we have perhaps four hundred standard, of which half is ours. With the odds at ten to one, Yufal placed two hundred standard on Yuilla to win, carefully, scattered among several bookmakers. We would have collected two thousand standard, two thousand! This is what you have lost me!'

'No…' Cianna began, only to scream in shock and pain as he brought the belt down across her bottom with all his force.

The blow jammed her forward on the saddle, face down, and a moment later his hand had twisted hard into her hair.

'It is not my fault!' she squealed. 'You are always changing your plans!'

'Silence!' Jelkrael roared and hit her again, full across the meat of her cheeks, once more to make her scream and buck.

The next caught her before she had readied herself, and the next immediately after, sending her into a thrashing, kicking panic, her bottom bouncing to the smacks, her legs and arms flying in every direction. Smack after smack rained down, until her heel caught Jelkrael beneath the chin. He staggered back, mumbling curses and rubbing his chin, also panting. Cianna turned her head, looking at him. Her bottom was aching dreadfully, and hot all over, but she could feel the wet juice between her thighs and the warm urgency of her sex.

'Why not fuck me?' she asked. 'It would make you feel better, I think.'

'Does no amount of pain get through to you?' he demanded. 'Klia would be in tears from less, begging me for mercy.'

'Then fuck me,' she urged. 'I am sorry for your loss, but it was no fault of mine…'

His mouth had set into a hard line, and she stopped, then wiggled her bottom, hoping to entice him. He lifted the belt and she tightened her grip on the horse, only for his grim expression to change suddenly, to a broad grin.

'You'll get your fuck, slut,' he said, 'but not from me. Now get down.'

Cianna climbed from the saddle, rubbing at her bottom. He was smiling, his fat face red and moist with sweat.

'This is ideal,' he said. 'People saw me drag you in here, they must have heard your screams. They'll know I beat you, though they won't know why. It doesn't matter. When you run, they'll think it because of the thrashing.'

'Run?' Cianna queried.

'Yes, run,' Jelkrael answered, 'You'll run now, and in a half-hour I'll set Glaucum on your scent. He'll have you before sunset.'

Cianna gave an uneasy glance at Glaucum, who had pricked up his ears at the mention of his name.

'That way,' Jelkrael went on, 'you can recoup at least some of the money you've lost me.'

'You will charge?' she demanded in horror. 'To let people watch me fucked by Glaucum?'

'No,' he answered, puzzled. 'Who would pay good money to see some slave slut punished? Such spectacles are common enough in the street. You'll be watched, yes, but at no charge. The money will come from Yufal's bets on where he'll catch you and how long he'll take with you. You'll hide in a tree, and he'll take the half-hour to which he has been so carefully trained. You get long odds on a half-hour.'

'And should I refuse to run? What will you do, sell me to the powdermills?'

'No, you are too good a fighter to sell. I will make certain adjustments to the saddle, have you fixed to it in the square, and leave you out for public fucking. In addition to cunt dogs, we Makeans make pets of the lesser wood apes, mandrills, some even own goblins for the discipline of their slave girls…'

'I will run,' Cianna stated, 'but do not be surprised if I am not caught.'

'You think you can out run Glaucum, sweaty and moist as you are? Even I can smell your cunt! You have fought twice as well, and can hardly be fresh. Now remember, up a tree, or it's the saddle in the square for you.'

Cianna nodded, making for the flap in the wagon. Outside the sun was moving close to the horizon, the shadows longer and darker than before. She jumped down, ignoring curious looks from the two male slaves, and padded into the alley beside the pit. At the end she turned, towards the sea, running faster, and faster still, down a long alley that wound between high houses.

She was seething with resentment, determined to escape, for all that she had no idea what she would do with her freedom, or how long it would last. What mattered was defying Jelkrael. Few people were out in the streets, and those that were gave her only curious glances. When she reached the broad esplanade that fronted the sea a few began to point her out, those who had watched her fight. None tried to stop her, but they watched as she crossed the beach and splashed into the sea, turning to run next to the shore.

Knowing full well that she could expect nobody to keep silent for her sake, she ran faster, with the ground rising to her left, to form a low, sandy bluff, then a shallow cliff. With nobody in sight, she left the sea, scrambled up the sandy face of the cliff by clutching at clumps of coarse sedge and salt plants. At the top she found herself clear of the town, on an open meadow. In the west the sun had touched the horizon, the light fading even as she dashed back towards the buildings of Ioto. Reaching the nearest, little more than a ruin, as the last trace of light faded from the sky, she swung herself quickly up into an ancient nuttop. To do as Jelkrael said was galling, yet if she was caught it seemed sensible to avoid as much of the public defilement as she was able. Clutching the gnarled trunk and panting with exertion, she prayed that the trick had been enough to fool Glaucum.

Listening, straining her ears for noises of pursuit, she waited, hearing nothing, seeing nothing. One moon swung into the sky, then another, both nearly full, bathing the rooftops in dull pewter and laying silver trails across the sea. Still there was nothing, and then, looking back along the shore, she saw the red flare of torchlight on the esplanade, moving her way. A lump rose in her throat as excited voices carried across to her, along with the urge to run blindly into the night. She fought it down, sure her only chance was to lie low instead of blundering through the dark.

Presently the torches disappeared behind the bluff, still moving along the shore. Straining her ears, Cianna watched the point where she had ascended the cliff. Nothing happened, her hope rising slowly, only to collapse as she caught a movement in the old garden beneath her and Glaucum trotted casually out of the bushes.

He came straight to the tree, looking up, his big eyes reflecting the moonlight. She looked down in dismay, realising he must simply have taken her scent on the air, not even troubling to attempt to follow the broken trail. He sat down, a shadow blacker than black, save for his eyes, and a pale shape that she realised was the tip of his cock emerging from his prepuce. She swallowed hard, knowing full well that he would wait until others came up, or possibly try and give the alarm.

There was no escape. People would come up, dozens, maybe hundreds, with torches to light the scene. One way or another they would force her down from the tree, where she would be fucked, kneeling on the lawn, to the sound of their laughter and betting calls.

A sudden realisation hit her, a way to defy Jelkrael, if not to avoid her fate. It was humiliating, agonisingly so, but less so than what was going to happen otherwise. She looked down in Glaucum's eyes, and with a strong catch in her she spoke to him.

'You want to fuck me, I suppose?' she said quietly.

He tilted his head to one side, another inch of cock emerging from his prepuce. He'd do it, she was sure, then and there, whatever she did. He was always playful, but his cock seemed permanently ready. With a sigh of utter resignation she began to climb down the tree. His interest increased, looking up at the view between her legs as she swung herself down.

She reached the ground and Glaucum growled, staring at her, his teeth just visible.

'There's no need for that,' Cianna chided. 'You can do me. Now.'

She got carefully to her knees, fighting down the agonising shame inside her. He move closer, sniffing, as she got onto all fours, her bottom lifted and her knees set apart, her sex on show. Glaucum hesitated. Cianna wiggled her bottom.

'Come on, fuck me. I'm ready.'

He moved close, pressing his face to hers, pulling back to trot round her. She closed her eyes, her bottom lifted high. She felt his skin, warm and hairy, the pressure of his nose, pushed into the hole of her sex, his tongue, lapping up her abundant juices. She sighed, unable to resist the pleasure, nearly coming as he licked at her sex.

Suddenly he was on her, jumping up, his coat tickling her back as he mounted her. His cock prodded her sex, rubbing up her clitoris, and she gasped, burying her face in the grass in a mixture of ecstasy and shame. Again it prodded, and then it was in her, up her, invading her vagina, starting to move, fucking her with short, hard thrusts. Immediately she was whimpering and crying into the grass, her mind burning with shame, her pleasure too great to be denied.

His legs closed on her body, his mouth took her gently by the neck, and she was being fucked, in full style, a mounted bitch, a bitch who had crawled to her mate, flaunted her sex for his cock. Hardly knowing what she was doing, she found she had reached back for her sex. Briefly she touched the swollen shaft in her hole, then began to masturbate. As she rubbed she concentrated on the feel of the cock in her hole, and of his long coat against her buttocks, tickling her. There was a constant image of how she must look in her mind, her pale curves, quite bare, with his black body on top of her, humping her in glee.

She cried out as she came, so far gone that she was wishing the others had come up, to watch her fucked like a bitch on heat, on all fours with Glaucum pumping away into her sex. She was thinking of their laughter, and of how shocked Babalyn would have been, of how Yuilla would have relished the sight. At that her ecstasy broke, and she sank down, squashing her face and breasts to the grass in abject shame for her behaviour.

For a moment there was nothing but burning humiliation, but Glaucum kept pumping merrily away, riding her bottom without the slightest thought for her emotions. She took it, knowing full well he'd only let her go once he'd finished, and before long she was masturbating again.

In the half-hour it took Glaucum to fuck her properly, Cianna lost count of the number of times she came. He kept moving, his cock prodding deep into her body, but it was the way swollen base of his penis filled her vagina that made it impossible to stop masturbating. She was full of cock, being fucked on her knees, her bottom turned up to his beastly attention, and it would not stop. Again and again she found herself rubbing at her clitoris, to come with a gasp of rapture. Each time, the climax was followed by a great burst of shame, but within minutes she'd be doing it again, rubbing at her sex with her whole mind focused on what was up her hole, on what was on her back.

When he finally lost interest, pulling back to leave her with his sperm dribbling from her open hole, she felt only regret that her half-hour of fucking was over. Exhausted, drained of both strength and emotion, she collapsed onto her side. He came round, taking her wrist very gently in his mouth and pulling. She responded, sitting up to stroke his neck, at which he let go.

'Later,' she said softly, 'for now, I need to be very sure of something.'

Moving her hands to his stomach, she eased him onto his back. He went, unresisting and she went down, kissing the firm, hairy flesh of his belly, then his cock. He gave a whimper of pleasure as she started to suck, swallowing down the salt and musk of his penis, along with the taste of her own juice. With one hand massaging his balls and the other gently masturbating him, she worked him into her mouth, sucking and swallowing what came out, until at last there was nothing to come.

Cianna sat back, wiping her mouth, feeling dirty, satisfied, also proud. She had fought, defying Jelkrael, denying him his pleasure too, if not Glaucum. For a moment she wondered if escape might not still be possible. The pursuers appeared to have continued along the shore, while Glaucum seemed both somnolent and trusting, watching her, but with no malice. He would stay with her, she was sure, but whether he would prevent her going where she wanted was another matter.

Then again, she considered, in Makea she stood out in a way that made concealment almost impossible. With her white skin, her red hair and her height, she was instantly recognisable, and would be all the more so with Glaucum beside her. She would be caught, and punished, probably in the way Jelkrael had described, tied for the amusement of an entire town.

Yet if she simply returned to the wagons, she could explain that Glaucum had caught her and herded her back before she'd had a chance to hide. She might still get strapped to the saddle, but of one thing she was certain, which was that Glaucum would not be ready to play his part for some time. Alternatively, she could wait for other men to come up with her, but it was impossible to predict what they would do, except that it would almost certainly involve her sexual debasement. Realising that there was no sensible choice, Cianna got up and began to walk back into Ioto, Glaucum padding beside her.

Chapter Five

Cianna lay face down in the wagon, her chin in her hands, barely awake. For two days they had ridden the wagons, from Ajad, a small sea port at the mouth of a river, through dense jungle and lush water meadows, moving slowly across a narrow neck of land towards Kea, the capital. In Ajad there had been a resident champion at the local pit, and Cianna had beaten her in a fair fight, her twelfth victory in a row.

Since the night she had run from Jelkrael her reputation had steadily grown, as had her ability to act as the savage the audiences wanted her to be. She now wore her body paint almost constantly, and did it herself, in the swirling patterns typical of Aeg art, to create a look that the earliest of those ancestors whose teeth she wore would have considered ancient and barbaric. The paint also seemed to protect her skin from the sun and made her feel marginally less naked, for which she was grateful.

With twelve victories to her name, Jelkrael had decided that he would make the most money by letting her challenge Moloa, the champion. With Cianna's reputation the gate was sure to be good, while Cianna had refused to lose on purpose, challenging Jelkrael to do his worst to her. He had tied her to the saddle and let Glaucum have her, but she had still refused. No threat he had been able to make had moved her, while it was plain that as strict as he might be he was not prepared to kill her. In the end he had given in, earning her grudging admiration even from Yuilla.

It was hard not to feel proud, while the fact that she was technically a slave seldom entered her head. Perhaps once a week Jelkrael would tie her to the saddle and fuck her from the rear, but more for the sake of variety than any desire to stamp his authority on her. In the same way Yufal, when he was with the wagons, stuck largely with Klia and would only occasionally demand Cianna's attention, or that the girls play together as he watched. Aside from that, she slept with Babalyn, curled together beneath a warm blanket, usually after licking each other to ecstasy.

On the bad side, Yuilla was still resentful, although after being repeatedly beaten and fucked in front of hundreds upon hundreds of gleeful spectators, she seldom did more than taunt. Worse than that, there was not so much as a hint of Sulitea and Aeisla, making Cianna wonder if they had in fact died in the mountains and that she might be truly alone. Despite these fears, she had continued to keep her ears open for information about the black powder, but had learnt nothing.

There was a river beside the road, a broad expanse of brown water, moving sluggishly through thick reed beds. Cianna had been watching it, idly considering the splashes made by jumping fish and the evil looking black-green reptiles that lurked at the water's edge. Beyond was jungle, and to their left, which again bore watching, with the occasional small ape appearing among the branches or the flash of plumage from some brightly coloured bird.

Abruptly the jungle on the far side of the river gave way, to a broad meadow, from which a great sluice emptied water into the stream. Beyond, set well back and well apart from each other, stood four high buildings of grey stone. Two also showed towering chimneys, and each was surrounded by a high walled coumpound.

'Julac Powdermills, Cianna,' Klia said suddenly from the edge of the wagon, where she was sitting. 'Your pet terror.'

Cianna lifted her head higher in sudden interest. A rank scent caught her nose, with notes of both dung and rotten eggs. She made a face.

'Smelly, aren't they?' Klia said. 'Imagine being one of the girls there, with that pong to wake up to everyday.'

'Revolting,' Cianna agreed. 'What is it? Dung, and it smells like bad eggs, or those magic sticks Jelkrael uses to light his cigars.'

'Magic sticks!' Yuilla taunted. 'What a barbarian! They are only splints tipped with brimstone, which burns when rubbed over coarse rock, or a badly shaved cunt. When Moloa has beaten you, she will do that, you know, and smoke her cigar with your tongue up her arsehole!'

'Don't be a beast, Yuilla,' Klia chided.

'What is brimstone then?' Cianna demanded, ignoring Yuilla.

'The yellow stuff on the end of fire splints, like I said, stupid,' Yuilla responded.

'And it is used in the powdermills, to make black powder?' Cianna asked.

Klia shrugged.

'There was a girl I knew in Ketawa,' Yuilla said. 'Who could smoke a cigar with her cunt.'

'I think we have all had Jelkrael's cigar up our holes,' Klia replied.

'No,' Yuilla said, 'I don't mean just stick it up and let a little puff of smoke out later. She could draw the smoke in, even blow out smoke rings. I always thought it would make a great signature, but you'd have to teach the girls to do it before the fights.'

'True,' Klia agreed. 'You've got a great signature anyway. I wish I had. Mine's boring. I want something ruder.'

'Change it,' Cianna suggested.

'Jelkrael won't let me,' Klia protested. 'He says it's bad showmanship for a girl to change her signature. Moloa's is best. Imagine how it would feel, having to lick her fat arse while she has a cigar, and with your cunt shaved!'

'Haven't you fought her?'

'No. I've seen her though. They don't call her the She Troll for nothing! She looks like one anyway, huge and fat, with no waist and this great square arse. She makes a real show of her signature too. With the girl I saw beaten, Moloa sat on her face while she did the shaving and had the cigar. It took ages, and the poor girl had to lick her arsehole all the time.'

'That's what you're going to get, Cianna!' Yuilla laughed. 'I can't wait to see!'

Cianna shrugged, pretending an indifference she didn't feel. Everybody seemed to assume that Moloa would beat her easily, so it seemed likely that the woman was simply too huge and too experienced to be overcome. If that was the case she would be beaten, and used in the way that gave Yuilla such delight. Yet to run, or do anything but try her best, seemed a greater dishonour than losing. Ignoring Yuilla's continued taunts, she pushed Moloa from her mind and watched as the powdermills gradually faded from site. There were four main buildings, each in a separate compound, so if the powder was made in the same way as in Aprinia, one would be for mixing, which left three, presumably for one ingredient each. One came from dung, the other from brimstone.

An hour later they reached a wide lake, from which the river seemed to spring. The jungle gave back, leaving rich farmland to either side of the water. Beyond the lake was a low ridge, and as they crossed it Cianna found the city of Kea spread out beneath them. It lay on a gentle slope around a bay, a sea of stone buildings set with trees, larger by far than any of the towns she had passed through, and richer.

'Kea,' Jelkrael declared, turning back from the lead wagon where Babalyn had been giving him his morning suck. 'You may safely gape in awe, Cianna. There is nothing like it in your homeland, is there?'

'Not that I have seen,' Cianna answered cautiously, not wishing to admit any hint of inferiority to the Makeans.

'And you, Babalyn?' Jelkrael continued. 'Now can you say our civilisation is backward?'

Babalyn lifted her head, glancing at the city, still with his cock held in her hand.

'How many people live there?' she asked.

'Over a hundred thousand, so I believe,' Jelkrael answered.

Babalyn nodded before speaking. 'In Opina, our capital, live some nine hundred thousand citizens, but then we have proper sewers.'

She sniffed the air and quite casually returned to sucking his cock, earning a gentle cuff from Jelkrael. He was smoking, his cigar in one hand, the other going back to rest on Babalyn's head, just firmly enough to keep her in place. Cianna watched, knowing the gesture from experience.

Drawing deeply on his cigar, Jelkrael closed his eyes. He blew a smoke ring, his mouth came slowly open, he swallowed hard, grunted and the expression on Babalyn's face turned briefly from resigned obedience to disgust. She too swallowed, and opened her eyes, still with his cock in her mouth and her cheeks sucked in, looking at Cianna, who giggled.

'Pull in,' Jelkrael puffed, gently pulling Babalyn off his cock. 'It is time Yufal went into the city, and we have much to discuss.'

The two male slaves obeyed the order, steering the oxen to the side of the road, where a stand of high palms provided shade. Cianna jumped down, Glaucum bouncing up to lick her face and rub his cock on her leg. She pushed him away, giggling, and hastily sat down. A rug was spread for Jelkrael and Yufal, who were served wine and a tray of sweetmeats. The girls gathered round them, sitting cross legged, Cianna with Glaucum's huge head in her lap, feeding him the sweet biscuits he loved.

'As you see,' Jelkrael declared, gesturing with his cigar, 'Kea lies ahead of us. In Kea there is more opportunity for accumulation than in the rest of our land put together. The question, as always, is how to maximise our profits.'

He drew on his cigar, took a swallow of wine, and continued.

'As you know, I had planned to have built up Yuilla as a prospective challenger by this stage, with a series of thrown fights, then to allow her to be bought, winning on both gate, bribes and betting. Matters have gone somewhat differently, with Cianna's twelve victories and bizarre appearance providing a reputation that no amount of bought matches could obtain.'

He grinned at Cianna, who found herself smiling and blushing, only to catch a dirty look from Yuilla.

'In Kea,' Jelkrael went on, 'are three pits, these being Faerdahl's Pit, the Dock Pit, where Moloa is resident, and the Great Pit itself, where the grand spectacles are put on for the Elite and the Exquisites. Now, as Cianna still refuses to throw a contest, the situation is not normal, yet somewhere there is money to be made.'

'There are good wrestlers in Kea,' Yufal suggested. 'Against Lia-Gau, or perhaps Ruamana, she might lose anyway, yet with enough rumourmongering I could probably get the odds well in her favour.'

'A possibility,' Jelkrael answered, 'but risky. What if Cianna wins? We take one-third of a big gate, yes, and a sixth of what might be a truly magnificent one when she fights Moloa, yet we lose our stake. No, there must be a better way. Cianna, stop playing with Glaucum, you are making him excited.'

Blushing, Cianna made a wry face and stopped scratching Glaucum under the chin, only to have him press his head eagerly to her belly.

'Think, all of you,' Jelkrael demanded. 'I wish to depart Kea a rich man.'

'How old is Moloa?' Cianna asked. 'And how confident?'

'Old? Perhaps thirty-five years,' Jelkrael answered. 'Confident? Absolutely. She is unbeaten across more bouts than I can remember.'

'Then what of this,' Cianna went on. 'In Kefra, before I went on, one woman fought two. Moloa, perhaps could be persuaded to take on both Klia and Yuilla, then me. She would be tired, at the least. In any case the gate should be excellent, and maybe I could win.

'More likely not,' Jelkrael objected. 'I have seen her defeat three at once, and have difficulty only in deciding whose head to sit on while she smoked her cigar. It is also too risky. The odds on you would be long, true, but I prefer to bet on certainties. No, in Kea there are a hundred bookmakers, allowing Yufal to practise his art as nowhere else. Gates are secondary. We must win on bets, and at long odds. In all truth, Cianna, you must overcome your scruples and throw a match. This honour code of yours had no meaning in Makea! Who would know?'

'Me, my ancestors,' Cianna answered, causing Jelkrael to throw up his hands in despair.

'Savagery! Superstition!' he declared. 'Yet still, this is not the provinces. Crowds are wary of match fixing and can turn violent. After your victories it would have to be a convincing opponent, and thus the odds would not be as good as they might. Again, think!'

'It is simple,' Babalyn yawned. 'You adopt Cianna's plan, only with a single opponent, perhaps Klia, who is more intelligent and also known to enjoy her defeats. Moloa will win easily, sit on Klia's head and begin to shave. Klia will lick eagerly at Moloa's anus, as she is expected to do, so eagerly in fact that she can push in a capsule and burst it with her tongue. In the capsule will be some powerful soporific. This is how distasteful medicines are taken in my homeland, up the bottom. Absorption rates through the rectal wall are higher than those in the mouth or stomach, which fact I assume is unknown in Makea?'

Jelkrael shrugged.

'As I thought,' Babalyn continued. 'Moloa will begin to feel the effects in minutes…'

'She will be instantly suspicious!' Yufal interrupted.

'No,' Babalyn went on, 'the thrill of her victory will carry her on, for a while at least, only when she is facing Cianna will the full effect be felt.'

'It is dishonourable to do this,' Cianna put in.

'Be quiet!' Jelkrael snapped. 'It is not you who will do it, but Klia, or rather Babalyn.'

'Me!?' Babalyn squeaked.

'Naturally,' Jelkrael responded. 'You understand the process. It is for you to complete it.'

Cianna fell back on the grass, laughing at Babalyn's change from smug superiority to shock. Instantly Glaucum was on top of her, his weight settling between her thighs as she gave a squeak of surprise and alarm. She tried to push him off, but it was too late. Very gently his teeth moved to her neck, and all she could do was lie back, helpless in his grip. His cock was already probing for her hole, then in, sliding deep up her vagina with a single, long thrust. She gasped at the sensation, her thighs coming high and wide by instinct as he settled down to fuck her.

In Kea they drove to an inn, the Five Moons, which Jelkrael felt would make a better base than the wagons, despite the cost. Leaving the girls in the long attic room he had taken, he disappeared into the city, to return at sunset, full of nervous energy and thoroughly pleased with himself.

'There will be little need for Yufal's rumourmongering!' he declared. 'Everywhere there is talk of the Ice Cannibal, much of it wildly exaggerated! I have seen Glaydrak, who owns the Dock Pit, and he states that Moloa will accept a challenge once Cianna has secured a victory actually in Kea. This is good for all of us, and I have booked contests at Faerdahl's Pit, in two days time. Klia, you will fight Zetina, in fair contest, as a rematch from our last visit. You, Yuilla, are to go against a first timer, Iphine, who is free, and sponsored by some Elite. They have paid fifty standard for the victory, but nevertheless, you are not to hurt her. Cianna, you will fight Lia-Gau, who is rated third or fourth in the city, depending on who you believe. So all is done. I have put posters in hand, and hired a crier, everything to hand! I have the laudanum you need also, Babalyn, and the sugar. So now food, Babalyn, the experiment, then rest. Tomorrow we parade!'

Finishing, he threw himself down on a couch, reaching out for his box of cigars. Klia hurried to help, rasping one of the fat yellow headed splints against the wall and lighting the cigar. Jelkrael drew on it and puffed happily. Babalyn hurried away to order the food brought up.

'There is more,' Jelkrael went on, 'if only gossip. Moloa has celebrated her two-hundredth victory, indeed, with a few more after. Hulak, for whom I was assistant once, has retired, selling off his stable, Lia-Gau among them. On an amusing note, a group of fishermen claimed to see a great winged demon some weeks back, flying across the sea against a low moon. Nonsense, of course, but apparently every sect in Kea is trying to claim it as an omen for their particular god! Priests!'

'A demon?' Cianna demanded.

'Probably a large gull,' Jelkrael answered dismissing the subject. 'So the experiment. Who wishes to have Babalyn lick her bottom hole?'

'It should be me,' Yuilla answered quickly, 'if I am to lose at Faerdahl's Pit.'

'What if the effects linger?' Klia asked doubtfully.

'True,' Jelkrael admitted. 'A possibility at the least. It should perhaps be me then.'

Presently Babalyn returned, greeting the news that she was about to have to lick Jelkrael's anus without too much shock. Their food followed her, baked meats and bowls of rice, both highly spiced, a soft, white cheese and bananas cooked in their own skins. Jelkrael ate with gusto, in the best of spirits, talking between mouthfuls, to expound his opinion on every subject that arose.

Their meal finished, Babalyn sat down to work, using candles, spoons and earthenware mugs. Cianna watched in fascination, Babalyn bending low over her work, her eyes near shut, a mannerism that reminded Cianna of Sulitea.

'Where did you learn such skill?' she asked. 'Have you studied with a witch?'

'A witch!?' Babalyn chuckled. 'Really, Cianna, do you know nothing? The powder is derived from poppies. The liquid is a distillate, a simple alchemist's trick.'

'You said you knew nothing of alchemy?'

'Every girl or boy of Aprinia who ever attended a party knows how to concentrate laudanum. The sugar glass is trickier, and is really a cook's skill. Pass me another spoon.'

A thick, clear golden liquid had been produced from the laudanum, which Babalyn set aside to cool.

Taking the new spoon and a fork, she began to heat the sugar as Jelkrael came over to them.

'What are you doing?' he asked.

'Making a capsule of sugar glass,' Babalyn answered

'A glass made from sugar,' he said, peering closer. 'Who would have thought it! You are clever, you Aprinians, it must be said.'

'Be careful, it is hot,' Babalyn cautioned him.

They continued to watch as she completed her work, creating a tiny cup of the sugar glass, into which she poured the laudanum. A few deft touches sealed the cup, which she licked when it was cool enough, leaving a smooth golden capsule no bigger than the end of her thumb.

'She will feel that going in, surely?' Jelkrael queried.

'Not once I have her juicy,' Babalyn answered. 'It is after all, a lot smaller than any cock. She will just think it a trick with my tongue.'

Jelkrael gave a sceptical grunt and began to undo his trousers. Pushing them down, he exposed huge soft buttocks, a shade paler than the skin of his face, then the dangling mass of his genitals as he cocked up a leg to remove a boot. Babalyn watched, her mouth slightly open and her huge dark eyes fixed to the bulbous bottom she was about to lick. When he was nude from the waist down she popped the capsule into her mouth and went to her knees.

'Stick it in only when I tell you,' he directed, sinking into a squat. 'I will see if I feel anything.'

Babalyn nodded and lay down beneath him, full length, casting Cianna a last rueful glance before her head disappeared beneath Jelkrael's massive dark buttocks. He settled himself on her face, pulling out one massive cheek, then the other, to spread them across it. As his expression changed suddenly to bliss, Cianna knew that Babalyn had begun to lick his bottom hole. He took his cock in his hand, tugging gently, his eyes closing in pleasure, the other hand moving to fondle one of Babalyn's breasts. For a long while he stayed still, masturbating lazily, with his big balls spread out over Babalyn's chin.

'Now try and get the capsule in,' he ordered finally.

Babalyn raised a hand. Jelkrael's expression became thoughtful, then pleased once more.

'It is in?' he asked, lifting his bottom a fraction.

'Yes,' Babalyn panted.

'Good,' he went on. 'I didn't feel a thing. Now continue, well up my arse. Cianna, climb on her, and suck my cock while she licks.'

Cianna obeyed, crawling quickly across and throwing a leg over Babalyn's body. He once more settled his bulk into Babalyn's face. Leaning down, Cianna took his cock into her mouth, sucking firmly to spare Babalyn any more anal licking than was necessary. He was already hard, and in no time he was groaning, his hand tightening in her hair, obviously near orgasm, only for his cock to start to shrink. She sucked harder, but it did no good. Instead his grip slackened in her hair, he sighed, clutched for the floor, and toppled slowly over. Babalyn lifted her head, looking at Jelkrael in surprise.

'A little less,' she said, 'or perhaps a weaker mix.'

Faerdahl's Pit proved to be a tall, narrow building in the oldest part of Kea, entirely made of wood, black with time and wax. Faerdahl himself greeted them, immediately extending invitations to a hall, where many of the more important spectators had been invited to drink and take their fill of the girls after the contest.

The pit was already crowded, with a great queue extending down the narrow street. More were arriving at every moment, and Faerdahl hustled Jelkrael and his party inside, quickly closing the door. Introductions were made to the other girls, Lia-Gau proving to be a lithe, broad shouldered woman the top of whose head reached Cianna's eyes.

Greetings exchanged, Cianna moved to the mouth of the corridor, where Jelkrael was looking out at the crowd from the shadows. The pit was tall, if no further across than others she had been in, with ranks of seating rising so steeply it appeared dangerous, and also a triple column of well appointed boxes, most of which were already occupied.

'Many of the Elite are here,' Jelkrael said quietly, 'Exquisites also. See, in the central box, Eudahl, who is brother to the King, and beside him old Velacqual, who commanded the fleet, and again, Ulourdos and his brother Nairgren, the King's nephews.'

'Will they come afterwards?' Yuilla queried.

'Not they,' he answered. 'Should any such wish to fuck you they will send for you. No, at our party will be merchants, officials, minor nobles. But look, Moloa herself, and Glaydrak beside her. See, the great slab faced woman beside the man in scarlet and blue? Have you ever seen such a monster?'

'I have seen true she trolls,' Cianna answered. 'The smallest could lift your Moloa one handed.'

'Undaunted, that's the spirit!' Jelkrael answered. 'Now there is one who should strike fear into your heart, you and Klia both. Observe the big man with the bald head in the box with the two women in blue. That is Bulzar, administrator at Julac mills. He will be there. Maybe I shall put you on the saddle and let him fuck you, if you do not do well tonight?'

'You do not need to threaten,' Cianna answered.

'I joked, only,' he said. 'You will win, I am sure of it. Lia-Gau's signature, by and by, is to spit in her victim's eyes, mouth and cunt, then to have her masturbate in the spittle.'

Cianna shrugged, glancing back to where Klia was talking to her opponent, Zetina, happily and openly. Faerdahl was beyond them, speaking to a green robed Elite who was Iphine's sponsor. Stepping back beneath the stands, she stretched, flexing her limbs, then began to tie her hair up into the tight topknot she wore when fighting. A new man appeared, apparently a clerk, to tell Faerdahl that the pit was full to capacity with many still outside.

'Fine indeed,' Faerdahl answered him. 'Perhaps we should have hired the Great Pit. So, to work.'

He strode for the corridor, Zetina and Klia coming behind him. Cianna followed, crowding around the entrance to join the other girls peering around Jelkrael's bulk. Faerdahl stood, at the centre of the ring, announcing the first pair with a flourish, his two placard girls beside him, and retreating into the mouth of the corridor with a bow.

Cianna watched with what had become a familiar pleasure as Klia and Zetina fought. They were well matched, and both experienced, executing complex moves, sometimes with grace, sometimes in a manner design to invite ridicule, but always to the best display of their bodies. The crowd were in festive mood, stamping and clapping until the pit shook, also showering coins down on the girls. At the end of the sixth round it finished, Zetina forcing Klia into submission with an arm lock. Jelkrael grunted in annoyance, but chuckled as he watched Klia urinated over, bottom up, then spanked on her wet skin, with droplets of pee and sweat flying in all directions, to the yet greater delight of the crowd.

After only a brief pause for refreshment, gathering up the coins and raking the sand, Faerdahl stepped out to make his second announcement. This met with more laughter than clapping from the crowd, with the wiry but small Iphine obviously no match for Yuilla. The crowd's amusement grew as the fight started, and rose to a crescendo of guffaws and catcalls when Yuilla finally submitted after deliberately giving up a dozen chances to take the match herself. Yuilla was duly made to kiss Zetina's anus to acknowledge her defeat and left face down in the sand with a small flag showing the Elite's house colours sticking out of her own bottom hole.

'A farce,' Jelkrael remarked, 'but a profitable one.'

Yuilla returned, making a wry face at Jelkrael, who sent her in under the stands with a slap to her bottom. Cianna stepped forward, her pulse rising fast as Faerdahl once more stepped out. Silence fell on the audience as he raised his hands to announce first Lia-Gau, as third ranked in Makea, then Cianna, as the challenger with her twelve victories behind her. To Cianna's surprise Lia-Gau kissed her before stepping out, something no opponent had done before.

'She seeks to make you friendly, thus an easier victim,' Jelkrael hissed. 'Ignore her. Now go.'

Cianna nodded and stepped out, raising her arms to the crowd and baring her teeth. There was a roar of approval, the first coins falling on the sand even as the placard girls ducked back. She turned, facing Lia-Gau, both ducked low, balancing on the balls of their feet. Cianna waited, eyes locked with her opponent, ignoring the roar of the crowd, with their demands for action and display. Lia-Gau came close, carefully, ducked, scooped sand up and hurled it at Cianna's face. Cianna danced back, eyes closed, dropped and swung her foot out, catching Lia-Gau's thigh to send her sprawling.

Again they faced off, Lia-Gau now slightly unsteady on one leg, and more cautious still. Cianna reached out, inviting a hold to test their strength. Lia-Gau took it immediately, tugging hard the instant she had her grip, pulling Cianna momentarily off balance. Cianna lunged forward, going the way she was pulled, head down, full into the softness of Lia-Gau's chest, to sprawl together on the sand. Both grappled for a hold, Cianna on top, the audience crying out in delight at the view of her spread bottom. A coin struck her thigh and she jumped up, allowing Lia-Gau to rise without interference. They circled for a moment, both wary, then stopped as the gong went to mark the end of the round. Immediately Lia-Gau stepped forward, patting Cianna on the shoulder, then kissing her and pulling her into a hug

'You are fast,' Lia-Gau whispered, 'and very strong, but a novice at heart. You are pretty too. After I've beaten you I intend to take you to my pallet, to smack your little bottom and have you lick my cunt. Two more rounds for show, then I'll have you.'

She pulled away, grinning. Cianna stuck her tongue out before accepting water from one of the placard girls. Again the gong sounded and she dropped into her ready crouch. Lia-Gau came on, wary, darting her hand out, pretending to scoop sand, only to hurl herself forward, shoulder down, meeting empty air as Cianna danced aside. There was laughter, mixed with demands for a better show of their bodies. In response Cianna flaunted her bottom, pushing it well out to show both her sex and her anus. Lia-Gau dived low, for Cianna's legs. Cianna jumped, kicked her legs apart, falling to land on Lia-Gau's back, only to tumble backwards, legs wide, onto the sand.

The crowd roared approval as Cianna jumped quickly to her feet. She was sweating, her paint smeared over her body, Lia-Gau's as well, making their skin slippery and hard to grip. Her tuppenny was wet too, as it always was during fights. Her nipples were also hard, in blatant erection, which Lia-Gau noticed, letting her eyebrows rise to show she had seen. Cianna wiped the sweat from her forehead, bracing herself once more. There was a little smirk on Lia-Gau's face as their eyes met, knowing, somehow taunting. Cianna responded with a shy smile, waiting, moving slowly, only to put her foot on a coin and slip. Lia-Gau was on her immediately, grappling to throw, one arm low to catch Cianna by her sex. Cianna hurled herself backwards, Lia-Gau coming down on top of her, to grapple, pulling up Cianna's leg and twisting. Cianna pushed back, lifting her body from the ground, her teeth set as she forced Lia-Gau's arm back and down. Lia-Gau leapt back even as the gong sounded, but offered a hand to help Cianna from the sand.

They embraced again, cuddling close, Lia-Gau's hand slipping between Cianna's thighs. Cianna gasped as a finger slid into the wet hole of her sex, fucking her quickly, to withdraw and rub at her clitoris.

'You're wet for me, you little slut!' Lia-Gau said, and pushed the finger at Cianna's mouth.

Cianna took it, eyes closed as she sucked up her own juice. Lia-Gau kissed her on the cheek, pulling close once more.

'One more round of play then, little one,' she whispered, 'and I'll have you. Later I'll tie you, spank you, fuck you with your own dildo, up your sweet little arse, then have you suck it clean. How you'd love me to do that, yes?'

'Yes,' Cianna sighed.

Lia-Gau stepped back, grinning openly. Cianna took another swallow of water, put her hand to her necklace to say a brief prayer, all the while struggling to fight down her arousal. Her nipples were straining, her tuppenny so wet that the juice was running down her thighs, her belly full of the urgent need to be filled. She blew out her cheeks, resting her hands on her knees as she gave Lia-Gau a weak smile and hurled herself forward even as the gong sounded.

Lia-Gau was taken completely by surprise, caught in the midriff by Cianna's shoulder and hurled back, winded, against the wall of the pit. Immediately Cianna was on her, slamming her down onto the sand, mounting her before she could regain breath. Two quick moves locked Lia-Gau's arms, twisted high behind her back. Rising, Cianna put a knee into her victim's spine, and pressed. Lia-Gau gasped in pain, frantically kicking her legs against Cianna's bottom. Cianna tightened the hold.

'Submit!' Cianna demanded, Lia-Gau shaking her head to spray out droplets of sweat.

Again Cianna tightened her hold, drawing a whimper from Lia-Gau. A coin struck her, hard, but she ignored it. Lia-Gau kicked up suddenly, but again her heel caught only the full flesh of Cianna's bottom.

'Don't!' Lia-Gau panted. 'Please!'

'Enough tricks,' Cianna snapped. 'Submit!'

Once more Lia-Gau shook her head, frantic with pain, but with her teeth set hard. Cianna set her knee in place, not wanting to risk the damage that would mean disqualification, nor to really hurt Lia-Gau. The crowd were demanding submission, calling for Faerdahl, cheering Cianna, and suddenly Lia-Gau was calling out her submission, over and over. Cianna let go and rose, slowly, to curtsey towards the boxes, then to Moloa, who returned a hard stare. At the corridor was Babalyn, holding out the dildo, which Cianna took, raising it to let the crowd see properly before starting to strap it into place.

Lia-Gau had not bothered to get up, but was crawling, still on her belly, towards the centre of the pit. Cianna stayed still, standing with her hands on her hips and the dildo sticking out from her crotch, until Lia-Gau reached her, to look up with big, moist eyes. Cianna ducked down, took Lia-Gau by the hair and kissed her on the mouth.

'My own dildo, in my bottom ring?' Cianna demanded. 'Was that not what you were going to do to me?'

Lia-Gau nodded weakly

'I think you know what to do then,' Cianna answered and dropped Lia-Gau's head.

As Cianna scrambled round in the sand, Lia-Gau lifted her hips, her knees wide, parting her sex. The noise from the crowd had died, to a delighted whisper, as Cianna adjusted Lia-Gau's thighs to the right height for entry. She laid the dildo into the sweat slick crease between the firm black buttocks, eased the head down, found the hole of Lia-Gau's vagina and slid up, deep in, then back. The dildo came out coated in thick white slime. Cianna put her thumb to the dildo, wiping up the juice, showing the glistening blob to the crowd, and smearing it onto Lia-Gau's anus.

Delighted gasps went up as the crowd realised that Lia-Gau was to be sodomised. More coins rained down. Cianna pressed the ball of her thumb to Lia-Gau's anus, watching the tight, fleshy hole give, opening to reveal a brilliant pink interior. Lia-Gau gasped, then gave a low moan as the full length of Cianna's thumb was pushed up her bottom. Cianna added a finger, then a second, stretching Lia-Gau's anus wide, to show the tube of moist pink flesh leading into blackness.

Grinning, Cianna put the head of the dildo to the straining bottom hole, pushing as she withdrew her fingers. Lia-Gau gave another broken moan as her anus filled with the thick, smooth head of the dildo, then grunted as Cianna began to jam it up. It went in, all of it, filling Lia-Gau's rectum until the fat, carved balls where pressed to her empty sex. With that, Cianna began to wiggle her hips, rubbing herself on the base of the dildo and the wrinkled balls against Lia-Gau's sex.

Lia-Gau gave a despairing moan as she realised she was to be masturbated as well as buggered. Cianna found herself giggling, and rubbed harder, watching Lia-Gau's buttocks wobble as the dildo moved in her anus. Her shame at masturbating in public had gone, and she knew she was going to come, as was Lia-Gau. Delighting in her victory, and the sodomy as well, she began to spank Lia-Gau, all the while squirming herself against the dildo.

The climax began, Cianna's pleasure rising high, her eyes focused on the quivering black bottom below her, a bottom stuffed full of thick wooden dildo, the anus gaping on the shaft. Suddenly Lia-Gau cried out in shame and ecstasy, coming against the rough wooden balls, a response that was too much for Cianna. Crying out her pleasure to the pit, she came, climax after climax tearing through her as she jammed the dildo in and out of Lia-Gau's bottom, mercilessly hard, wringing out breathless screams in response as they came together.

Cianna giggled, staggering and clutching at the arm of Bulzar, who was supporting her through the lamp-lit streets of Kea. At the party thrown by Faerdahl after the contest, she had signalled him out as soon as the small ceremony that gave her an official rank had been completed. With some eight men to each of the girls, he had been delighted by her attention, and the more so when she had refused to let any others lead her aside.

Bulzar had suggested leaving while the party was still in full swing, gaining a purely formal permission from Jelkrael to use her as he pleased. Jelkrael had laughed, sending Cianna off with a firm swat to her bottom and remarking that he would never understand women. She had simply giggled, high on the excitement of victory and the numerous goblets of strong red wine that had been pressed on her.

As she left, her last view had been of Babalyn, equally drunk, being tied firmly to a frame as six men stood behind her, ready cocks in their hands. Now, despite the cool breeze blowing on her bare skin, she found her head spinning and her steps uneven as Bulzar helped her up the long, shallow slope of one of Kea's main thoroughfares. As he put his arm around her his hand went to her bottom, clutching one full cheek, his little finger delving into the crease between them.

'Is that where you mean to put your cock?' she giggled. 'Up my bottom ring? Did you like it when I buggered Lia-Gau? How she squealed!'

Immediately his hand delved lower, a finger tip prodding at her anus.

'Here?' she said. 'Go on then. Bugger me in the street. Let everyone see me, with your fat cock up my bottom. I bet you've a large one, haven't you?'

She made a grab for his crotch but he caught her wrist, then gave her bottom a resounding smack.

'Patience,' he said,' it will not do for a man of my station to be seen buggering slave girls in the street, wrestling champions or not. Besides, I have something else for you.'

'You do?' Cianna asked.

'Something to satisfy even you,' he replied. 'Now come on.'

As he spoke he had ducked down. Catching Cianna under her bottom, he lifted her, up across his shoulder, so that her bare rear end was sticking out to the front, with the lips of her sex pouting out between her thighs. She gave a squeak of alarm at the sudden rude treatment, but made no attempt to fight, allowing herself to be carried, head down, with passers-by laughing and making suggestions as to what Bulzar should do with her.

Showing considerable strength, he carried her much of the length of the road, to a villa set back in a grove of palms. Within, she was dumped onto a couch, Bulzar quickly dismissing the two slaves who had come to greet him at the door.

'Now,' he stated, his hand going to the hem of his robe, 'for my pleasure.'

'As you like,' she sighed. 'Shall I finger my ring, to make myself ready?'

'Wanton slut,' he answered. 'No, not yet. Wait.'

He pulled up his robe, exposing a massive, stocky body, heavy with both muscle and fat, and quite hairless. He wore a breechcloth, no more than a twist of linen, which he left on, walking from the room. Cianna sighed and stretched, reaching for a grape from a nearby bowl. She felt ready, moist and wanton, eager for cock for its own sake, and to come herself while one was in her. In moments Bulzar returned, holding on his hand, on which rested a wad of some kind of grease, thick and greenish brown

'For your cunt,' he explained, 'your anus too. You will need it for lubrication.'

'I am moist from the fight, thank you,' she giggled, 'although perhaps a little for my bottom ring, as you mean to bugger me.'

'You need it all, I assure you,' he insisted. 'Come, pack your cunt. I like to watch it done.'

Reluctantly, Cianna took the wad of grease, wondering if Bulzar truly had a cock so vast that all the lubricant was needed, or if he was merely boasting, as all Makean men seemed to. The grease felt cool, and slimy, with a smell she remembered from the heavy oil used to grease the axles of the wagons. She made a face, but cocked up her legs and slid forward on the couch, exposing her sex and the crease of her bottom.

Bulzar watched, grinning, as she slapped the thick wad of muck to her sex. Some went up her vagina, then more as she pushed it in with her fingers, filling herself until her hole was stretched and she could feel the irregular mass plugging the open mouth of her sex. What was left she pushed down further, between her buttocks, finding the tight dimple of her anus and slipping her finger inside. He began to touch himself as he watched her finger her bottom, squeezing what was obviously an already erect cock through his cloth.

'There you are, I'm ready,' she announced, taking hold of her ankles to make herself easily available for penetration. 'Fuck me then, or straight up my bottom if you'd rather.'

'You are bold for a slave,' he answered, 'and yes, you'll get your fucking, and my cock up your arse as well. Presently.'

He stepped back, pushing at the door he had just come through, giving a peculiar call as he did it. Cianna watched, expecting that a servant or slave had been invited to share her, even a cunt dog, only for her mouth to drop open as a vast, yellow-grey troll shambled out into the room. It stood, tiny eyes slowly registering her presence, nose wrinkling to the smell of her sex. Her eyes went down, instinctively, to its crotch. A cock hung down, vast beyond all human proportions, both thick and long, and as gnarled and uneven as the rock the creature resembled.

'Meet Voqual,' he said. 'Normally he lives in my villa at Julac, to guard against intrusion and keep the slaves in proper awe. By good fortune I brought him in today, to have his tusks capped. Fine are they not?'

Cianna managed to nod, unable to speak, as Bulzar pushed up the troll's thick grey lip, exposing twin tusks, each capped with golden filigree. In response its eyes turned slowly towards him, then back to between Cianna's still open thighs.

'Don't be scared,' Bulzar went on. 'He's quite tame, so long as you don't try and thwart him anyway. Voqual, fuck cunt.'

Bulzar pointed to Cianna, who simply lay there, staring open mouthed at the monster. Voqual gave a low growl, his massive hand closing on his cock. Cianna lay still, thighs wide, knowing full well that it was pointless to try and close them. Bulzar stepped back, grinning broadly as he pushed his hand down the front of his cloth.

The troll came forward, his cock already stiffening in his hand, a great pillar of grey flesh, grey-pink where the prepuce had began to roll back. With a quick prayer to her mother, Cianna rolled up her thighs, offering her grease filled sex. Voqual sank down, the floor trembling as he went to his knees. Poking out his cock, he touched it to Cianna's sex, rubbing the head in the grease flesh. With the firm, rough cock head right on her clitoris, Cianna could only gasp in pleasure, a sound that changed abruptly to shock. The massive head had been pushed to her greasy hole, and was going in, stretching her wider, and wider still. She was gasping and shaking as her tuppenny filled, sure she would tear at any moment, while her whole body seemed to be crammed with cock.

Only when she found the courage to look down did she realise that the full width of the monstrous thing was in her, her vagina stretched wider than she had every expected it to go, save in childbirth, yet unbroken. Much of the grease had been pushed out, over the troll's cock and down over her buttocks, adding a fresh obscenity to the sight of her penetrated ring.

She sighed, lying back as Voqual's massive hands took her thighs, clamping her in place as he very slowly began to fuck her. Panting, helpless to the short, hard thrusts, she could only let it happen, her body jerking on the massive penis, her head swimming with the sensation. Bulzar watched, his own cock standing proud from his cloth, thick and meaty, with a big, purple-brown head, but nothing compared to the one inside her.

The fucking was getting faster, shock after shock going through her body, her breasts wobbling back and forth, the huge cock jamming ever deeper up her hole. She was crying out, and gasping, her vision blurred, her hands clutching at the smooth surface of the couch. It got faster and faster still, until suddenly her whole belly seemed to expand as the troll came up her hole, his sperm bursting out inside her. Cianna screamed, clutching at her sex, feeling the straining ring of her vagina, the taut bud of her clitoris. She was coming, slapping at herself, over and over as Voqual jammed his penis in, deep in, one last time, until his balls squashed into the cleft of her bottom.

It stopped, abruptly. Voqual pulled back, sperm bursting from her sex as he vacated the hole, more squeezing from her vagina as it slowly contracted back to a normal size, grease too. She collapsed, back onto the couch as he let go of her legs, her body limp, her thighs going slowly down, but still wide.

Weak, exhausted, she looked at Bulzar. Grinning back, he tugged at his cloth, which fell away, leaving him nude but for his boots. Voqual lumber away at a word, all interest lost with his sperm discharged. Bulzar came close, to take Cianna by her legs, rolling her body up, his cock prodding between her buttocks. He found her anus, and pushed, Cianna managing only a weak groan as her ring stretched to take his cock head. Holding her legs wide and high, he watched as he wedged his erection slowly up her bottom, inch by inch, until the full length was in her rectum, stretching her just short of pain.

She let it happen, panting gently as she was buggered. Even when he put his thumb to her clitoris she made no effort to resist, merely taking her breasts in her hands to feel them as he casually masturbated her. She was brought to orgasm once more, so that her anal ring contracted on his intruding penis, then again, grunting and panting in her helpless ecstasy as he buggered her. With the second orgasm he came himself, pushing his cock in and out of her straining anus with the ring still pulsing from her climax. It was done up her, deep in her rectum, before he pulled slowly out. Taking her by the hair, he thrust his dirty cock at her mouth. She took it, too far gone to care, sucking up the salty sperm along with the earthy taste of her own bottom. He kept it in, making her clean it properly, then sat back with a satisfied grunt.

Cianna rolled from the couch, onto all fours. She was dizzy with lust, vagina and anus sore and gaping, her breasts swinging heavy beneath her chest. Not really sure what she was doing, she crawled across the room, to where a great mirror covered half of one wall. Turning, she stuck up her bottom, looking back to admire the view. Everything showed, her pale buttocks, high and wide, her twins holes, red rimmed, troll sperm dribbling from one, human from the other, grease from both. Her breasts were filthy too, from where she had fondled them during the fucking, and her belly as well, the grease mixed with come in a slimy mess. Her clitoris was showing, a pale bud in the middle of the filth that coated her tuppenny, taut and urgent. Beyond, she could see Bulzar reflected, watching her, his limp cock lying across one big thigh. The troll was visible too, eating fruit, apparently indifferent to her wanton display.

Rolling onto her back, she spread her thighs to the mirror. She found her sex, flicking at the little bud. That single touch was too much, too good to resist, and she began to masturbate, all the while with her legs rolled high, watching the mess ooze from her well used holes. After a while her spare hand went under her bottom, finding her vagina, then her anus, fingers pushing into the greasy cavities. Her flesh felt loose, slimy and open, and as she watched she could see the mess squeezing out around her fingers.

On sudden impulse she let her bladder go, pee spurting out, to spray the mirror and floor. Watching it, she held back a little, to let the warm fluid trickle down between her sex lips and buttocks, into the gaping holes of her vagina and anus. As her holes filled with urine she thought of the way Yuilla peed in girls' mouths to show her victory, and how Klia sometimes masturbated as it was done to her.

As her pee ran out she snatching up a good handful of the mess from between her bottom cheeks, slapping it to her sex. Her bottom was in a pool of warm pee and slime, her clitoris burning as she rubbed, her whole body greasy and foul, providing an unutterably deliciously feeling as she came, screaming out her ecstasy with her back arched and her fingers working frantically up her filthy, aching holes.

Her challenge to Moloa accepted, Cianna found herself with a week to wait before fighting. After her defeat of Lia-Gau, odds of as little as ten to one were being offered on her, to Jelkrael's irritation, as twenty to one was more normal for the champion's opponents. Despite that he remained in high spirits, with a handsome profit from the fight at Faerdahl's Pit and the attention of the fashionable clique in the city.

Each night entertainments were held, with Cianna in constant demand. Always at his most unctuous, Jelkrael did his best to stop her being used too heavily, explaining even to Elites that it would spoil her chances against Moloa. Despite his efforts he was forced to capitulate occasionally, allowing Cianna twice to be taken back for fucking, and also to be made to lick a female Exquisite to orgasm in front of a large audience. Bulzar she saw frequently, but never alone, and with no more sexual contact than a brief suck of his cock as one among several other men.

With a full day to go before the contest, Jelkrael and she retired to the room at the Five Moons, leaving instructions that all who came for her where to be told she was elsewhere. All afternoon she lay quietly on Jelkrael's couch, thinking of the situation she was in, and how strange it was beside her home life in Boreal. In the evening she ate lightly, and retired early, only to spend much of the night staring out of the window to watch the moons swinging slowly by through the sky.

She awoke to brilliant sunlight, and Babalyn seated beside her with a tray of meat pastries and sweet jellies. Learning that it was nearly noon, she ate and prepared herself quickly, with Babalyn, Klia and even Yuilla fussing around her and doing their best to boost her confidence.

Finally Jelkrael returned from the Great Pit, declaring that Cianna was expected there within the hour. They set off, riding the open wagon, with Cianna standing naked but not collared, and proud, her head held high, no longer embarrassed at the public exposure of her body.

A thick crowd had gathered around the pit, greeting her mainly with cheers, along with a few taunts from Moloa's more ardent supporters. The building was some twice the size of any other pit she had seen, but of the same design, only with a double set of public doors, for the commonality and the nobles. Within was again familiar, with a great dim chamber underneath the stands, which were already packed, with the massive beams that supported them groaning beneath the weight.

Among the pit officials within she recognised Glaydrak, who greeted Jelkrael with a professional yet slightly condescending nod. Beyond him stood Moloa, a vast woman, nearly Cianna's height, but broader, heavy with muscle and fat, her broad, flat face showing a cruel grin. Cianna gave her a nod, which only caused the grin to twitch up at one corner. A pit official approached Jelkrael, leaving Cianna alone with the other girls.

'Have you seen her?' Babalyn said, glancing back at Moloa. 'She is a monster! Look at her eyes!'

'Don't be alarmed,' Klia urged. 'She does it to terrify her opponents. She is as human as you and I.'

'Give her a quick victory,' Yuilla advised Babalyn. 'Don't get her temper up, then in with the capsule and she is done!'

'Quiet!' Klia hissed. 'She is likely to toy with you for one round at the least, Babalyn, perhaps two, simply to warm her muscles, but if you don't resist she won't hurt you badly.'

'Stop it, please!' Babalyn said. 'I'm terrified as it is! Look, what's she doing?'

'Stropping her cunt razor,' Klia answered. 'You wouldn't want it blunt, would you?'

Babalyn frantically shook her head as Cianna put an arm around her shoulder. In Babalyn's bush of frizzy hair was the capsule, ready to be placed in her mouth before she stepped out onto the sand. Again and again they had rehearsed the manoeuvre, until Babalyn had brought the insertion to a precise art, using a capsule no larger than a pea.

'Truly superb!' Jelkrael declared as he joined them once more. 'Never have I known so high a gate! Even at a sixth share we would stand to make as much as in three ordinary contests, four even. With a third of the gate and Yufal's bets, I will be rich! He is in the stands, and signals odds of eight up to twelve.'

'You are ready?' Glaydrak enquired, appearing at Jelkrael's shoulder.

'As ready as I can hope,' Jelkrael replied.

Glaydrak nodded, stepping towards the corridor. Jelkrael followed, holding Babalyn by the hand. In the narrow mouth of the corridor, Cianna found herself shoulder to shoulder with Moloa, their flesh touching, the champion's arm as thick and solid as a man's. Pausing, Moloa looked at Cianna.

'How old are you?' she demanded suddenly. 'You seem little more than a girl, for all your height.'

'Seventeen winters,' Cianna answered.

'Seventeen?' Moloa replied. 'Run back to your nursery, little one.'

Cianna stuck her tongue out, lost for a better response. Moloa made to reply, but Glaydrak was already on the sand, his hands lifted for silence. Cianna listened as he made a respectful address to the King and various nobles, then announced Moloa with a sweeping gesture to the corridor. Moloa stepped out, raising one massive arm to shake her fist at the audience in a gesture of utter contempt. Quickly Babalyn ducked down, then rose, winking at Cianna. Again Glaydrak spoke, announcing Babalyn, who walked out slowly, her jaw trembling. The audience cheered and laughed, many throwing coins. Glaydrak retreated, two placard girls stepped forward, made their pirouettes and once more crouched down, leaving the pit to the contestants.

Moloa flexed her arms, not even bothering to crouch. Babalyn backed away, drawing ribald comments from the crowd. Moloa came forward, walking casually, only to suddenly lash out with an open handed slap. Babalyn jumped back, squeaking, as Moloa spun on her heel, snatching. Babalyn cried out, caught by the wrist, to be dragged in, grabbed around the waist and lifted bodily, her legs kicking madly as she was upended. Laughing aloud, Moloa threw up a knee, tossed Babalyn over it, delivered a dozen hard swats to the wiggling black backside and dropped her into the sand.

Slowly Babalyn climbed to her feet, rubbing at her bottom. Moloa put out her hands, beckoning Babalyn forward, an invitation that was ignored. Instead Babalyn backed away, Moloa coming forward, great arms spread. Babalyn ducked, rolled, only for Moloa to dance back, planting a foot on Babalyn's stomach. Immediately Babalyn was gasping out her submission, but Moloa merely laughed, reached down to fondle one fat brown breast before stepping back.

Babalyn stayed down, Moloa standing over her, hands on hips. The crowd began to yell, calling on Babalyn to fight. Slowly, Babalyn pulled herself up, onto her elbow, onto all fours, only to have Moloa plant a foot on her hip and kick her over. Babalyn scrambled away, Moloa following, hand out, reaching down to slap at Babalyn's bottom, once, twice, setting the full dark flesh quivering and leaving rich purple marks.

The gong sounded, and immediately Babalyn collapsed into the sand. The placard girls ran out, holding water flasks, one going to tend to Babalyn. Refusing the water with a gesture, Babalyn pulled herself up, resting her arm on the pit wall. She was breathing hard, her skin wet with sweat and dark with bruises on her buttocks and thighs. Cianna made a sign, clenching her fist in encouragement, to which Babalyn responded with an exhausted shake of her head.

As the gong sounded once more the placard girls skipped back. Moloa came forward, cracking her knuckles with her fingers locked together. Babalyn turned, ducked low and suddenly charged. Moloa stood firm, barely moving her body, but enough to lock one great arm around Babalyn's waist. Again Babalyn was hauled squealing into the air, plump black bottom stuck out to the audience. Again she was spanked, hard, her legs kicking in desperation, her thighs and buttocks wide to show every detail of her sex and anal region.

At last Babalyn was dropped, to lie panting on the sand. Her face was streaked with tears, her lower lip pouted and trembling. Throwing a leg across Babalyn's prone body, Moloa looked down in disgust. Cianna saw the muscles of the big woman's belly twitch, and a great gush of urine spurted suddenly from the thick forest of her pubic hair, full into Babalyn's face. Babalyn's hands came up to shield her eyes. Moloa laughed redirecting the stream to urinate in Babalyn's hair, over her chest, her belly, and lastly her sex.

Babalyn was left in a pool of steaming piddle, soaked from head to toe. Again she offered submission, and again Moloa refused, reaching down to pull

Babalyn up by the hair. Gripped tightly, two fat fingers were pushed into Babalyn's vagina and she was lifted, high over Moloa's head, then sent crashing to the sand in a spray of droplets of piddle and sweat. Moloa lifted her hands in triumph, stamping across to Babalyn, who once more offered submission. Moloa gave a harsh chuckle and accepted it, the signal for ringing laughter, clapping, cheers and a shower of coins from the audience.

Glaydrak stepped out, bowed briefly to the King and passed Moloa a box. Moloa took it, pushed a toe under Babalyn's body and rolled her over, face up. Cianna found her hand going to her mouth as Moloa sank down, into a squat, huge bottom poised over Babalyn's face, then in it. A roar of delight went up from the audience, which Moloa acknowledged with a wave.

Opening the box, Moloa extracted the folding razor she had been stropping earlier. Babalyn was taken by one ankle, her legs hauled wide, spreading her sex to the audience. Moloa spat, full into the curly mass of Babalyn's pubic hair, then set to work, shaving.

Cianna watched as Babalyn's sex was denuded, the thick dark hair quickly scrapped away, to leave the plump brown mound she had kissed so often naked and shiny. The main mound done, Babalyn was rolled up, to have the hair between her bottom cheeks and on her sex lips shaved away, until her whole underside was entirely nude. By then, Babalyn's sex was wet, white juice running from the hole, her nipples hard too, drawing yet more raucous comments from the crowd.

The shaving done, Moloa made an elaborate show of lighting her cigar, striking the match on Babalyn's newly shaved skin and blowing a triple smoke ring with the first puff. Beneath her, Babalyn had lain inert, allowing her body to be handled to Moloa's amusement. Now, as the big woman wiggled her bottom, Babalyn's arms came up, taking hold of Moloa's huge thighs. Cianna realised that Babalyn had began to lick, and after a moment Moloa reached down, spread her sex with two fat fingers and quite casually began to masturbate. As Moloa rubbed herself she continued to smoke, also the flick ash onto Babalyn's breasts and belly. When at last she came it was with no more than a low sigh.

Eventually Moloa dismounted and stood up, revealing Babalyn's juice smeared face. Slowly Babalyn rose, falling back twice but finally managing to stagger to her feet and stumble to the corridor entrance.

'You did it?' Jelkrael demanded. 'The distillate is in her?'

'No,' Babalyn gasped. 'I didn't. I swallowed the capsule, when she threw me…'

Babalyn went limp, falling into Cianna's arms. Looking up, Cianna found Jelkrael white in the face.

'Over three thousand standard Yufal has on you,' he said weakly. 'Our whole fund! Promises from our gate also. I am ruined!'

Cianna gave him a weak smile, even as Glaydrak appeared, giving Jelkrael a nod, then a puzzled look as he stepped past them onto the sand. Cianna watched him, suddenly confused, still holding the sleeping Babalyn.

'Lord King,' Glaydrak began, making a sweeping bow to the royal box, 'Exquisite nobles, Elite gentlemen, men and women of Kea and Makea beyond. I trust you have been amused by the rapid despatch of our haughty little Aprinian girl, which, while a mere taster, had, perhaps, a certain style. Now though, I give you no over cultivated weakling for the She Troll to devour, no soft product of a society in decline, but a true barbarian, a creature of the northern wastelands! With thirteen victories to her name, and undefeated, I give you, Cianna, the Ice Cannibal!'

He made a sweeping bow, gesturing towards the mouth of the corridor. Seeing her cue, Cianna hastily dropped Babalyn and ran out. A cheer greeted her, and a few coins, then sudden, expectant silence. She turned, to where Moloa was lifting her bulk from the sand, grinning. Glaydrak retreated, the placard girls skipped out and back. Cianna was alone with Moloa.

Moloa stood, spreading her great arms, then crouched low. Cianna touched a finger to her necklace, drawing a picture of her grandfather to her mind, then also ducked down, waiting. Moloa came on, a pace at a time, stamping, and lashing out with her open slap. Cianna caught the arm, wrenching, only to be thrown off her feet. Rolling, she bounced back upright and danced away before Moloa could touch her.

Once more Moloa spread her arms, moving forward. Cianna ran immediately, ducking as Moloa moved to cut her off, only to twist back, kicking out hard at Moloa's midriff. Moloa staggered back with a grunt, snatching for Cianna's feet, an instant too late. Cianna scrambled away, jumped up, amazed that Moloa had not gone down to the blow.

Twice more they came together, both times with Cianna striking by pure speed, but with no effect on Moloa. After the second Moloa was grinning, her eyes bright as she again fell into her crouch. Cianna fell back, glancing at the placard girls from the corner of her eye, even as the gong struck. Breathing deeply, Cianna stood away, taking a flagon from a placard girl. Moloa was not only heavier, but stronger than her, unlike every other girl she had fought in Makea. To bring her down by skill was highly unlikely, by force impossible. Moloa would also know every trick, every facet of Makean wrestling. In sheer strength she was no match for Moloa, yet she was faster, more agile. She could hold her own, but only for so long, then the huge buttocks would be settling over her face and the razor scraping at the hair of her tuppenny.

The gong sounded and again they faced off. Cianna began to dodge, using her speed to avoid Moloa, a tactic that quickly had the crowd frustrated, yelling for more contact and more display. Ignoring them utterly, Cianna continued to twist and duck, run and leap, until at last the gong rang again. Moloa was chuckling as she drank her water, draining the flagon, then spreading her sex lips to Cianna. Cianna swallowed, remembering how Babalyn had been urinated over on the ground, but returned the gesture, then spun, spreading her buttocks to show Moloa her anus and briefly allowing the ring to pout. The crowd laughed, clapping too, but Moloa merely grinned.

The third round started, Cianna again ducking and weaving, occasionally putting in a kick or a slap, but doing her best to avoid contact. With Moloa's reactions always a fraction slower than her own, she began to grow confident, adding the occasional rude gesture, somersaults, or flaunting her bottom to the crowd. Moloa failed to rise to the bait, steady, determined and patient.

In the fourth round Cianna began to strike in more, wondering if she might not wear Moloa down by sheer persistence. Twice she got good kicks in to Moloa's midriff, although with little effect. On the third attempt her heel came down on a coin buried beneath the sand. For an instant she was off balance, and Moloa was on her. Slammed hard into the sand, Cianna's leg was twisted up, and locked. Red pain hit her, and anger. Striking back at Moloa's neck, Cianna hit out, twice, but the blows where ignored.

'Submit!' Moloa grunted, shifting to bring her face clear of Cianna's reach.

Cianna hit out, lashing frantically at Moloa's arm and hip, to no effect. The hold tightened and Cianna cried out, gritting her teeth in pain. Again the hold tightened. She closed her hand on her necklace, praying, forcing herself to push the agony from her mind. Moloa chuckled and tightened the grip yet more.

'Submit, little one,' she grated, 'and maybe I won't piss on you after all.'

Cianna said nothing, mumbling prayers through a haze of pain, her vision blurred, her hand gripped tight on her necklace, everything concentrated on thoughts of her family, until she seemed to be in Boreal, but above it, high over Sulitea's meadow, floating in silence…

Suddenly she was back on the sand in the Great Pit at Kea. Moloa was sitting back, the hold released, the placard girls coming out from the corridor.

'Tough little brat, aren't you?' Moloa said.

Cianna said nothing, filled with anger as she imagined her brothers laughing at her, or her grandfather turning away to hide an expression of shame as she lay defeated in the dirt. Stretching out her leg, she reached up for a flagon being offered by one of the placard girls. Sat up, she took water, drinking some and pouring the remainder over her head. The tone of the crowd had changed, voices raised in doubt, hissed demands for the bookmakers to take money on Moloa, derisive grunts in response.

She got up, wiping sand wet with sweat from her legs and buttocks. Opposite her Moloa had her hands raised to a section of her supporters among the crowd, who returned a cheer. Cianna touched her necklace, uttered a prayer. The gong sounded and she bared her teeth, wiped a tendril of hair from her face and crouched down, her eyes locking with Moloa's. Moloa returned the grin, squatting to begin her stamping advance. Cianna screamed, hurled herself forward, driving a fist into the centre of Moloa's chest even as the great arms closed on her. Moloa grunted in pain, but held, crushing Cianna into herself, only to scream as Cianna's teeth clamped into her neck.

Hurled back, Cianna sprawled on the sand for an instant, bouncing up and once more darting forward. Her fist drove up, her knee also, Moloa staggering back, unable to keep the hold. Immediately Cianna darted back in, hacking and kicking, throwing herself down to avoid a crushing back handed slap, then up, driving both fists into Moloa's ribs. Moloa screamed in pain and fury, clutching for Cianna's body, catching her and hurling her away, to strike the wall, following with a roar of pure fury. Cianna ducked, twisted, planting her foot hard into Moloa's bottom to send her crashing into the pit wall.

Not waiting, Cianna hurled herself onto Moloa, punching, kicking and biting, only for the assault to be returned with equal fury. The crowd forgotten, they tore at each other, rolling in madden frenzy on the sand, one on top, then the other, without thought for holds, let alone displaying themselves. Cianna was screaming, her vision red, her pain faded to heat, indifferent to everything but Moloa's body, striking and clawing and biting, until at last hands were gripping at her shoulders, pulling her back, Moloa also. She stood, finding Jelkrael and his two male slaves clutching onto her. Glaydrak had Moloa, also a pit official, pulling her up from the sand.

'The gong went,' Jelkrael explained.

Cianna spat at him, catching him full in the face, and wrenched herself back. A gasp went up from the crowd, Jelkrael standing pop-eyed in astonishment. The male slaves let go of her and she snatched a flagon from a placard girl, upending it over her head. Across the pit Moloa was with Glaydrak, her body wet with sweat, Cianna's war paint and also blood, her face set in fury. Cianna laughed.

Jelkrael stepped quickly back. Cianna shook out her hair, which had come lose in the fight, and bared her teeth at Moloa, her mouth wide to show the sharpened points and red blood on her lips. Moloa gave back a hard, set look, angry, with none of the amusement she had shown before. Raising her arm to her mouth, Cianna clamped her teeth into her own flesh, bit, to feel the skin burst and the sharp pain. Sucking, she showed her blood filled mouth to Moloa, swallowed her mouthful and pointed at Moloa's neck.

Moloa motioned to Glaydrak, beckoning him back from the corridor mouth. Briefly they conferred. Glaydrak signalled a pit official, who listened to Moloa, then glanced at Cianna and back. Nodding, he walked to Cianna.

'A point of rule,' he announced. 'Attempting to kill your opponent leads to disqualification, in the same manner as the breaking of bones. It will also be treated as murder. Do you understand?'

Cianna laughed and spat sideways, leaving a red mark on the sand.

'I understand, and I laugh in the Feast Hall, Makean pig,' she answered.

He gave her a puzzled look and backed hastily away, but nodded to Glaydrak and Moloa. The gong sounded, the men hastily departing the sand. Cianna shook her hair out once more, screamed and lunged. Moloa met her, arms up, face protected, striking out with her fists. A punch caught Cianna's shoulder, spinning her around even as he knee came up into Moloa's side. They clung tight, Moloa frantically defending her face from Cianna's teeth, falling, to crash to the sand, Cianna on top.

Moloa's hands lashed out, a double fisted blow, driven straight to Cianna's face, missing to the side. Darting her head in, Cianna buried her teeth in Moloa's arm, evoking a scream and a frantic bucking motion that sent Cianna sprawling into the sand, teeth still locked in place. Moloa hurled herself away, rolling in the sand, kicking and punching in blind panic, to strike Cianna's face.

Cianna rolled back, dazed, cursing herself as she struggled to clear her vision, kicking out wildly as she scrambled back. Her leg cut through air, the blur clearing to show Moloa on one knee, clutching her bleeding arm, her huge chest shivering to quick, hard breaths. Cianna bared her teeth, crawling forward. Moloa swallowed, bunching a fist, her face setting in determination, but also fear.

'You're not human!' she babbled. 'You're a beast! A man-ape!'

Cianna nodded her head and licked a fang, braced herself and lunged, her arm out to parry Moloa's furious punch, crashing together, head to neck, her teeth locking across Moloa's throat…

'Submit!' Moloa screamed. 'Submit! Get her off me! Glaydrak, help!'

Immediately Cianna bounced back, and up, laughing to the ceiling high above her, a wild, uncontrolled sound of pure, feral glee. It lasted only a moment, before her strength went, fading to leave her weak kneed. She struggled to stand, the stands spinning around her, noise and faces blurring, clutching for the pit wall. All around her was noise, cheering and the furious stamping of feet, voices raised in salute, or anger. Someone touched her and her head snapped round, teeth bare, only to see that it was Babalyn, holding out a flagon of water.

Cianna took it, her hand shaking as she poured the full contents down her throat. Slowly her vision cleared, if not her hearing, her ears buzzing with sound. Across the pit Moloa was still sprawled on the sand, Glaydrak standing over her, expostulating. Two pit officials stood by them, frowning.

'Are you all right?' Babalyn asked, her arm going around Cianna's shoulder.

'Yes,' Cianna answered weakly. 'Let me stand.'

Drawing in her breath, she forced herself to let go of the wall, turning to find Jelkrael coming towards her, the dildo thrust out before him.

'Fuck her!' he said, pushing it at Cianna' chest.

'Fuck her?' Cianna managed.

'You must!' he hissed. 'For the victory, for your title, for my money!'

'I spit on it.'

'Then for our team! For honour!'

'Moloa is beaten. There's your honour.'

'Then for Babalyn. Think how Moloa abused her! She pissed on her in the sand! This is not her signature!'

'For revenge, yes. Revenge for a friend is good.'

Cianna snatched the dildo from Jelkrael, holding it up. A great cheer rose from the crowd, coins showering downs, demands ringing out that Moloa be made to kneel, or sodomised, or urinated on first. Cianna ignored them, still struggling to stand up properly as she strapped the dildo into place.

'A moment!' Glaydrak shouted. 'Lord King, I dispute the victory and ask your judgement.'

'On what grounds!?' Jelkrael demanded, his voice loud in the sudden quiet as every face turned towards the King. 'Damage? Not so! Moloa lives, with no bones broken!'

'I challenge on the grounds that Cianna is not fully human,' Glaydrak said evenly. 'Look at her, Lord King. She is unnaturally tall, her skin white, her hair red. No others have such characteristics. Jelkrael may claim she is from the northlands, but there is no proof of this. I say that somewhere in her ancestry there is Red Ape!'

Cianna's mouth came open in protest and she started forward, pulling against both Jelkrael and Babalyn. The King raised his hand, then put his fingers together, his eyes flicking to Cianna, then the crowd. An angry murmur began, but died as the King once more raised his hand.

'Is there a rule on this matter? he demanded. 'A precedent perhaps?'

'Neither, Lord King,' an official responded.

'Then the savage girl has her victory,' the King answered.

Wild cheering broke out immediately. Glaydrak bowed and quickly stood away, leaving the centre of the pit clear. Cianna stepped forward, beckoning to Moloa, who pulled herself to her knees, crawling slowly to the centre of the pit with a look of consternation set hard on her face. Head towards the king, she went down, lifting her vast ash-black buttocks. Cianna took a deep breath and stepped behind Moloa, looking down at the fat, hairy sex lips. The skin of Moloa's tuppenny was near black, the lips plump and heavy, also swollen, with the pink centre moist and puffy, the huge clitoris taut in excitement, the hole pooled with white fluid.

Cianna gave a chuckle and squatted down, over Moloa's huge bottom, putting the dildo to the wet hole. She pushed, and the thick head went straight in, without difficulty. Grinning maniacally, she began to fuck Moloa, posed to make sure as many of the audience as possible could actually see the dildo going in and out of the sopping, quite obviously aroused vagina.

The position hurt her aching muscles, but she kept it up, and after a while reached down, to rub on Moloa's outsize clitoris. Immediately Moloa gave a moan of shame, but she held still, and in seconds she was coming, with the same low sigh as when she had been sat on Babalyn's face. Cianna rose immediately, pulling the dildo from the gaping hole of Moloa's sex. Raising her hands, she flourished the juice stained cock to the crowd, stepped back, staggered and collapsed onto the sand.

Chapter Six

Jelkrael sat, his hands folded over his ample stomach, a huge cigar clamped between his teeth. Babalyn was beside him at the table, counting gold and silver coins into little piles. Yufal stood, looking happily over her shoulder, with the three girls seated cross-legged on the ground, Cianna with Glaucum's head in her lap, as usual.

In the three days since her victory she had done little but rest. The fight had left her whole body aching, with barely an inch of skin unbruised. Even at the parade Jelkrael had organised in her honour she had done nothing more than stand to accept the plaudits of the crowd. All offers to have sex with her had been denied or delayed if the gap in social status made it impossible for Jelkrael to refuse outright.

It had also taken Yufal two days to gather in the bets, but it been done, and in the early hours of that morning the money had at last been brought to the rear door of the Five Moons. Since then, Jelkrael had been in an irrepressibly good mood.

'Done,' Babalyn declared, dropping the last coin into place. 'Forty-one thousand, seven hundred and twenty-eight standard.'

Jelkrael's hand went to his cigar. He drew on it, removed it from his mouth and blew a thick yellow smoke ring towards the ceiling.

'Say that again,' he ordered.

'Forty-one thousand, seven hundred and twenty-eight standard,' Babalyn repeated. 'It's correct, I assure you.'

'I don't doubt you for a minute,' he answered. 'I merely wish to hear the words. That is enough, you may not realise, to allow me to sell up and retire. A villa in the hills, I think, with an orange grove and pond where I will keep carp.'

'Sell up?' Klia asked in shock.

'Not you, my Warrior,' he said. 'None of you. I shall keep you all, and we shall talk of the old days while pretty Vendjomois girls serve us tea in the most delicate of porcelain.'

'You mean to free us?' Cianna asked.

'That I cannot do,' he said. 'A slave is a slave, and besides, I would still wish to command obedience when I wanted my cock sucked or to have a girl on the saddle. Or, if you do not wish to join me in a life of ease, I will sell you to Glaydrak at the Dock Pit and you may seek to hold your title. There is much of your precious honour in it, ease too. Moloa has her own apartments, beside Glaydrak's, in the attic of the pit. It is said that no slave lives so well.'

'I'd rather go home,' Cianna said quietly.

'An idle hope,' he answered. 'How would you get there? Wherever she goes a girl as pretty as you will be taken as a slave, save Aprinia, and their ships do not touch here. I would let you though, in gratitude, if there was a way. You also, Babalyn.'

'What if we found a way?' Babalyn asked. 'Buy a fishing vessel, perhaps? The coast of Cypraea is no more than four hundred leagues away, the southern border perhaps six hundred. It could be done.'

'Well…' Jelkrael began doubtfully, only to stop at the sound of a sharp rap on the door.

'Glaydrak, probably,' Jelkrael said, 'with an offer of a rematch.'

'If Moloa dares!' Klia laughed, rising to open the door.

Cianna turned to see who it was, finding a young man in a robe of brilliant turquoise blue standing outside, evidently an Elite. Jelkrael stood immediately and hurried over, then out into the passage, closing the door behind him. A brief conversation could be heard, before Jelkrael returned, now downcast as he addressed Cianna.

'The Exquisite Ulourdos has offered a thousand standard for you,' he sighed.

'A thousand?' Cianna answered. 'What of it? It is little enough for you now, surely?'

'True,' Jelkrael admitted, 'but one such as Ulourdos is not to be refused. He is an Exquisite, and stands in line for the throne. He has boasted that he will be the one to tame the Ice Cannibal, to his royal relatives apparently. He will not be denied. I am truly sorry.'

'I don't want to be sold!' Cianna complained. 'Besides, what of my title?'

'All that matters to Ulourdos is that he gets his way,' Jelkrael answered quietly, with a glance to the door. 'That is his aide. He himself is downstairs. You had better go.'

'Now?' Cianna demanded.

'Now, please,' Jelkrael insisted. 'If I keep him waiting he is likely to have me whipped for insolence, or to drop the price! Come on.'

'What of me?' Babalyn demanded.

'What of you?' Jelkrael answered.

'I must be with Cianna!'

'You must? Very well, if you can persuade Ulourdos to buy you as well, you may go.'

Babalyn got up hurriedly, knocking over some of the piles of coins. Cianna also rose, reluctantly, shocked at the sudden change in events. They trooped downstairs, after the aide, who never so much as glanced back. Stopping in the main room of the inn, the aide crossed to a tall, slim young man, his robe brilliant golden cloth set with jewels, who Cianna recognised as Ulourdos. His bearing was erect, his expression of amused contempt as Jelkrael and the aide fussed around him. Four guards followed him, also young, and in extravagant blue, crimson and gold uniforms.

As he came towards them Cianna gave him a sulky look, feeling instant dislike. There was a cruelty in his eyes, a callousness, which if typical enough of Makean men, seemed far more intense in his case. As the others fell to their knees she remained standing, hoping that he would be put off by her failure to show proper respect. He crossed to her, stopping a foot in front of her, his eyes lifted fractionally to stare full into hers, full of arrogant certainty. She bared her teeth, but he responded with an amused chuckle.

'Wild indeed,' he remarked. 'She is unbroken, you say?'

'Many times I have whipped her, Exquisite,' Jelkrael answered hurriedly, 'many times she has been put to the dog. Still she refuses to plead, or to show proper respect. You saw, perhaps how she spat on me in the pit?'

'I did,' he answered. 'It amused me. Clearly she needs to be trained by a more skilful hand. Yes, a thousand, why not?'

He snapped his fingers and the aide quickly gave Jelkrael a bulging leather bag, which vanished into the folds of his smock. Again Ulourdos snapped his fingers, turning for the door, only to stop as Babalyn snatched at the hem of his robe. He turned, looking down on her with amusement in his eyes.

'Take me also!' she begged. 'Please, Exquisite, please! It makes me shiver just to look at you! My cunt is wet and ready, my breasts are straining!'

'This is usual, when women meet me,' Ulourdos answered.

'I am her lover too,' Babalyn went on. 'We will perform for you, the lewdest of tricks! Please, I beg you!'

'A hundred standard for the little fat Aprinian,' Ulourdos said suddenly. 'She grovels so prettily.'

'A gracious offer, Exquisite!' Jelkrael answered.

'My aide will fetch the money,' Ulourdos said.

'Yes, Exquisite. I am honoured, Exquisite,' Jelkrael stammered.

Ulourdos ignored him, signalling to a guard. The man stepped forward, holding out a chain. Numb, Cianna allowed it to be fixed around her neck. Jelkrael had been on the verge of giving in to Babalyn's argument, granting them freedom. Now, minutes later, she had been sold to some hateful new master, with no choice whatever in the matter. The guard pulled and she stumbled after him, Babalyn following, both glancing back as they were pulled from the inn.

Outside was a carriage, of elaborate design, painted in a complex pattern of gold, dark blue and crimson. A guard helped Ulourdos into this, while Cianna's chain was clipped to a hook in the rear. The carriage set off, Cianna and Babalyn running behind with the guards, save for the one who drove.

They left the square, travelling slowly through dense traffic, to Cianna's relief, along one crowded street, into another, and at last to a broad avenue with great houses set behind high walls to either side. The traffic had thinned, and Cianna found herself forced to run once more, with the collar jerking at her neck. Only when she was sure she would fall did the carriage slow and turn, past two guards in the same livery and into the grounds of the largest house she had ever seen.

With the carriage parked outside the house, Cianna's neck was unclipped. Ulourdos alighted, walking up the broad marble steps and inside, to dismiss his aide and the guards with a wave. Despite her feelings, Cianna could only stare, open mouthed, at the expanse of marble, brilliantly polished wood, rich fabrics and features of gold-leaf. A magnificent double staircase led up to a higher level, which Ulourdos climbed, the girls coming behind. From the landing huge doors opened into a room hung with drapes of crimson and gold, the colours mirrored in the carpet. They crossed it, and into another beyond, larger still, with a vast bed at the centre, wide enough for six or seven people. Cianna stopped, looking around, still with her mouth open. Beside her Babalyn had sunk to her knees.

'Never have you seen such riches, is it not so?' Ulourdos demanded.

'Never,' Cianna admitted.

'You see,' he said. 'I know your very thoughts!'

'You are a warlock?' Cianna asked.

'Never have you met a man such as me,' he went on, ignoring her question. 'Be sure of it. Now, the fat showman said that you have never been broken? Never made to beg for mercy while under the lash?'

Cianna nodded uncertainly.

'Excellent. To tame you will be a pleasure indeed!'

'Why break me?' Cianna asked. 'I will do as you ask.'

'Why break you? Why break you, she asks! For the pleasure of it, my little one, and because it is needed. You stand before me, when you should think it a privilege to kneel. You do not address me by my title! Insolence, sheer and bold! Oh you need to be broken, make no mistake, and you will break with me! You will grovel, begging for mercy, on your belly in your own sweat and urine! Just wait!'

He cut a caper, a flurry of legs and robe that left Cianna wondering if he was entirely sane.

'You will be whipped,' he went on, 'by me, the most skilled of men! In hands such as mine the whip becomes as an artist's brush, able to cause ecstasy or agony, a whimper or a scream! It is the ideal implement. All women, slave and free both, understand the whip. Not so men, to whom brave defiance is natural!'

Again he cut a caper. Cianna and Babalyn exchanged worried looks.

'Should the whipping fail to break you,' he continued, 'which is unlikely, it will be down to the dungeons, for a little play with knives and fire! In fact, it might be anyway, if it amuses me. Now, let us begin. First, slaves should be naked, completely. Remove your jewellery.'

Babalyn moved to comply at once, her fingers going to one of the ornaments in her nipples. Cianna did nothing.

'Your necklace, remove it,' Ulourdos said. 'You must be naked.'

'I cannot,' Cianna answered. 'It is part of me.'

'Ha, ha,' he crowed, 'resistance, and so soon! Now, I could easily have you held while it is removed, but this misses the point. You must take it off yourself, to my order.'

'No,' Cianna answered.

'You will, soon enough!' he laughed. 'Remain here, you have a lesson to learn in humility. Presently I will return, and you may fight me, yes, me, the Exquisite Ulourdos, with swords! And when I have defeated you, and put a few swats across your impudent behind, I will fuck you. Once fucked by me, be assured you will be begging for more, and naked.'

He strode from the room, leaving them together.

'What I am supposed to do?' Cianna hissed.

'Do?' Babalyn demanded. 'Nothing! You are supposed to get beaten and fucked!'

'But swords!'

'He wishes only to humiliate you. To show the gulf which exists between him, a man of Makea, and you, a barbarian slave girl.'

'He does not seek to slay me?'

'No, although he might inflict a cut or two, enough to leave you begging for mercy on the floor. He will then use the flat of the sword to spank your bottom, down across his knee. This is the way it is done.'

Cianna nodded doubtfully, entirely unsure what to do, expect that nothing would make her take her necklace off. Putting her hand to her necklace, she squeezed a tooth, a fang from the one grandfather she had known. It seemed to pulse between her fingers, throbbing, like a heartbeat.

Ulourdos returned, closing the door behind him. He was carrying two short swords, one of which he passed to Cianna with a mocking bow, then stood back to make an elaborate flourish in the air with his blade. Cianna looked at her sword, which was blunt and so light she wondered if it was hollow, nothing more than a toy. A glance at his showed that it was the real thing, sharp and well made. He made a pirouette, spinning to push out his blade towards her.

'Ha!' he cried. 'There I could have had you, and so easily. Come, defend yourself, learn what it means to fight a man, I, the Exquisite Ulourdos!'

Cianna braced herself as Babalyn made a hasty retreat to the furthest corner of the room. Ulourdos came forward, with a prancing, flamboyant step. Cianna gave back, still hesitant, and he rushed forward, eyes blazing, mouth wide to drive the sword at her shoulder. She danced aside, dodging his body, reluctant to make contact. He wheeled on her, his sword low, ready for a cut. She put out her hand, the palm flat towards him, a pacfic gesture. Low, mocking laughter seemed to run through her head.

Ulourdos slashed out at her fingers, which she snatched back an instant before the blade would have cut through them. Anger flared, the laughter in her head rising to become cruel, taunting. Ulourdos pranced forward, his sword thrust out. Cianna gave back, hurled her sword into his face, snatched his arm as it came up by instinct, twisted, dragging him forward, her mouth coming open to catch his neck, her teeth sinking into the soft flesh. He screamed once, she felt the spurt of hot blood in her mouth, and as her teeth met, she heard her grandfather's laughter, clearly, just as she remembered it from before his death, now joyous, revelling in her act.

Ulourdos clutched at her, shuddering, his sword dropping to clatter on the floor. He gave a single, choking gasp, then went limp in her arms. She dropped his body, spitting blood from her mouth as she stood back. His face was still frozen in horrified surprise, his eyes wide and staring. Cianna stood looking down on him, filled with elation, the blood hammering in her veins, her breathing hard. Across the room, Babalyn was making little whimpering noises, but she stepped forward as Cianna stood to her full height, stretching.

'Do you wish a trophy?' Cianna enquired.

'A trophy!?'

'Some hair? Perhaps a tooth?'

'No, I do not!' Babalyn exclaimed.

'You are right,' Cianna admitted. 'He was no warrior, to be slain so easily. It would not be fitting to take trophies. Still, he was a man of some rank…'

'Just leave the horrid thing!' Babalyn cut in. 'We must run, now!'

'Why?'

'Because you've killed him!'

'I was supposed to fight. He said so himself.'

'You were supposed to lose! Will you ever get that into your head!'

'But…'

'You have killed an Exquisite! You, a slave girl! What they will do to you does not bear thought! To me also!'

'Do you think so?'

'I know! What would they do in your country, if some… some serving girl killed a noble?'

'Nothing, if it was in fair combat. A noble so weak would not deserve his rank.'

'Well that is not the way in Makea! Look, I know a way to get out of the mansion. There is a trick, played on slave girls to make them look stupid. Say we are sent for chicken's milk.'

'Chicken's milk? But…'

'Just follow me! Quickly.'

'I had to fight,' Cianna protested as she followed Babalyn, wiping blood from her mouth. 'He would have made me take my necklace off, and with it part of my soul would go.'

Babalyn didn't answer, unfastening the door and peering outside, then beckoning Cianna to follow. Nobody was in the outer chamber, with only one guard at the bottom of the staircase. He rose at their approached, with a questioning glance.

'We are sent to buy chicken's milk,' Babalyn said quickly. 'With a whipping if we fail. Please tell us where we should go?'

'The market, naturally,' the guard answered, and laughed. 'Be sure to choose a good quality!'

The guard's laughter followed them down the stairs. As they reached the bottom he called out to share the joke with his comrades at the door. They gave sweeping bows as Cianna and Babalyn hurried out, and added suggestions as to how the girls should go about their errand. Beyond were the gates, which they passed with no greater difficulty, out into the streets of Kea.

'We are as good as dead,' Babalyn moaned. 'It is only a matter of time! They will take us!'

'Then we fight, and die,' Cianna responded.

Babalyn merely looked at her as if she was mad, then once more hung her head. They were in deep jungle, some way to the south and east of Kea, having run and walked until finally Babalyn had been able to go on no longer and sat down, weeping on a decaying log.

'We must at least go on!' Cianna urged.

'Why?' Babalyn wailed. 'Where to? Already the dogs will be on our scent. They will find us, for all your tricks at the irrigation ditches. They are wise to such things! I should have stayed, with the guards at least it would have been quick.'

'What of sanctuary?' Cianna suggested. 'We might loop around the city, following the ditches, come in along the shore at night. Jelkrael would shield us, surely, if we can only reach the Five Moons, the wagons even.'

'The first place they'll look,' Babalyn sighed.

'Julac then,' Cianna said. 'Administrator Bulzar is an Elite, and not easily cowed.'

'Why would he help us?' Babalyn demanded.

'He has loved me…'

'Loved you!' Babalyn broke in. 'He has fucked you, Cianna, that is all, because you are beautiful and exotic and it brings him prestige to have a leading fighting girl as his plaything.'

'Perhaps, but always he sought me out, and would have had me more often, had the chance offered. After the victory parade he demanded that I be sent to him.'

'So he wants to fuck you again. Do you think that would make him take the risk of sheltering you, who have murdered an Exquisite!'

'I did not murder him…'

'I have heard your explanation! It won't stand! What can I do!?'

'We stand, or we try Julac,' Cianna insisted. 'Or the hills, if we can reach them. There is a way to hide, for girls, if they truly must. In a goblin burrow.'

'A goblin burrow! Do you know what they do to girls?'

'Of course, but none will follow. It is awful, I know, but…'

Cianna broke off. From somewhere far off had come the sharp, staccato bark of a dog.

'Julac,' Babalyn said suddenly, jumping to her feet. 'We can surrender ourselves to Bulzar. At least we avoid the dogs.'

She ran with new energy, Cianna following.

For hours they pushed through the jungle, splashing through the shallow, muddy ponds when they could, heedless of leeches and the scratches of twigs and thorns. At sunset, more by luck than skill, they came out above the lake beside which the road to Ajad ran. Two hours later, after what seemed an eternity of groping and stumbling in the semi-darkness, they reached the low ridge which looked down over the four squat grey buildings that made up the powdermills, each within its high wall. Nearer to them, a scattering of other buildings showed dull pewter in the moonlight, two with lights in their windows.

'Bulzar has a villa,' Cianna said quietly. 'Which do you think it might be?'

'That highest up the slope,' Babalyn answered. 'Where the smell is least offensive. It is also the largest, surely fitting for the administrator?'

Cianna nodded in agreement. Moving carefully forward, they made their way down the slope. Reaching the garden of the villa, they went more carefully still, creeping into the garden on all fours, to peer in at one of the lit windows. Inside was a large, square room, sparsely furnish with heavy wood and a few thick drapes. Nobody was visible, and Cianna ducked down again, to whisper to Babalyn, only to freeze as a vast shadow loomed over them.

Babalyn screamed and went abruptly silent. Cianna kicked out, only to meet a leg that felt like a tree trunk. A great hand came down, snatching her up by her waist and lifting her without effort, Babalyn also. Realising that it was the troll, Voqual, Cianna forced herself to go limp, allowing him to carry her into the villa, to be dumped on the floor. As she pulled herself up on one elbow Bulzar appeared.

'Cianna?' he demanded. 'And Babalyn too? This is not the orthodox way to visit me, nor the time. You're covered in mud, and scratches! Did you lose the road?'

Cianna shook her head, prodding Babalyn with her foot to make her come round. Babalyn's eyes opened and she crawled quickly back into a corner, staring at the troll.

'Do not be alarmed by Voqual,' Bulzar said. 'Cianna has told you about him, surely?'

Babalyn shook her head in terror.

'I didn't mention it,' Cianna admitted, blushing.

'He is quite tame,' Bulzar said. 'Voqual. Leave.'

The troll lumbered off. Both girls got to their feet, slowly, Cianna sitting on a couch, Babalyn hastily coming close beside her. Bulzar gave them a quizzical look.

'There is much to explain,' Cianna said. 'Babalyn, you are better with words.'

'She has killed somebody,' Babalyn said. 'We seek shelter from you, Elite Master.'

'Killed somebody? Who? In a contest?'

'No. An Exquisite, Ulourdos.'

'Ulourdos, the King's nephew!?'

Babalyn nodded her head. Bulzar blew out his cheeks.

'Spare us,' Babalyn said weakly. 'For mercy?'

'Tell me what happened, exactly,' he demanded.

Babalyn began, relating every detail from their purchase in the Five Moons to their escape. Bulzar listened wordlessly, his face set, emotionless.

'Were you seen, coming here?' he demanded as she finished.

'No,' Cianna answered.

'You are certain?'

'It is dark, we came through the jungle. A dozen times we have followed drainage ditches, doubled back through ponds. We have not heard dogs in hours, and when we did they were distant.'

Bulzar grunted, then spoke, more to himself than the girls.

'I should give you to the authorities, but I ask myself, why should I? They will be looking for scapegoats, and I am unpopular with certain cliques among the Exquisites. It is well known that I took you to my house in Kea, Cianna, and it is not impossible that I would be accused of hiring you as an assassin. By coming here you compromise me seriously, you realise this?'

'No,' Cianna answered. 'I sought only protection.'

'Such an accusation would be an absurdity!' Babalyn exclaimed. 'Ulourdos bought us of his own choice!'

'Such inconvenient pieces of logic are easily overlooked,' Bulzar answered.

'What will happen?' Cianna asked.

'Scandal, outcry, accusation. The public adore such things. Still, for all the outcry, the death of Ulourdos will not be greatly mourned.'

'No?' Babalyn queried.

'By the public perhaps, for whom he was something of a model,' Bulzar went on. 'To the Elite and the other Exquisites he was an embarrassment, vain and confident to the point of insanity. You met him, can you imagine him in charge of a fleet or army? It would be a calamity, and yet he had the rank to command just such a post, and expected to.'

'Then I should go back to Kea and claim him for my escutcheon,' Cianna stated. 'As my reward I can demand freedom for Babalyn and myself.'

For a moment Bulzar looked astonished, then laughed and continued.

'In your savage land this might be the case. Not in Makea. Yes, the Exquisites would be grateful for his death, and the more grateful for your return. That way they could provide a dramatic public execution, calming the public anger, and all would be well.'

'Why?' Cianna demanded. 'He demanded that I fight. I killed him, fairly. I am innocent!'

'Innocent indeed!' Bulzar laughed. 'He was an Exquisite, you a slave girl, his property. You are his to do with as he pleases, including kill. Not surprisingly this does not work in reverse!'

'And you call me savage!' Cianna answered. 'You Makeans have no more honour than trolls!'

'Barbarians!' Babalyn spat. 'In Blue Zoria she would be given a fair trial, and might claim self-defence.'

Bulzar laughed again and shrugged, taking up his goblet of wine.

'What of my title?' Cianna demanded. 'I was popular also.'

'Indeed you were. So was Moloa. The crowd are fickle, and would relish nothing more than the drama of your execution. It would be the talk of Kea for years! Many would sympathise, perhaps, but they would still come to watch. Still, given the character of Ulourdos, I for one drink a toast to you. Long may he rot!'

He swallowed his wine.

'You will shield us then?' Babalyn queried.

'I will,' he answered. 'Why not? This is my Domaine. None come here without good reason. No Exquisite has set foot in the works for twenty years. Why should they, with the stink and the danger? My Supervisors come, but by invitation, and never to the upper story of the villa. My little Vendjomois pretties will know, but there is no harm in that, while I will be able to take my full enjoyment of both of you, freely given, which I personally prefer. For now, under the house with both of you. If dogs come on your trail, I had no knowledge of you. If they have not come by noon tomorrow, then we may safely assume they never will.'

Lying on her pallet in the attic space of Bulzar's villa, Cianna peered down through a grill at the powdermills below. Since the first night spent huddled beneath the pilings that supported Bulzar's house, she had done her best to discover what happened there. It had been her initial intention in singling Bulzar out for her attention, and despite her situation she was determined to continue. After so much time it seemed more than likely that Sulitea and Aeisla were either dead or in close captivity, yet she clung to hope, and she knew that abandoning her quest would mean abandoning part of that hope also.

For three days they had remained in the roof space of Bulzar's villa, firmly out of sight, with his two Vendjomois slave girls providing for them. Bulzar had travelled to Kea, returning with the news that the city was in uproar, that Jelkrael had been arrested, but released, and that her endless detours along irrigation ditches and through ponds had paid off. Dogs were still out, criss-crossing both fields and jungle, but on the second night there had been heavy rain, finally destroying the chances of being followed to the mills.

Day after day she had watched, following the movements of the slow, methodical men who worked there, and of the great covered wagons that came and went. Some she had identified, including the Supervisor of the mixing mill, Maerdrhen, who was second in authority only to Bulzar. Despite that, all she had learnt was that a great deal of water and wood was needed, but the various activities, buildings and machines were entirely meaningless to her. Finally, she had abandoned her obedience to Sulitea's demand for secrecy and explained what she was doing to Babalyn, who now lay beside her. Babalyn's response had been surprise, even disbelief, but that had not stopped her offering any help that did not risk punishment.

Below them, the river was clearly visible, and the road beyond, on which they had travelled to Kea. Nearer were the four mills, each with its high stone wall and cluster of subsidiary buildings. Two of the mills had chimneys, from one of which smoke was still rising, in a thin white tendril.

'The building which stands alone, with the ponds behind, is where the powder is mixed,' Babalyn said.

'How do you know?' Cianna asked.

'I have been watching the wagons,' Babalyn answered. 'They never come in to that building, but they always leave from it. Hence it must be where the finished powder is made. Also, there are no slave houses and thus no slaves. Mixing is a task too dangerous from any but the most careful and dedicated.'

'That is clever,' Cianna answered.

'Simple logic,' Babalyn said. 'So, there are three other buildings, each apart, and in each an ingredient must be made, or processed. Which do most wagons go to?'

'The largest,' Cianna said, 'with the chimney that is not smoking.'

'Then that is your nitre plant. A lot of dung is needed. At home it was always a joke, because the officials would urge us to make more.'

'I see,' Cianna replied doubtfully.

'The smallest, with no chimney, will be for brimstone,' Babalyn went on, 'or so I imagine.'

'Why?'

'Brimstone comes from volcanoes. There are only two in Makea, Ura and Agura, at the far end of the island. The last wagons to arrive there came in a convoy, and so may have travelled a long way. No wagons go to the third plant. Also, brimstone must be kept away from fire, and I imagine none is needed in its preparation, it being so combustible anyway. Thus there is no chimney.'

'The third plant?'

'I don't know. They are burning something, and use a huge quantity of faggots. It is the same in Blue Zoria, with whole thickets used for the mills. Maybe they melt something, or boil something. Bulzar must have books. Perhaps if we are allowed down into the house you could find out.'

'I can't read.'

'Show me then, but be careful. I don't want a whipping for your curiosity.'

'He'll probably whip us anyway, just for sport. He'll certainly have the troll fuck us.'

Cianna took a sip from her goblet, swallowed the rich red wine and went back to the task of sucking Bulzar's cock, which she was sharing with a Vendjomois girl, Ki'Lae. The three of them were on the couch, Bulzar seated at the centre, the girls lying to either side, their heads in his lap, drinking and paying court to his genitals. In front of them, Babalyn lay, tied across a chair, pop-eyed and slack mouthed, drool running from her open mouth, her big breasts swinging and slapping against the chair to the motion of Voqual's pushes as he fucked her.

It had been her turn to be fucked by the troll, a fate allotted to a different girl each evening, while the others served and attended to Bulzar's needs. In addition to having his cock and balls sucked, these included a great deal of fondling, watching them play together, fucking them and as often buggering them. They were also beaten frequently, with brisk, across the knee spankings, sometimes beltings or the cane, if he felt a heavy punishment was in order.

Each evening the program changed, but it invariably included one or other of the girls being tied down for the troll. Babalyn had been terrified, and had had to be gradually coaxed into taking her share. At first she had not even been able to touch Voqual's skin, but within three days she had found the courage to touch, then to lick at his monstrous cock, and at last to take it in her vagina. Now, tied securely in place, with her bottom raised and spread by the chair and ropes, she was panting out her second fucking by him.

It was a view Cianna found it impossible not to enjoy, just from the state of breathless, helpless ecstasy girls got into with the huge cock up their tuppennies. Voqual was always gentle, holding the girls by the hips with hands so large that even with Babalyn's ample bottom his thumbs where able to hold her crease wide while his finger were beneath her body. He also made a point of fondling her breasts as they hung down over the edge of the chair, and of tickling her anus and clitoris with his nails, either by instinct or training. In either case, the treatment made the girls come.

Once fucked, with the vast amount of sperm Voqual seemed capable of producing each evening well inside her, the girls would be released and allowed to join in the games. Often this would involve licking up the mess on the fucked girl's body and also the floor, which was what Cianna was anticipating as she sucked on Bulzar's cock.

Voqual was getting there, humping his cock into Babalyn's rear with ever greater urgency. Her mouth went wider, hanging loose, spittle running out freely. She began to pant, clutching at her breasts, pushing her buttocks up to the thrusts. Voqual grunted and she screamed, even as thick, yellow-white fluid exploded from around his cock.

'Lick them clean, Cianna,' Bulzar order casually. 'Zae-Sha, on my cock.'

The second Vendjomois girl took Cianna's place. Voqual's cock was out, standing proud over Babalyn's bottom. Cianna crawled quickly over, and began to lick it, up the shaft, then sucking the fat head into her mouth to drain out the sperm. Voqual took it calmly, allowing her to clean his cock and balls without more than a low grunt. Licking up the sticky sperm from the rough yellow-grey flesh, Cianna found her own need growing higher and higher. She had not been fucked, or licked, giving her full attention to Bulzar's cock.

With Voqual's cock and balls quite clean, Cianna turned her attention to Babalyn, whose whole rear was sodden with come, smeared across her bottom and up between her cheeks. It had pooled in her anus, with a thick clot of it hanging from the mouth of her sex and drips hanging among the half-grown stubble of her pubic hair. Cianna could smell it, and Babalyn's sex too, strong and musky. Poking out her tongue, she leant close, dabbing at one full dark cheek. Babalyn sighed, pushing her bottom further out. Cianna began to lick, cleaning the smooth brown skin of sperm, swallowing at intervals as she went.

Soon Babalyn's whole bottom was a wet, shiny ball, glossy with Cianna's saliva, only the crease still filthy. Her legs were wide, stuck out to either side, her bottom a fraction lifted, giving Cianna access to every crevice of her body. Now fully aroused, with a strong, rude need, Cianna pushed out her lips, making sure Bulzar and the Vendjomois girls saw, before kissing Babalyn full on the open hole of her sex. Sucking, she drew out the troll sperm, until it filled her mouth, sat up, showed the others what she had done, and swallowed.

Bulzar grinned, the girls giggling and pushing closer to their master, who had a trim brown bottom in each hand, his fingers inside wet, open holes. Cianna went back to Babalyn's sex, burying her face in the wet flesh. Licking hard, her set her own thighs apart, touching herself, gently, stroking her pubic mound and beneath her buttocks, teasingly close to the yet more sensitive areas of her vagina and anus. Her nose was in Babalyn's hole, her lips around the big clitoris, kissing it. Babalyn screamed at the treatment, then again as Cianna sucked on the little bud, mercilessly hard, all the while wiggling her nose in the slimy hole.

With Babalyn coming under her tongue, she could no longer resist her own need. Her fingers went to her sex, one up the sopping hole, another to her clitoris. She began to rub, still feeding on Babalyn's sex, only to be overcome by a sudden, desperate urge to fuck her friend. Snatching at one of the thick, beeswax candles that illuminated the scene, she blew out the flame and jammed it unceremoniously up Babalyn's hole. Babalyn squealed at the rough treatment, and gasped as Cianna began to fuck her, pushing the candle well in.

Bending down, Cianna buried her face between Babalyn's buttocks, linking the tight black anus and burrowing her tongue into the hot, slimy hole at the centre. She reached out, grabbed another candle, blew and pushed it to Babalyn's spit-wet bottom ring. It went up, Babalyn crying out again in protest, of which Cianna took no notice, stuffing the thick candle well up, until perhaps a hand span protruded from the straining ring.

Cianna climbed to her feet, settling herself above Babalyn bottom. The angle was wrong, but two hard slaps took care of that, and she slid herself down onto the candle in Babalyn's sex, pressing her clitoris to the anal one and holding it in place. She began to rub, herself and Babalyn at the same time. Her spare hand went back, to her own bottom and between the cheeks, finding her bottom ring and tickling it as she masturbated, looking down at Babalyn's bouncing buttocks.

Babalyn was panting, almost as far gone as she had been with the troll's cock up her. Cianna laughed at the sight, delighting in her control of her friend's bound and helpless body, in the thought of the twin holes straining around the candle shafts, the fat breasts bouncing and quivering to the motion, the equally fat bottom, wobbling as it was fucked. Her finger went up her bottom, deep in, to find the cavity slimy and hot, and she was coming, crying out in ecstasy, jamming her clitoris onto the smooth wax of the candle, calling Babalyn's name and at last sinking slowly to the floor, the candle pulling from her sex.

When she looked up, it was to find Bulzar smiling happily and both the Vendjomois girls with sperm on their faces and in their hair. They were still licking at his cock, and masturbating, both of them, with one hand each back between their thighs and their bottoms cocked up, the holes penetrated on Bulzar's fat fingers. Cianna watched them come, then set to work on Babalyn's ropes.

Wine was drunk, the flagon passed from hand to hand rather than served, while the girls cleaned themselves up, taking turns to lick up what mess remained on each others bodies, and Bulzar's. Finally Bulzar stood, stretched contentedly and jerked his thumb towards the stairs. Zae-Sha and Ki'Lae scampered up immediately, followed by Cianna and

Babalyn. As she reached the landing Cianna heard Bulzar giving a terse order to the troll, and Voqual's grunt of understanding. A moment later the door to the villa slammed shut.

Cianna walked into Bulzar's bed chamber, a square room, comfortably furnished, in which he had now decided all four girls should sleep as well as he himself. Cianna guessed that this was done merely for the pleasure of having his playthings to hand, as he would occasionally fuck one or another of them in the night, and also liked his morning erection sucked.

She took her turn at the wash stand, then curled herself onto the mat, watching as the others got ready. All seemed satisfied, and presently the breathing of Ki'Lae beside her had become low and rhythmic, then Zae-Sha's, even as Bulzar began to snore gently. Reaching out, Cianna prodded Babalyn. In the dimness she saw her friend shift, then rise to one elbow.

Both rose, padding slowly to the door, where the landing was bathed in the dull orange glow of a night lamp. Babalyn took the little oil lamp and scampered quickly down the stairs, Cianna behind her. At the bottom they paused, listening for a moment, then quickly pushed through the beaded curtain that closed off the room in which Bulzar worked. Scrolls lay on the desk, and carefully stacked pieces of charta, each indicted with symbols meaningless to Cianna. Babalyn glanced at each, frowning.

'Inventories, pay roll, a recommendation for a post at another mill,' she read out. 'These are the work of the normal running of the mill, no more.'

'What of this?' Cianna asked, pointing to a massive cabinet of polished wood.

Cianna moved the lamp, illuminating the spines of books within the cabinet, visible through the carved screen of the doors. Briefly she ran her eyes along the shelf.

'Ideal,' she announced. 'Here, the original designs for the mill. Here, a handbook on the manufacture of black powder. Here, another, listing the characteristics of different mixtures.'

Cianna reached out, tugging at the handle, to find it locked.

'His keys are in his robe,' she said, 'I'll fetch them.'

'A moment,' Babalyn answered her, 'there may be more here.'

She returned her attention to the table, scanning quickly through the pieces of charta. Cianna watched, envying Babalyn's ability to take in at a glance what she could not understand with any amount of study. Babalyn stopped, holding a piece of charta.

'Here,' she said, 'a letter Bulzar was writing earlier, to the head of public works in Kea. It states that he can take no more dung unless he is allowed to clear an area of jungle for the growing of something, a tree I think. Yes, it must be. That is it. To take more dung he needs more wood.'

'So?' Cianna demanded.

'So,' Babalyn replied. 'That is your third ingredient, and explains why no wagons arrive at the third plant, only carts carrying faggots. The ingredient is wood, but we know they burn it, so it must be ash.'

'Or charcoal,' Cianna answered, 'or even smoke. Smoke is probable. Sulitea uses smoke for several effects.'

'If it was smoke, they wouldn't use wagons to take it to the mixing plant,' Babalyn pointed out.

'Look further,' Cianna said, only to stop abruptly as a creak from elsewhere in the house.

Quickly they pushed out through the bead curtain and in at another. A wooden bench ran across the far wall, with a single round hole at the centre. Babalyn nodded at it and Cianna quickly climbed up, sinking into a squat over the hole. Holding up the lamp, Babalyn leant herself casually against the wash stand. Footsteps sounded on the stairs, and a moment later Bulzar appeared.

'You, the Ice Cannibal, need a friend to hold your hand in the dunny?' he chuckled. 'Never would I have thought it! And what a remarkable position, showing everything. Do you normally pee like that?'

'Yes,' Cianna answered, blushing faintly. 'How else would I?'

'Seated, like everyone else,' he replied. 'Or am I being foolish. Perhaps you are down here for another purpose.'

'No,' Cianna answered quickly. 'We merely needed to go at the same time.'

'You don't fool me,' he went on. 'You came down here to watch each other, and to play a little, didn't you? Don't think I don't know the sort of dirty tricks girls like you get up to.'

'You're right, we did,' Babalyn said before Cianna could answer. 'We're sorry.'

'No cause for apology,' he said. 'Still, fucked by Voqual and licked to climax yet eager for more. That is remarkable. Continue then. It would amuse me to watch.'

'What we were going to do?' Cianna asked.

'Naturally,' he said, 'I adore the sort of intimacies girls bestow upon one another. What were you planning, to take it in each others hands as it comes out? Mouths even?'

'Hands,' Babalyn said quickly.

'Do it then,' he laughed, 'but turn first. Pretty though your cunt is, I prefer the rear view, so that I can see every detail.'

Now blushing hot, Cianna swung herself around, sticking her bottom out over the hole. Her bladder felt ready, if not full, and she tensed herself, letting go to hear the tinkle of her pee in the pot beneath. She had her eyes shut, and she could feel the heat of embarrassment in her cheeks.

'Come, Babalyn,' Bulzar said. 'Get ready.'

The tinkling noise stopped. Pee spattered Cianna's bottom. She looked back, finding Babalyn behind her, squatted down with her hands stuck out. Bulzar was grinning, and his cock was hanging out of the side of his breechcloth. Squeezing again, she forced her pee out into Babalyn's cupped hands. Her anus had started to pout, and she stopped abruptly. Look back, she found Bulzar grinning, his cock now half stiff in his hand.

'Do it,' he said, 'there is no room for shyness here.'

'I have,' Cianna answered.

'You have peed, yes,' he said. 'You sadden me, Cianna. I understood I was to have full and willing use of you.'

'You do,' she answered.

'Then do it,' he went on. 'Dung in Babalyn's hands, as I'm sure you intended.'

'You want to watch me do my dung in Babalyn's hands?' Cianna asked in disbelief.

'That is what you intended, wasn't it?' he asked, now with a slight irritation in his voice.

'It was,' Babalyn said softly. 'Come, Cianna, do it. He is right. We should hold back no secrets from him.'

Cianna nodded, her face burning hot, unable to find words. Her anus was already pouting, and she could feel the load in her back passage, eager to get out. With a sob, she let go, feeling her ring open and a heavy, firm piece squeeze out. Unable to stop herself, she looked down, to see it coiling into Babalyn's cupped hands, beneath the lips of her sex, on which two drops of piddle still hung.

She squeezed again, pushing out her full load into Babalyn's hands. Bulzar was now masturbating a full erection, his eyes glued to her rear view, her gaping bottom ring and the filth that Babalyn was holding. Her anus closed, and she looked down again, to find the full, steaming mound in Babalyn's hands.

'Now do it,' Bulzar grunted, 'in with your bottom, and rub your cunt.'

Cianna hesitated, shaking her head in her shame and to fight down the lewd feelings that the sheer intimacy of what she was doing had triggered. Bulzar's cock was pointed right at her, furiously hard. Hanging her head, she reached down, for her tuppenny, parting the lips to find her clitoris, then to dip a finger into her hole, finding herself shamefully wet. With a sigh she began to rub, firmly, bringing herself quickly towards climax. Her resolve snapped, and she found herself doing as she had been ordered, lowering her bottom, slowly. Her bottom cheeks touched the squashy, warm mess in Babalyn's hands. She sank lower, and it was in her crease, oozing up between her buttocks and over her sex, and she was coming, sitting down firmly in

Babalyn's hands as it hit her. The hot, slimy dung squashed out over the fullness of her bottom. She cried out in ecstasy, wiggling herself in it, squirming her filthy buttocks into Babalyn's hands, peak after peak of her orgasm tearing through her, until she could hold it no more. Her knees slid apart and she sat down on the hole, her eyes closed, her head hung in shame. It had felt glorious, too good to be denied, knowledge that made the sting of her shame stronger still.

She looked round, to find Babalyn making a wry face at her. Bulzar had come, splashing sperm across Babalyn's hair and over Cianna's buttocks, and was already at the washstand.

'Wash me, please,' Cianna asked.

Babalyn nodded and went to fetch a bowl, washing Cianna's bottom as Bulzar looked on, apparently simply enjoying the intimacy of their act.

The following morning, Bulzar once more went to Kea, returning two days later. Immediately Cianna and Babalyn were called to him in his work room. His expression was worried, and Cianna found a lump rising in her throat.

'Matters are worse than I had feared,' he stated as he settled himself onto a couch.

'How so?' Cianna demanded.

'The King has played a clever gambit,' Bulzar went on, 'one which not only satisfies the lust of the rabble for a bloody revenge, but allows them direct participation. It also minimises his own expenses, both in terms of cost and the use of men. He has offered a boon, of one thousand standard, to whoever brings you in alive, both of you, but eight hundred for you alone,

Cianna, as it is assumed that you committed the actual murder.'

'Killing,' Cianna corrected him, 'of a torturer, a mad animal.'

'As you say,' Bulzar went on. 'Now, having been a fighting girl, it will not surprise you to learn that this offer has been taken up with enthusiasm, with every bravo in Kea and beyond keen to win the prize. There is also extensive betting.'

'Jelkrael will be placing his bets as we speak, I imagine,' Babalyn managed.

'Jelkrael has left Kea, immediately on his release,' Bulzar told them, 'but his dog has been sequestered, as it knows your scent well. It is to be used by that hunting party organised by the brother of Ulourdos, Nairgren, a party, incidentally, who are the favourites to bring you in, at three to one.'

'What are the odds on us defying escape?' Cianna asked.

'Some offer twenty, more thirty,' Bulzar replied. 'I have had placed a hundred standard, spread among a dozen bookmakers.'

'Thank you for your confidence,' Babalyn answered him.

'You show remarkable resilience,' he said, 'but more importantly, I am in a position to ensure that you win. This is the way to bet, on certainty.'

'This was Jelkrael's attitude,' Cianna remarked. 'So, you will protect us, here?'

'I fear not,' he said. 'With so much interest, the risks become inordinately high. I doubt even the best of cunt dogs could pick your scent out above the stench of the powdermills, but many will doubtless be passing down the road, and who knows, with the wind in an unlucky direction. More importantly, my own supervisors intend to sponsor two teams. Indeed, I am to lead one, Supervisor Maerdrhen the other. This will mean cunt dogs, here at the mills.'

'So how are we to escape?' Cianna demanded.

'What if we are caught?' Babalyn added.

'Nothing good, I fear,' he said. 'You have been sentenced in your absence, to death, by being staked out on ant hill, a choice made by Nairgren, who feels it is fitting that you die by a multitude of bites. They will use jungle ants, which you may have seen? It will be the larger species, with the red abdomen and the dark thorax, whose bite is actually less severe then their smaller relatives, making your death more agonising...'

'I do not wish to know!' Babalyn exclaimed.

'He is like his brother, this Nairgren?' Cianna demanded.

'No,' Bulzar answered. 'He is a sensible young man. Capable, and strong, his apparent vindictiveness is more to please the crowd than to revenge his brother. They never really got on. He is right too, because the method of execution has proved popular, while again there is extensive betting.'

'What on?' Cianna demanded in horror.

'On how long you last, on how much the ants devour...'

'No, no, be quiet, please!' Babalyn exclaimed. 'I can't stand it!'

'Be brave!' Cianna urged. 'Death comes once, then eternity. We will laugh together in the Feast Hall of Heroines!'

'You have your beliefs,' Babalyn said miserably.

'You do not?' Cianna asked.

'The philosophers in Aprinia state that gods are illusory concepts created by the human mind,' Babalyn answered. 'After death comes nothing.'

'Nonsense,' Cianna answered, 'the soul survives. When I killed Ulourdos I felt my ancestors urging me to the deed. I heard my grandfather's laughter as my teeth met in the pig's neck, as clearly as I hear you now.'

Babalyn made a wry face, but said nothing.

'In any event,' Cianna went on. 'We shall not be caught. Bulzar is going to help us evade detection, and remember, he has a hundred standard on our escape.'

'How then?' Babalyn asked.

'This is my council,' Bulzar advised. 'They will have your scent. From the wagons you rode in, from the bedding at the Five Moons. Each dog team will be given a little cloth. They will reason that as you would be immediately spotted in a town or village, you will stick to open country. In the fields your scent will be picked up easily. Even to me your juices taste unlike those of a Makean girl, so for the cunt dogs it will too distinctive to miss. Avoid the fields, and all cultivated land. Instead, take to the wilds, preferably high jungle. There it rains more often, while there are many streams to follow, also strongly scented beasts to distract the dogs. In due course you will see the volcanoes, Ura and Agura. Make for their northern slopes, where the jungle is wild and dense. Hide there. The search is unlikely to go so far afield.'

'And what then?' Babalyn demanded.

'They will eventually abandon the search,' he said. 'Ulourdos will be quickly forgotten once some new diversion arises to claim the attention of the rabble. Not that you will be safe. Live as best you can. Return here in perhaps a half year. I have enough to buy a longhouse in the hills, where you might be safely installed.'

'You are generous,' Cianna answered.

'It would amuse me to keep you,' he said, 'while your gratitude is worth more than any amount of fear or natural subservience.'

'What of clothing?' Cianna asked. 'The suits your workers wear perhaps?'

'Difficult,' he said. 'Yes, in the mills the male slaves work in tough suits of canvas, but they are brilliant orange in colour, with a bold black circle to front and rear, to make them distinctive in event of escape. Also, if you were caught, questions would be asked as to how you came by such suits. However, this had occurred to me, and I have purchased ordinary peasant clothing in Kea, old, cheap and designed for men, but it should serve well.'

'Very well,' Cianna said. 'When do we leave?'

'Tonight, late. Once I have had my fill of you. I will miss our nightly amusements, as will Voqual. Ki and Zae cannot accommodate his cock properly. Still, in due time you will be back. For now, wash and perfume your cunts, I want you ready as soon as we have eaten. It is safe. I have left instruction that I am not to be disturbed, and Voqual will patrol the garden. Tonight, neither of you go on his cock, you may be glad to learn, or sad.'

Cianna and Babalyn retreated, to wash and perfume themselves, as Bulzar liked. Cianna found herself trembling at the prospect of flight, beside which performing lewd acts for Bulzar seemed trivial, indeed, a more than fair exchange for their sanctuary. Not that she had a choice, while she had still failed to uncover the full details of what went on at the mill.

Clean and perfumed, they went to join Bulzar, who was lying on his couch, picking at the carcasses of a pair of jungle fowl, from which he would occasionally throw a bit for the Ki'Lae and Zae-Sha. Knowing what was expected of them, Cianna and Babalyn went straight to their knees on the floor, waiting for morsels to be thrown so that they could catch them in their teeth.

Bulzar nodded appreciatively at their prompt obedience and threw each a full leg. Cianna caught hers as she was supposed to, but held it instead of eating it from the floor, as the Vendjomois girls were. Bulzar gave her an indulgent smile, but said nothing. Babalyn also picked up her fowl leg from where she'd dropped it, leaving a greasy smear on one plump breast.

They ate, the fowl, apatta, baked fruit and pastries, Bulzar for once permitting the girls to have as much as they wanted. Cianna stopped when she was satisfied, not wishing to feel bloated, and sat back on her heels, waiting as Bulzar and Babalyn consumed the dishes and the wine. Finished, he took a slow cup of sweet wine, then sat back on his couch with Ki'Lae and Zae-Sha cuddled to either side of him.

'Time for our farewell bout,' he declared. 'Now, I realise you are unlikely to be in the right frame of mind for such pleasures, so you may simply display while Ki'Lae and Zae-Sha attend to my cock, something rather special.'

'Anything,' Cianna answered. 'It is the least we owe you.'

'Also a better way to spend the evening than in morose reflection,' he said. 'I have considered, and decided on a sight I will long hold in my memory. I have always delighted in watching girls in the extremes of emotion, on a troll's cock, or under a dozen of the lash. Don't be concerned, I won't whip you tonight, as I have no wish to leave you sore. No, but I was amused the other night, at the way you played on the dunny. Tonight, I wish a similar show, but in the place of the pot you may use each others mouths.'

'Not to dung in, please,' Cianna answered.

'Not if you don't wish to,' he said casually. 'As the other night, it is a pleasure to watch moments you would normally guard as your most intimate. I understand slave girls, you see, always wishing to have some part of their lives held back from their masters. Naturally I will have none of it, however considerate I may be in other matters. So, roll up the rug. Ki, Zae, clear the table, then put your pretty mouths to my cock.'

They obeyed, removing the rug to expose the bare tiles of the floor. With Bulzar's cock in Ki'Lae's mouth and his balls in Zae-Sha's, Cianna lay down spreading her thighs wide as Babalyn came to kneel beside her. For a moment they waited, watching the Vendjomois girls suck, until Bulzar's cock had begun to stiffen. Babalyn then climbed on, swinging her leg over, to poise the ripe bulge of her sex above Cianna's face.

'You will lick, naturally,' Bulzar instructed.

Babalyn immediately settled onto Cianna's face, sex to mouth. Cianna kissed her friend's sex, full on the lips, and took hold of the big, meaty bottom, gently squeezing both cheeks. Babalyn returned the favour, cupping Cianna's buttocks, her thumbs tickling at vagina and anus as she began to lick.

With a tongue on her clitoris and the hot musk of Babalyn's sex strong in her head, Cianna found her body responding where her mind wouldn't. She could feel her nipples stiffening, and the familiar ache in her belly. Bulzar was watching them, his cock now rock solid, with both girls licking at the shaft, one to either side.

'Do it then,' he ordered.

Cianna swallowed, her last view of the tiny pee hole at the heart of Babalyn's sex starting to pout as she shut her eyes. An instant later the stream erupted in her face, full up her nose before she managed to catch it in her open mouth. Blowing bubbles through her nose, she frantically tired to swallow, gulping down the hot, musky piddle, with more spilling from her mouth, onto the floor and into her hair.

Bulzar groaned, Ki'Lae giggled and Cianna let her pee own go, her fountain spraying out, into Babalyn's face. Babalyn kept licking, even though Cianna's spray was gushing hard into her face. It felt exquisite, with the hot pee running down between her sex lips, into her open vagina and down between the cheeks of her bottom. Pulling up her head, she returned the favour, burying her face in Babalyn's pee soaked sex with the urine still trickling out into her mouth.

Cianna's fingers went to Babalyn's sex, two burrowing into the moist hole, another to the pouted anus. In response Babalyn's hands spread Cianna's thighs wider still, one thumb poking up the vagina, another invading the wet anus. Cianna moaned, still peeing, with it gushing into Babalyn's mouth and over her face, and spreading out on the floor beneath her. Her vagina was full of it, her bottom in a warm, wet pool. A second finger went up her bottom hole, spreading it, and she felt the hot piddle start to trickle inside.

At that it simply became too much. Everything else forgotten, she started to come. Her climax hit her and she screamed, then went silent as she buried her face in Babalyn's wet sex once more. Coming, she was licking frantically at the pee soaked flesh, burrowing her tongue into the juicy vagina, hauling the big black buttocks wide apart. Her finger went deeper up Babalyn's bottom hole, even as her own closed tight, squirting out the pee that had run in. Her climax reached a peak, her muscles in frantic spasm, full in Babalyn's face, spraying piddle everywhere, a long moment of pure ecstasy, until at last it began to fade. Jamming her fingers as deep as they would go, Cianna touched something solid, deep up Babalyn's bottom, touching off a final, lewd peak to her climax.

She kept fingering, and licking, bringing Babalyn to a state of gasping, squirming pleasure before suddenly sucking the big clitoris into her mouth. Babalyn screamed, coming instantly, a second time, and a third, until at last Cianna took mercy and pulled her face away. Babalyn sank down, gasping, to kiss Cianna's tuppenny.

As her head cleared, Cianna looked round, to see what effect their show had had. Bulzar was frantic, his eyes glazed in passion, the head of his penis shiny with engorged blood. He was on the edge of orgasm, and they had come a moment too early.

'Do it,' she sighed. 'Dung on my titties. For him.'

'For you, slut,' Babalyn answered, and sat up, moving forward to poise her ample bottom directly over Cianna's chest.

Mouth wide, Cianna watched, her eyes glued to the full spread of Babalyn's magnificent bottom, and the tight, dark dimple between the big, rounded cheeks. A little pee dribbled out, to run down Cianna's cleavage as she squashed her breasts together, making a soft, pink valley beneath Babalyn's bottom.

'I'm going to do it,' Babalyn sighed.

Babalyn's tight black anus began to pout, pushing out, bulging, opening, to show the brilliant pink centre, then darkness. Slowly, a fat, solid piece of dung squeezed out, to fall full between Cianna's breasts. She felt its weight, lying heavy on her soft flesh, warm too, with the full heat of Babalyn's insides. Bulzar grunted, and from the corner of her eye Cianna saw his cock erupt, full in the two girl's faces.

'He's done,' Cianna sighed. 'Stop.'

'I can't,' Babalyn sighed. 'Stay still.'

Cianna could only watch as once more Babalyn's anus opened. Another lump was laid into her cleavage, and more, until her breasts were surmounted by the full, steaming pile of dung, while piddle was running down between them and over her belly. Babalyn wiggled, her bottom ring closing, a hand going between her thighs. The big buttocks began to jiggle, and Cianna realised that Babalyn was masturbating over what she had done. It took moments, and as Babalyn cried out in ecstasy once more, she sat down, full in the mess, squashing it out over Cianna's breasts and her own bottom, then wiggling in it as she finished herself off.

'You call me a slut?' Cianna said.

Babalyn giggled and gave her bottom another wiggle, then lifted herself stickily off Cianna's chest. Cianna sat up, drawing her breath in as she looked around her. Bulzar was sat back in contentment, his cock lying limp against one thigh. Both Ki'Lae and Zae-Sha has their faces smeared with sperm, with strands hanging from noses and chins, both with one eye shut by blobs of the sticky white fluid. Babalyn was a mess, her hair sodden, her skin glistening wet, pee dripping from her mouth and even her nose, her whole bottom filthy. Cianna grinned at her friend, knowing she looked no better herself. Kneeling forward, she kissed Babalyn, open mouthed, sharing the taste of each other's bodies, until the sound of Bulzar's voice interrupted them.

'Enough,' he announced. 'Wash and dress. It is time for you to leave.'

Cianna nodded, getting up carefully, with pee dripping from her body. There was a knot in her stomach immediately, as Zae-Sha came to help her, bringing a ewer of water, while Ki'Lae went for the clothes. Bulzar watched, fingering his chin and taking an occasional swallow of wine. With his goblet drained, he left the room.

With her body dry and her wet hair tied up into a knot, Cianna began to pull on her clothes. Being dressed after so long naked felt strange, especially in the male clothes, which she had never worn before. The trousers especially felt odd, uncomfortably tight across her buttocks, but sagging over her tuppenny. The shirt, at least, gave ample room for her breasts, although Babalyn's looked distinctly over filled.

'We do not look like men,' Babalyn remarked, 'not at all.'

'We do not look like slave girls either,' Cianna added.

'Peasant woodcutters, I hope,' Bulzar said, appearing at the door, 'who often dress in male clothes. You could pass, save for Cianna's colouring, and for that I have a remedy, if a crude one.'

He swung forward a bucket, showing them a black powder.

'Rub this into your face and hands,' he instructed.

'What is it?' Cianna asked, peering into the bucket.

'Charcoal,' he answered, 'from the mill. I have axes too, old and rusted, but sharp enough.'

'I thank you once more,' Cianna said, slipping a foot into one of the crude boots he had provided.

'Do not forget that I have a hundred standard on your escape!' he answered.

She smiled, pulling on her second boot and knotting the thongs that held them closed. Dipping her hands into the bucket of charcoal, she quickly smeared her face and neck, then, more reluctantly, her hair.

'At a distance you might pass for a Makean,' Bulzar said doubtfully. 'Never close to.'

Cianna made a face and stood up. Bulzar opened the door, Cianna kissed him, took Babalyn by the hand, and together they slipped out into the night.

Chapter Seven

For two full days Cianna and Babalyn made their way gradually west, ever deeper into the jungle clad heartland of Makea. Every stream they crossed was followed, often for miles, and inland more often than not. Gradually they rose, until the huge trees and lush undergrowth had begun to thin, to dense scrub, while the ground had become increasingly broken.

They saw no buildings larger than the occasional hunter's cabin, which they gave a wide berth. Twice dogs were heard, but never close, and once, far below them, they saw a clearing in which slaves were working to cut great orange blossoms. On neither occasion were they followed. Twice it rained, leaving them wet and steaming as they dried, but thankful.

On the morning of the third day they reached a gully, a great split in the land, with a sheer drop of some three times Cianna's height to a stream rushing among huge boulders. Without discussion they turned to the south, higher into the mountains. For an hour they walked, the gully beside them gradually growing shallower, until they reached a great thicket of cane, coating the sides of the gully and much of the slopes.

'We might climb down here,' Cianna suggested.

'Maybe,' Babalyn answered doubtfully, peering over the side. 'Perhaps a little further, it seems to widen beyond that outcrop.'

Cianna nodded and they pressed on through the cane, moving behind a jagged pinnacle of grey rock, then back toward the gully. Close to the edge Cianna paused, sniffing the air. There was a strong scent, male, slightly rank. A noise sounded ahead, the snap of a stick. Carefully, she peered out from the foliage.

Across the gully, not more than thirty paces away, an ape was seated on a rock, a split cane in its hands, from which it was sucking the sugary sap. It was big, its hair long and straight, a brilliant red, not unlike her own, only covering the entire body save for the face, part of the chest and the belly. All these areas showed pale flesh, as did the ample set of genitals that hung between its legs, leaving no doubt whatever that it was a male. Watching it, Cianna found herself blushing, realising that the creature could only be a Red Ape, the man like beast that both Gaidrhed and Glaydrak had thought she resembled. Babalyn pushed in beside her, took one look at the ape and giggled. Cianna gave Babalyn a warning look and put her finger to her lips. Carefully, they moved back.

'Is he dangerous, do you think?' Cianna asked.

'Only if attacked, if it is anything like the Forest Apes we get in Cypraea. They are black, but similar in form. They eat only plants. They have been known to chase people who run, but I think really in sport.'

'Do they fuck girls?'

'I don't think so.'

'Good. Let's go a little further, then down. His scent is strong. It might help to hide ours, or distract dogs.'

They moved on, then down, descending the wall of the gully without difficulty. Glancing back, Cianna found the ape as before, chewing cane and paying no attention to them whatever. Both removed their boots, tied them around their necks and splashed into the stream, enjoying the feel of the cold water on their feet. For some time they walked, treading carefully on the slippery boulders, until the gully split, a shallow valley cutting into the hill.

'A false trail here, I think,' Cianna said, putting down her axe.

'A moment,' Babalyn replied. 'I need to pee.'

'In the stream, as always,' Cianna reminded her.

Babalyn nodded and began to undo her trousers. Pushing them down, she stuck her bottom well out to avoid urinating in them and let go. Cianna watched the thick yellow stream spurt out into the water, remembering how it felt to take it in her face. Looking back, Babalyn smiled, then giggled clearly thinking the same.

'My turn,' Cianna announced as Babalyn wiggled her bottom to shake the last few drops free.

Squatting down, Cianna stuck her bottom out, as Babalyn had done. Relaxing her bladder, she let go, enjoying both the sense of relief and the exposure of her position. She let it flow out, her eyes shut, only to open them abruptly at a gasp from Babalyn. She turned, expecting to see men and dogs coming up the gully. There were none, only the Red Ape, no more than thirty paces away.

Still peeing, she hesitated. Babalyn was moving backwards, slowly, and gesturing her forward. As the last of her pee trickled into the stream, Cianna began to rise. The ape was close, making soft little noises, his mouth pushing out in a strange kissing gesture. There was no hint of aggression, but plenty of interest, and sexual interest, to judge by the way his cock was growing, the head already half clear of the prepuce. Cianna smiled nervously. Immediately the ape's expression changed, his thick lips peeling up to show big, yellowing tusks. Quickly she changed her own expression, pouting her lips out in imitation kissing motion it had been making.

Standing straight, she realised that she had made a mistake. To pull up her trousers she needed to bend, effectively flaunting her bottom. Yet if she stepped out of them she risked losing them. Hesitating, she threw Babalyn a desperate look. Babalyn shrugged, looking back from where she had stopped, some twenty paces up the gully. Biting her lip, Cianna bent, clutching for her trousers. As her cheeks came wide she caught her own scent. Immediately the ape became more interested, moving quickly forward, close behind her, looking down on her naked bottom, his cock half stiff with blood. Cianna swallowed, not daring to move. The ape sniffed, dropped suddenly, into a squat, directly behind her. Soft hands took her bottom, feeling the shape of her cheeks and hips.

She stayed stock still, trying not to enjoy the gentle fondling of her bottom, then telling herself that if she was going to be fucked it was pointless not to take pleasure in it. With a fresh flush of shame she stuck out her bottom, letting it fill his hands. Something firm and slightly damp nudged between her buttocks, pushing to her anus. Quickly she moved up, offering her vagina. The hands tightened on her hips, the cock slid up and it was done, she was being fucked, the ape's penis deep in her body, his long hair tickling her buttocks where it touched.

It began to move in her, rutting happily away in her hole, all the while its hand stroking her body, her buttocks, her hips and waist, them her breasts, cupping them with a puzzled sound. Cianna moaned, her head hung down, her mouth open, unable to take in what she was doing, or how nice it felt. He began to play with her breasts, bouncing them in his hands and slapping them together, all the while making joyful little hooting noises, and never once slowing the motion in her hole.

His cock was big, and her vagina felt nicely full, not straining, but well stretched. She could feel his balls too, the big sac slapping against her sex. His pace was good, making her pant and gasp. At last she was unable to resist the pleasure. With a groan of pure shame she reached back, caught up the fat, squashy mass of his scrotum and began to rub it on her tuppenny. He grunted, pulling himself in closer, his cock jamming to the hilt in her hole. She sighed, rubbing harder to bump the big testicles over her clitoris, sending little shocks of ecstasy though her body. The shocks built, blended, and she was coming, sobbing and gasping with her head hung in utter shame, but also in ecstasy as she felt her sex squeeze tight on the full, hot length of his penis.

The pleasure faded, slowly, dying to leave her weak kneed and gasping. She looked up, to find Babalyn staring down, open mouthed. At that moment the fat cock in her hole jerked and she was filled with sperm, sticky fluid erupting from her hole to splash over her hand where she still held her grip on his balls.

Unlike the troll, the Red Ape did not lose interest once it had come. Instead, it watched as Cianna quickly douched herself and dressed. Babalyn kept her distance, waiting until Cianna joined her, then giggling and throwing sidelong glances as they moved on. The Red Ape followed them, slowly up the gully, then into a wood of sequacia and another tree strange to Cianna.

'You seem to have found an admirer,' Babalyn remarked.

'Somebody,' Cianna replied, 'is risking being held down for my admirer's amusement.'

'I apologise,' Babalyn said,' but it was funny, the way he mounted you. The look on your face when his cock went up!'

Cianna stuck out her tongue, unable to feel resentment in the face of Babalyn's attitude to what had happened. Babalyn continued.

'It may be to our advantage. In Cypraea, the Black Apes defend their harems ferociously. They're incredibly strong, like trolls. Even five men would be no match for one. Also, if he thinks you are his mate, he may provide food. I for one am fed up with climbing banana palms.'

'You may be right,' Cianna admitted, blushing as she imagined the regular dose of thick cock she seemed likely to get. 'In any case, if he wishes to follow, there is little we can do.'

Making the best of the situation, they made no effort to lose the creature. Even thirty paces away they could smell his musk, which they knew could only be to their advantage. Nor was there any doubt that his shaggy bulk would offer protection, a sure deterrent for any small group of men, and even dogs. By noon they had become used to his presence.

They had risen higher, the trees thinning further, with long grass between them. It was also possible to see the twin volcanoes in the distance, and tors of grey rock on the ridge above them, and Cianna realised that they were close to the place where she had fallen from the demon.

The Red Ape had paused, at a thicket of thorn trees, each of which bore clusters of a waxy yellow fruit. As the ape was eating them it seemed reasonable to hope that she and Babalyn would be able to as well, so she joined in, finding them sweet, but with an odd prickling sensation to the taste. They ate their fill, paying little attention to the ape, only to finish and find him approaching them, holding his genitals in one big hand and stroking his thumb over the flesh of his penis.

'Your turn,' Cianna said, nodding to the rapidly stiffening cock.

'Mine!?' Babalyn demanded.

'Yes, why not?'

'Why not!? He's an ape!'

'So? What of Voqual?'

'He is a troll, half-human. Besides, I was tied down. I always made sure I was tied down. You did it unrestrained!'

'So it would be all right if I held you for him?'

'No!'

Babalyn's answer had held more than a trace of a giggle. Cianna beckoned with a finger. Babalyn shook her head, glancing at the Red Ape's now stiff penis. He had began to make the same little hooting noises he had before, and there was no doubt at all of his intentions. He looked at Cianna, then Babalyn, and back.

'He prefers you,' Babalyn stated. 'It's your hair. He thinks you're his mate.'

'Say that again and I will hold you down for him,' Cianna replied. 'Come, Babalyn, play fair. I let him have me, so must you. Turn your back to him, pull down your trousers and stick out your bottom. He'll be up in a moment.'

Babalyn threw Cianna a dirty look, but dropped slowly to her knees. Her big bottom formed a round ball in her over tight trousers, a target on which the ape's eyes were fixed, unblinking. Babalyn looked back doubtfully.

'You see, he likes you too,' Cianna said. 'How could he resist that bottom? Come, he's more gentle than Jelkrael and no more selfish than Bulzar. You'll enjoy it.'

Hesitating, Babalyn turned Cianna another dirty look. Her hands were at the fastening of her trousers, but motionless.

'Come, Babalyn, down with your trousers and stick it out,' Cianna instructed.

Babalyn bent forward, making her bottom rounder still. The ape moved closer, his erect cock held in his hand. With a last dirty look to Cianna, Babalyn pushed her trousers down over the ripe swell of her bottom. Cianna immediately caught the scent of aroused female, as did the ape. Wasting no time, he got down behind Babalyn, took her by the hips and plunged his erection into her body. She gasped, going down onto all fours. Her mouth came open and her eyes glazed as he began to fuck her, with strong, deep pushes that made the meat of her buttocks wobble and quiver. Cianna watched, open mouthed, imaging how she herself must have looked, puffing and gasping her way through sex, with the great red ape mounted on her upturned buttocks, cock deep in her hole.

He was getting faster, making Babalyn's breasts swing in the tight shirt, with the nipples sticking out, hard and proud. Babalyn had her eyes closed, her mouth wide, a trail of spittle hanging from her lower lip. Suddenly she was pulling at her shirt, fumbling with the buttons, tearing one, to spill her fat brown breasts out into her hands. She caught them, feeling and squeezing the plump flesh, her nipples sticking out between her fingers. One had went back, to her sex, and she began to masturbate, shaking her head in her ecstasy as she brought herself towards climax with the huge ape humping ever faster on her bottom.

Cianna's own hand was between her thighs, feeling her sex lips through the tight material. She felt wet, and swollen, ready for her own share of cock. The decision was immediate. An instant later she was struggling to get the trousers down, pushing them off her hips, falling to all fours, crawling close, only for the Red Ape to grunt and jam himself hard into Babalyn's body as he came.

He pulled back straight away, extracting his cock from her hole, sticky with come and juice, leaving her with a beard of sperm hanging in her pubic hair. Cianna crawled forward, cuddling Babalyn, kissing her, on the mouth, on her back, on the full swell of her bottom. Giggling, they fell together, going head to toe by instinct, Cianna's tongue burrowing into Babalyn's sperm slick sex. Babalyn sighed in pleasure as Cianna lapped up the thick come.

Tongues to each other's clitorises, hands on each other's bottoms, they licked urgently, both eager for her orgasm. Cianna's face was smeared with come and Babalyn's juice, filthy and slimy as she rubbed it between Babalyn's thighs and buttocks. For a moment she let her tongue probe the wet anus, deep in, to get the taste. With that she started to come, going back to Babalyn's clitoris, licking hard. Their peaks came together, in perfect unison, to leave them panting on the grass, wet with sweat, sodden with come, and thoroughly satisfied.

'There, was that so bad?' Cianna asked as Babalyn finally rolled off her.

'No,' Babalyn admitted. 'Not so bad.'

Cianna laughed and hugged Babalyn to herself, kissing her. The kiss was returned, their mouths opening together in a long, sticky exchange, sharing the sperm in Cianna's mouth. When they broke apart a long streamer of it remained between their lips, which snapped at their giggling response. Again they came together, Babalyn's hands now going to Cianna's breasts, Cianna's to Babalyn's bottom, their passion rising once more, to be abruptly cut off by a distant sound that set the hairs prickling on the back of her neck.

Cianna stopped, listening. The sound came again, more clearly, the bark of a dog. Babalyn threw her a worried glance and they jumped to their feet. The Red Ape also rose, looking to the south and east. Another bark sounded, closer, and from a different direction, immediately down slope from them. The ape sniffed the wind, growled and loped quickly off towards the trees, climbing into a huge sequacia.

With no more than a shared glance, the girls began to move off to the west. Alternately running and walking, they made there way along the fringe of the trees, only to reach the lip of a deep valley. It ran clean across their path, a wide belt of farmland cutting through the jungle and up into the hills. Far below, people could be seen working in the fields. With no choice, they turned yet further inland, pushing through the long grass of the highlands, half-crouched and feeling dreadfully exposed. Reaching a stunted thorn tree, Cianna risked looking back. Grass stretched away, down to the fringe of trees, empty, until a sudden movement caught her eye, near the sequacia the ape had climbed. There were men, five, and a dog. They ignored the tree the ape had climbed, dispelling that last hope that they might be hunters.

'They have our scent,' she said, to which Babalyn responded with a little whimpering noise.

They ran on, higher still, ducked low. Twin urges warred in Cianna's head, to run in blind panic and to turn and fight. Barking sounded behind her and she looked back quickly, to see the dark shape of the dog coming at them at a run.

'Run for the tors,' she urged.

'What use?' Babalyn panted. 'Let's not anger them further. Let's give in.'

'There are goblins up there,' Cianna answered. 'Don't you smell them?'

'Yes,' Babalyn answered. 'I can't...'

'You can,' Cianna said, grabbing Babalyn's hand. 'Come on.'

Once more they ran, now upright. The tors loomed above them, grey against blue sky. Again Cianna risked a backward glance. The dog was coming, streaking through the grass towards them, far faster than they could run, its great black back rising and falling as it bounded through the grass. In despair, she turned, clutching the axe and waving Babalyn to run on. Babalyn hesitated a moment, then went, leaving Cianna to hiss a prayer through grated teeth as she braced herself.

The dog came closer, racing across an open space, and Cianna recognised Glaucum. Suddenly the axe felt heavy in her hands. Hesitant, she forced herself to keep her grip on the shaft. He bounded up, leapt, and she found she could not strike, going down under his weight, his huge tongue licking her face, his nose pressing to her neck, her breasts, his cock pushing on her belly, to her vagina, and up her.

'No, not now,' Cianna gasped, as he began to fuck. 'No biscuits. No biscuits, Glaucum.'

Immediately he stopped, his cock pulling from her hole, allowing her to roll clear. He sat as she quickly stood up, his great tongue lolling from his mouth, his eyes huge and pleading.

'Biscuits soon,' she said, holding out a folded hand. 'Biscuits.'

She ran, and he followed, bounding beside her and jumping for her hand, which she held up, away from his mouth. Ahead, Babalyn was close to the rock, then at it, Cianna joining her, to collapse panting against the rough grey stone. The men were still far below them, but coming on at a run, yelling orders to the dog.

Cianna began to search, looking for the goblin burrow with the scent strong in her nose and her tuppenny growing rapidly moist. Almost immediately she found it. A narrow slit opened under one of the rocks, with footprints in the mud at its mouth, small and strangely shaped, with abnormally long toes. The reek of goblin was strong, make Cianna weak at the knees and filling her with the urge to lift her bottom into a position for mating. Glaucum growled at the scent, pawing the ground and pointing at the burrow with his nose.

Babalyn looked down the slope, with fear in her eyes, her lower lip trembling. The men were spreading out, into a crescent, and unlimbering equipment from their backs, bows, nets and spears. The leader was yelling at Glaucum, his voice angry, pre-emptive. The dog whined, sniffing at Babalyn's sex. Babalyn ducked down, squeezing herself into the goblin burrow. With a final prayer to her mother, Cianna followed.

Immediately the scent became overwhelming, far too strong to resist. She could hear herself whimpering as she squirmed her way down into the dank earth, her need for sex rising to push everything else aside. The darkness meant nothing, nor the closeness of the passage, nor the thought of the men outside, but only the urgent, overwhelming need to have her tuppenny filled with fat, rigid penis.

Scrabbling at the earth, she pulled herself lower, all light gone, her body filthy with soil. Rough stone bruised her arm, but she took no notice, nor when the passage flattened to a pool of thick mud, leaving her filthier than ever. She sat up, her body swaying drunkenly, lurching into Babalyn as she too fell into the pool. Immediately they clung together, kissing and licking at each other bodies, tearing at the fastenings to their clothes. Babalyn's huge breasts spilt free. Cianna clamped her mouth to a nipple, sucking, as a noise came to her ears, a faint, staccato chittering.

It grew louder, the goblin musk rising until she was conscious of nothing but the urgent need of her body, a last flicker of rationality winking out as long fingers closed on her hips. Her bottom came up, instinctively, to meet the goblin as it mounted her. Something fat and round nudged her sex and slid up, its cock. Other hands closed in her hair, over her breasts, on her buttocks, her legs, her waist. She collapsed, beneath a pile of writhing creatures, their cocks prodding for the openings to her body. Her mouth was filled, gaping wide around two bulbous penis heads that had been jammed in simultaneously. Hands took her breasts, squeezing them around a thick shaft, to jiggle them against it. A finger invaded her bottom, deep up her rectum, to wriggle around in the hot, slimy flesh. Her hair was taken, and used to masturbate with. Both her armpits were used, fat cock tips prodding at the shallow, sweaty cavities.

She resented nothing, not even when the first of them came inside her and was replaced by two others, one forcing her anal ring with its companion's sperm as a lubricant. She merely pushed her bottom back as her rectum filled with cock, and a moment later another had got below her, finding her vagina. With every hole full and penes rubbing on every part of her body, she was went limp, allowing herself to be shaken, slapped, groped and pulled in every direction, aware only of her desperate desire for yet more attention.

More started to come, in her mouth, a great gout of hot sperm delivered deep in her throat, choking her, making her gag, and bursting from her nose and out around her lips. An instant later, a full, slimy load was delivered into one of her armpits, another into her hair and face, splashing in her eyes. The one between her breasts came, smearing them with thick sticky come, another immediately replacing it in the wet slide of her cleavage.

Her own first orgasm came when a second goblin tried to invade her sex, on top of its comrade, probing for her hole. It failed, sliding the head of its cock over and over in the wet mush of her tuppenny, full against her clitoris. She came immediately, her body bucking on their cocks, the tightening of her anus in orgasm triggering the one up her bottom to fill her bowels with sperm.

With her climax done, she became lost in a forest of cocks, poking into every orifice, and a sea of sperm, coating her body, filling her mouth, her vagina, her rectum. She came again, over and over, every time her clitoris was prodded, but without volition, her body jerking and shivering, used, without the need for her to do more than keep her bottom stuck out. Time and again her vagina was filled, her anus too, more often than not at the same time. Her mouth was used repeatedly, often by cocks that had been in her other holes. Not an inch of her was spared, the groove of her spine, the soles of her feet, even the backs of her knees used to rut in, and all of it in an ecstatic haze, taking her far beyond conscious thought.

Even when it began to subside her proper awareness did not return. Most had come, many twice. The weaker individuals and late comers where taking advantage of the sloppy holes into her body, letting her slump down, thighs spread behind her. When the two that had been fucking her from underneath finally crawled out, she collapsed into the mud. One was still in her mouth, holding her head up by the hair to make her suck. Another was up her bottom, seated upright on the firm globe, its cock jammed to the hilt in her anus, buggering her with urgent, sudden pushes.

The one in her mouth came, and her face was dropped into the mud, only for her head to come up again, mouth open in the hope of being filled once more. It didn't happen, and when the cock in her rectum jerked to empty a final load into her body it was over. Even as the erection was pulled from her anus she was collapsing into the pool of mud and sperm beneath her, utterly exhausted.

She had been come in, and over, uncountable times. Her vagina was a gaping hole, running sperm and juice, her rectum packed with it, bubbling out as her anus struggled to close in a series of wet farts. Her mouth was full, her face plastered, with a thick coating in her hair, a slimy beard of it hanging from her chin and a thick tendril suspended from the tip of her nose. Her breasts were also covered, her cleavage slimy, the plump globes squashed out in the filthy mixture of mud and come which coated the passage floor.

Half-conscious, still dizzy with musk, she gave no resistance as long, spatulate finger took her by her arms, her legs, her hair. She was dragged, through the slime and filth, along narrow tunnels, down shafts, through open chambers, all in total darkness. Occasionally a goblin would mount her, up on her bottom, fucking or buggering her depending which hole it chanced to find. Each time she stuck up her bottom, eager for more, her body sensing nothing but pleasure.

At last she was dumped, face down on wet earth. There was a final flurry of use, one goblin fucking her, another in her mouth, and she was left. Crawling to the edge of the chamber, she set her back to a slope of earth and grass roots, cocked up her legs to spread her sex and began to masturbate. She came, twice, before warm flesh pressed beside her. Her arm went out, between Babalyn's plump thighs and down, to a tuppenny as swollen and sperm sodden as her own, finding the big clitoris even as the favour was returned, to masturbate each other to repeated ecstasy, and finally to oblivion.

Cianna awoke from lewd dreams to an urgent need for sex. Dimly, in the back of her mind, she was aware that she was down a goblin burrow, creating a lingering spark of fear insignificant beside her need. Her head was on someone's leg, a human leg, and with barely a thought she moved to press her face into the V at the top. She found a plump, moist sex, female, which she began to lick, evoking a moan of pleasure.

Moving higher, she twisted her body, straddling the girl's face. A tongue found her clitoris immediately, lapping at the little bud. She did the same, only vaguely aware that her partner's sex was less opulent than Babalyn's, the lips not so plump, the clitoris smaller. It made no difference. Wrapped together, they brought each other to orgasm. As Cianna came, she sensed an increase in the strength of the musk. Hands took her by the bottom, a cock pushed between her thighs and up, the balls dangling into the mouth of the girl who'd been licking her. She was fucked, briefly, pre-emptorially, the cock stuffed in, pumped, faster, and jerking inside her to fill her hole with sperm, which the girl beneath her lapped up from her sex and the goblin's balls.

The goblin took her body, rolling her off her partner. Something pressed to her lips, a skin bag. She tasted water, cool and fresh, and drank, swallowing down gulp after gulp until, until the bag was pulled away. Propping herself up on the wall, she lay in her dizzy, musk induced haze, idly toying with her tuppenny and breasts as she wondered when she was next going to get a fucking. Around her she heard others drink, of interest only in that there would be other girls, to lick and to lick her when she wasn't full of fat green penis.

Time passed, a haze of half-waking urgency, of touching, of being licked, of licking at other girls' bodies, of being mounted, of cocks in her vagina, her mouth, up her bottom. When she needed to pee she simply let go, enjoying the feel of the wet stream gushing out of her sex and running down her thighs to the soil beneath. Water was given, and food, more often than not in the form of a helping of goblin sperm down her throat. The chittering noise of the goblin's became something welcome, something to signal a new round of fucking, greeted with no fear or regret, but only lust.

Again and again it happened, the same routine of cocks and tuppennies, or water and sperm, until the sound of excited chittering was not immediately followed by her being mounted, but by angry, panicked noises. A new noise penetrated her mind, a scrapping. Light hit her eyes, blinding after the long darkness. Goblins screamed, full of rage and fear, dragging at her legs, dropping her as new, brighter light burst in on her. Voices reached her, male, full of excitement and revulsion. A surge of cool, fresh air caught her face.

Her mind began to clear, slowly. Earth walls became apparent, thick with grass roots, her chamber, and a passage, through the roof of which light broke, far off. A goblin screamed in rage and she glimpsed a green head, vanishing down a shaft in the passage. Voices sounded again, and a spade head appeared in the hole, knocking down earth.

Still dazed, but with the goblin musk clearing in the fresh draft blowing through the chamber, she looked around her. Babalyn sat to her side, naked, plastered with filth, eyes unfocussed, mouth hanging open with goblin come still running from one side. Other girls were beyond, two, both stark naked. Red hair was visible in the dim light, blonde curls, white skin, all encrusted with dirt. A new waft of air caught her, fresh and clean, and she struggled to find her voice.

'Sulitea, Mistress?' she asked. 'Aeisla?'

The mop of filthy red hair turned. Aeisla's face appeared, the eyes blank, then slowly filling with recognition. Her mouth came open, but no sound came out, then a hoarse croak. Cianna forced herself to move, shaking Babalyn's leg, then crawling across it. Aeisla reached out, their hands met, clasping tight together. Cianna came close, hugging Aeisla to her in a brief, passionate embrace, then Sulitea, whose eyes were shut. A muffled thud sounded along the passage, the hole expanding suddenly as new earth collapsed into the passage. Again voices sounded, now clear.

'It's a burrow all right. I can smell them.'

'The right one, do you think?'

'Must be. There'll be a maze under half the hill. The problem is where the girls are hidden. There'll be a lot of digging yet.'

'A thousand standard buys all the digging it takes.'

Cianna's memory came rushing back at the words, Ulourdos, dead on the floor, flight, Julac, the long journey through the hills, the ape, being chased, and finally the goblin burrow.

'Men?' Aeisla asked groggily. 'Oh father…'

'Men who mean to kill me,' Cianna babbled. 'Quiet, please! Babalyn, wake up! Sulitea, Mistress, it's me, Cianna. Can you see me?'

'Babalyn?' Aeisla asked. 'Babalyn N'Jukolana? Why is she here?'

'She was with me,' Cianna answered, 'as a slave. Mistress, Sulitea, wake up!'

Sulitea's mouth had come open, her tongue lolling out. Babalyn whimpered. Cianna shook Sulitea, whose eyes came slowly open, blinked, and slowly filled with recognition and awareness.

'Cianna?' she said. 'You too? Why is it light?'

'The goblins have gone deep down,' Cianna said quickly. 'Men are digging out the burrow, bad men.'

Sulitea shook her head, reached up to wipe dirt from her face. Aeisla had risen to a crouch, Babalyn turning towards them, looking on without apparent comprehension. A fresh clod fell in the passage, some twenty paces away. A boot appeared, kicking loose a clump of earth and grass roots. Cianna looked frantically around, to find that their chamber ended in a narrow vent, too narrow for her.

'I killed a man, an important man,' Cianna said quickly. 'These here, they mean to take me, Babalyn too, for death. Can you summon, Mistress?'

Slowly, Sulitea pulled herself into a kneeling position. Again she shook her head, then raised one hand and drew in a deep breath. Aeisla took a water bag from where it lay on the floor, pressing it to Sulitea's lips. Sulitea drank, sat back on her haunches. Returning the skin, she began to take deep breaths, then to move her hands in slow, precise motions. More earth fell from the passage ceiling and Cianna felt her heart jump. Sulitea stopped, gasping.

'I can't,' she panted. 'The air, the musk. I'm too dizzy.'

'Try, please, Mistress!' Cianna urged.

'It's not possible,' Sulitea sighed. 'I just can't. I can barely think at all.'

'What will they do, these men?' Aeisla asked, glancing to the hole, now a long slit of brilliant sunlight in the passage roof. 'Kill us?'

'No,' Cianna answered. 'They mean to execute me in Kea, a great city, Babalyn also. You they will make a slave.'

'Then we go out,' Aeisla said. 'Be defiant. Mock them, fight, anything to draw their attention from Sulitea.'

'They have bows,' Cianna said, 'nets, spears.'

'Then do nothing until Sulitea emerges. Sulitea, feign exhaustion.'

Cianna nodded, fighting down the bubble of fear in her throat. Slowly she began to crawl down the passage, Aeisla following. At the opening she clutched for her necklace, muttered a prayer and stood, blinking in the light. Men stood back, exclaiming in surprise. As her vision cleared she found one with a crossbow trained on her. Another was pointing a tube that looked uncomfortably like a miniature bombard, a third had his sword drawn, standing close to the trench at the bottom of which she stood. Two more, with spades, stood in the actual trench. Beyond was Glaucum, laid out in the grass.

'Out,' he ordered, 'and no tricks.'

Slowly, Cianna crawled up the slope of the trench, pulling herself to the lip on clumps of grass. The man with the sword moved back, keeping it levelled at her chest. His face was familiar, like that of Ulourdos but firmer, harder. Realising that it was Nairgren himself, she backed carefully away.

'Hands behind your back,' he ordered. 'Raigos, tie her. Gag her.'

The bowman came close as she put her hands behind her back.

'Another!' one of the diggers called out.

Nairgren took a step back, turning, but never taking his eyes from Cianna. Aeisla climbed from the trench, the gun moving to cover her. Standing her full height, the top of Nairgren's head barely reached her chin.

'A giant!' Raigos said.

'Tie her like the other,' Nairgren ordered. 'Aqual, up.'

One of the diggers scrambled from the pit, moving to tie Aeisla's hands. Cianna watched as her own were lashed off, seeing Aeisla clealy for the first time, the tall, slim figure, long legs sheaved in muscle, high, proud breasts, broad shoulders, firm, tight bottom, belly rounded out in the first stages of pregnancy. Cianna gasped in horror, her mouth falling open.

'Where is the Aprinian?' Nairgren demanded.

'Here,' Babalyn sighed, standing up in the trench.

'Up,' Nairgren ordered as Raigos pulled the thong on Cianna's wrists tight. 'Tie her, Telak.'

The man with the gun put it down, reaching to pull Babalyn from the trench. Meekly, she put her hands behind her back, allowing them to be tied.

'One more, stranger still,' the digger still in the trench announced, 'white skinned, with hair like an elf's.'

Sulitea began to climb from the hole, dragging herself, only to fall back. The digger took hold of her, pulling her to the lip, where she collapsed in the grass.

'Tie her,' Nairgren ordered. 'They are not to be trusted, these savages.'

Cianna ran, instantly, wrenching herself free of Raigos' grip as he attempted to fit a gag to her. She saw Aeisla kick out, and Aqual go down, clutching his side in pain. Nairgren moved, pushing his sword point to Aeisla's neck, but Cianna was already free, bounding through the grass in great leaps.

Glaucum gave voice behind her. Male laughter rang out. She tried to look back, stumbled, tripped, going down hard, struggling to her knees, only for Glaucum to crash into her. She went down, kneeling, the breath knocked from her body. He was on her back, panting, his cock probing for her hole, sliding between her buttocks, probing again, to find not her vagina, but her anus, still slick with goblin sperm and her own juice. Frantically she bucked her bottom, trying to get his cock to the proper hole. It was too late. Used to wriggling girls, he stuck to the hole he'd found, pressing, streetching out her slimy ring, bursting it. She gasped as her rectum was invaded, the full, fat length of Glaucum's cock jammed inside her with three firm pushes.

He began to bugger her, his balls slapping her empty sex, his hairy belly rubbing on her upturned bottom. The men were laughing, and as they came close they realised what had happened.

'He's in her arsehole!' one called. 'Raigos, look, Glaucum has put it up her arsehole. He's buggering her!'

'I've seen plenty get it in the cunt,' Raigos answered, 'but never up the arse. Will you look at him pump though!'

'And the way his balls slap her cunt,' the first man said. 'A standard says she comes before he's done his load.'

Cianna felt a stab of shame at his words, knowing he was likely to win his bet. Glaucum's heavy ball sack was smacking over and over on her sex as he buggered her, the coarse hairs tickling her clitoris. She could do nothing to stop it either, her body pressed hard down by his weight, her hands tight in the small of her back, beneath his belly. She was helpless, and as his cock moved in her rectum his knot was swelling, straining out her anal ring. The feeling was impossible to resist, even with the leering men watching and making remarks on her obscene sodomy.

'I'll not take that,' Raigos said. 'Fat Jelkrael says he is trained to take half-an-hour in their cunts, never less. How can she not come?'

'She will regret running, come or not!' the first laughed. 'Ho, Aqual, come and watch. Glaucum has his cock up her arse!'

Cianna shut her eyes, trying to block out their voices, and the feelings in her own sex. It was impossible, each slap on her clitoris brining her closer, and closer still. Nor was that all, with the knot swollen to full size in her anus and the big cock moving in fast, hard jerks in her rectum, putting her in a breathless ecstasy over which she had no control whatever. She was panting, then whimpering, and at last screaming out in an unbearable mixture of shame and ecstasy as her orgasm hit her, peak after peak, with each slap of the meaty, rough scrotum on her spread tuppenny.

The men called out in delight to see her come, clapping and slapping at their legs. Glaucum took no notice, humping away up her bottom, faster and faster, his cock squelching in her slimy cavity, the knot filling her anus to bursting point as she gasped out her passion into the grass. Her body was collapsing slowly lower, onto the ground, jammed down by his weight and the thrusts of his cock in her rectum. Dizzy, drool running from her open mouth, juice from her gaping sex, Cianna let it happen, jolt after jolt of orgasm running through her as she was buggered. Glaucum began to come, pumping hot sperm into her gut to make it swell, but never stopping, never even slowing, and again a climax hit her.

Faintly, she heard Raigos laugh as Glaucum gave a wriggle to push himself yet deeper up her bottom. She felt her anus close on the shaft, beyond the knot, and knew that the fat cock was well and truly trapped up her bottom. Galucum was going to bugger her, for his full half-hour, with the men watching and laughing on how often she came, on how badly she degraded herself.

'I wonder if he can bugger all four?' Aqual said, provoking laughter from his companions.

Raigos answered, his tone jocular, changing suddenly to alarm, and to a scream of unreasoning terror. Instantly Glaucum was scrambling off her back, his knot popping from her ring to make scream in sudden pain. She went over as he leapt free, sperm spurting from her well buggered anus. Glaucum fled, whimpering, down the slope. Cianna looked up, back towards the girls.

Above her, not thirty paces away, a hideous apparition hung in the air, writhing tentacles with a grotesque, half-human face at the centre, the eyes burning scarlet orbs, the mouth a black hole, ringed with needle teeth. Raigos had run, Aqual too, and the other digger. Telak stood, lifting his gun, which roared out, spitting flame, to tear one great tentacle from the demon's body. The head began to turn, slowly towards Telak, the maw widening. Telak dropped the gun and fled.

Nairgren stood alone, screaming at his men to come back. His sword was clutched in both hands, his face white as he backed from the demon. Sulitea called out a word and the demon struck down, enveloping Nairgren, who screamed, hacking desperately with the sword, babbling in insane terror as the tentacles wrapped around him. The sword flew from his hand, full into the demon's face. The tentacles jerked, shivering, loosening for an instant. Nairgren broke loose, and fled, his screams mixing with those of Babalyn, who was cowering terrified in the grass, also the open laughter of Aeisla and Sulitea. Cianna rose, weak kneed as she stood, to walk back to the others. Ignoring the demon, she went to Babalyn, taking her gently around the shoulders.

The four girls sat in a wide pool, bathing themselves in cool stream water. It had been their first desire, once Babalyn had been brought out of her hysteria and persuaded that the demon was no threat to her. By then the five men and the dog had long vanished into the distant trees.

After collecting the men's equipment, they had begun to search for a suitable bathing place. Sulitea talked all the while, explaining how she had landed the demon on the night they became separated, only to be swarmed over by goblins and dragged down, overcome by musk. Like, Aeisla, she was pregnant, her belly rounding out, which Cianna found it hard to keep her eyes away from.

Finding the little gully between two sharp tors, they chose a pool and plunged into the water to rinse the accumulated filth from their bodies and hair. Five times Cianna washed out her hair, then sat on a rock below the surface to douche herself and clean her bottom.

'What of you, Cianna, Babalyn?' Sulitea asked.

Cianna nodded to Babalyn, who began to speak, telling her own story, and Cianna's, to the point of seeking shelter in the goblin burrow. Sulitea and Aeisla listened attentively, slapping their hands on the water surface in recognition of Cianna's wrestling achievements, and at Babalyn's description of the death of Ulourdos.

'Fine,' Aeisla stated. 'You should be proud.'

Cianna shrugged, smiling and blushing at the praise.

'How long did all this take?' Sulitea asked. 'I truly do not know much time has passed?'

'Over three months,' Cianna told her.

'Three months! It seems like hours, or years, I don't know. Three months, wasted!'

'Not so,' Cianna said. 'I have your knowledge, or most of it. There are three ingredients for the black powder. The first is nitre, a substance gained from dung. The second is brimstone, a yellow powder found in the vents of volcanoes. The third is simply charcoal.'

'And it's preparation?'

'They are mixed together, which is dangerous. Water is involved.'

'This is all you know?'

'Is it not enough?'

'This is good,' Sulitea answered. 'You have done well. Not well enough sadly. We need more knowledge. How it the nitre prepared from dung? From what wood does the charcoal come? What proportions of the three ingredients are needed? How must they be mixed? Are cantrips needed to prevent explosion, or to ensure the efficacy of the process?'

'I don't know,' Cianna admitted, suddenly close to tears.

'The water is to prevent it exploding prematurely,' Babalyn put in. 'Otherwise she knows as much as I do.'

'To have discovered what you have is a great achievement,' Aeisla cut in. 'Better anyway than ours.'

Sulitea made a face, her hand going automatically to her swollen belly.

'You are… pregnant?' Cianna asked cautiously.

'How could we not be?' Aeisla answered. 'Three months, and fucked every day. My poor tuppenny will never be the same, nor my bottom ring! As for the pregnancy, I wouldn't be the first.'

'I have preparations for these things,' Sulitea said, 'both the pregnancy and slack flesh. I can make us virgin if I wish, back in Boreal. What matters is the powder. You have come close. We need only the final details, at least enough so that the sages in Thieron may start to experiment.'

'You wish to continue?' Cianna asked.

'Naturally,' Sulitea answered. 'Have we come all this way to fail?'

'But I am pursued,' Cianna objected. 'Every man in Makea seeks the reward for bringing me in, and when Nairgren brings news of your demon, they will come here in full force, with archers, bombards, warlocks…'

'Not warlocks. Not in Makea,' Babalyn said. 'What you do is unknown, Sulitea, in Aprinia too. When Cianna said you would summon a demon, I thought it only the hopeless wish of a trapped slave.'

'It is how we came,' Sulitea answered, 'and how we will return, once we have the full secret.'

'Then there is a simpler answer,' Babalyn went on. 'Bring me back to Blue Zoria. My father will have all the knowledge you need, or at the least he will know those who do. In his gratitude he will gladly tell you whatever you ask. Also, it will be to the standards of Aprinian science, far superior to the primitive techniques of Makea. We make guns, bombards, that you can hold in your hand, and which fire six or eight shots, each one from its own capsule. There is nothing like that here.'

'I will bring you back to Blue Zoria,' Sulitea said, 'and gratefully accept whatever your father will tell us. What I can not do is go to my uncle, who is King in Thieron, and tell him that my maid has obtained a crucial secret while I have spent three months being endlessly ravished down a goblin burrow!'

'Why not?' Babalyn asked. 'You should be proud of Cianna.'

'I am,' Sulitea said. 'I am also ashamed of myself.'

'I also,' Aeisla added.

'Why so?' Babalyn insisted. 'No woman can resist the scent of goblins. Once we have it in ours heads we are lost. This was not your fault.'

'In Mund,' Sulitea explained, 'a high-born girl is expected to resist, at any cost. Already I am thought an irredeemable slut, simply because I allowed myself to get carried away once or twice. I had hoped to restore my place. Now I will be a laughing stock!'

'Then don't tell them.'

'I have to say something! Cianna or Aeisla must tell the saga for me, and I for them. To leave out a few embarrassing details, such as Cianna and her dog, maybe, but I must have something to my credit.'

'Claim the deed for yourself.'

'Claim an honour due to Cianna! Unthinkable! Better to admit to the goblins!'

'What do you intend to do then?' Cianna demanded.

'I must consider carefully,' Sulitea answered her. 'First, describe this place Julac again, in greater detail.'

Cianna felt her flesh crawl as the great clawed hand pulled from her waist. She shook herself, fighting down her fear, and scuttled into the shadows, pressing between the comfortingly warm and human bodies of Sulitea and Babalyn. Above them the long sinewy arm of the lank demon withdrew, reappearing a moment later to set Aeisla gently on the earth.

'Well?' Sulitea hissed.

'The great building with the chimney is the nitre plant,' Babalyn answered quietly. 'To the side, the long, low sheds are for the slaves, the wider ones I am not certain of. Otherwise there are stables, a wagon shed...'

'No matter,' Sulitea cut her off. 'To the nearest slave shed, come.'

Sulitea moved forward, going carefully in the near blackness. Cianna followed, her own confidence rising in reaction to Sulitea's calm certainty. The idea was to offer freedom in exchange for the information they needed, a proposal they were certain no slave could refuse.

For five days they had stayed hidden in a cave high in the mountains, preparing and waiting for a night with the right conjunction of moons. While the others discussed the details of their plan, she had spent much of her time constructing clothing from the equipment abandoned by Nairgren's men. As a result, each of them now wore a short, tight skirt and a crude chemise, both of coarse green material. They also had weapons, Aeisla with Nairgren's sword, Cianna with another, although Babalyn had refused to take the gun, declaring it primitive and as dangerous to the wielder as the target.

They reached the shed, crouching down in the shadow of the wall. Cianna wrinkled her nose against the reek of dung, which they had been able to smell long before they reached Julac. She had imagined it would be unbearable in the actual plant, but it now seemed less strong, and she realised that she was actually getting used to it. Aeisla ducked down beside her and they looked back, finding neither movement nor light.

Moving to the front of the building, they found the doors bound shut. The rope was cut and they slipped inside, in near blackness. Cianna got down on all fours, crawling slowly forward with her fingers stretched out before her. A new smell caught Cianna's nostrils, an acrid, male tang, of sweat and unwashed bodies. There was sound too, breathing, small movements, a sudden muttering noise, immediately stilled. She hesitated, thinking of the goblins and wondering just how many men were in the building, men who had not had sexual contact with a woman in years. Behind her the door creaked shut, and the blackness became absolute. Forcing the images of what the goblins had done to her from her mind, she moved carefully forward. Her fingers touched cloth, then skin.

'Here,' she said quietly, reaching back to touch Babalyn.

A questioning grunt sounded from the darkness, followed by a rapid shuffling noise.

'Shh,' Sulitea's voice sounded, soft and calm. 'Do not speak.'

'Who?' a voice demanded. 'You are a woman!'

'Shh!' Sulitea repeated, more urgently, 'let go of me! Be quite, we are here to bring you free!'

'Why are you here?' the man demanded, aloud. 'Have the pushers sent you for us?'

'Be quite!' Sulitea hissed. 'And get your hands off my breasts! We are here to bring you free, do you understand? To free you, in return for knowledge!'

A second voice sounded, and a third, one grumbling, and the other inquisitive. Light flared, dim and red, leaving Cianna blinking as her eyes adjusted.

Suddenly there was silence. She looked up, finding herself on a dirty floor, looking down between a long line of crude wooden pallets, on each of which lay a man, perhaps fifty in all, some still asleep, most stirring or already sat up. At the end of the room one stood, his hand still on the cover of the nightlamp.

'Ice cannibals!' the nearest man spoke, clutching his blanket to his chest in terror. 'Spare me! Do not eat me, I pray!'

'Eat you?' Sulitea demanded. 'I can think of nothing more repulsive! We are here to free you!'

'Free us?' another man asked. 'We are slaves.'

'Now you are slaves,' Sulitea went on. 'Only tell me what I need to know, and we will free you, all of you. You have my word on this, and I am a High-Demoiselle and the niece of a King.'

They looked back blankly, some still in terror, others in apprehension, some curious. All were now awake. Sulitea stood, raising her hands, a gesture that strained the fabric of her makeshift chemise against her big breasts.

'I will explain,' she said. 'Will this light draw attention?'

There was no answer. Cianna glanced around again. The men looked hesitant, scared, but cocks were stirring beneath the thin blankets as lust rose up in the face of fear.

'Sulitea, Mistress,' she said quietly, plucking at Sulitea's chemise.

'Be quiet,' Sulitea answered, 'we have little time. Now, you men, listen. I am Sulitea Mund, a powerful witch. Outside the wall of your compound waits a great demon, able to lift you over the wall with ease. To whoever wishes their freedom, I grant it, and in return I ask only that you tell me what you do, here at Julac. You, tell me?'

She pointed at the man they had first spoken to, who was still staring blankly at her breasts. Beneath his blanket his cock was erect.

'What do you do?' Sulitea demanded. 'You process nitre, yes?'

'I am a dung boiler,' he answered.

'A dung boiler?'

'I boil dung.'

'To what purpose?'

'If I do not, the pushers will beat me.'

'What of you others?' Sulitea sighed. 'A trifle of knowledge for your freedom.'

'We are slaves,' one said.

'Beyond the wall is jungle,' Sulitea said, 'enough to hide in for years, or band together, raid a harbour, steal a ship.'

'We are slaves,' the man repeated.

Beyond him another man had pushed back his blanket, exposing a big, dark cock, close to erection. Sulitea gave a hiss of frustration and a nervous glance at the window. A second man threw back his covers, taking hold of his cock, to masturbate blatantly, his eyes fixed on the girls.

'They are Makeans and Vendjomois,' Babalyn said quickly. 'There are no Aprinians here. Slavery is all they know.'

'They must want freedom!' Sulitea hissed.

'Quickly,' Aeisla urged. 'Someone will see the light. They may investigate.'

Sulitea hesitated, biting her lip. More men had exposed themselves, making no effort whatever to conceal their cocks as they masturbated over the sight of the girls near naked bodies. Sulitea cursed, Babalyn moved close to Cianna's side.

'If you are so gutless, then,' Sulitea said, 'and so lustful, I offer my maid, to suck the cock of any who will tell me what they do to prepare nitre.'

Cianna's mouth came open in protest, but shut it as Sulitea gestured to her. None of the men spoke.

'Is she not beautiful?' Sulitea said, gesturing to Cianna. 'Cianna, open your chemise, pull up your skirt. Come on, this is no time for modesty! We must hurry!'

Reluctantly, Cianna put her hands to the fastening of her chemise, tugging it to let her breasts spill free. A quick jerk had her skirt up to her waist and she was showing everything. Immediately the men's masturbation became more urgent, their attention more focussed. One came, a great jet of sperm erupting from his cock to splash over his thin body. Others started forward, most of them.

'Remember the bargain,' Sulitea said, retreating quickly. 'Come, Cianna, give Aeisla your sword and get down on your knees.'

'I…' Cianna began, only for her protest to turn to a startled squeak as a hand took hold of her bottom. 'Help me, Babalyn!'

'How?' Babalyn demanded.

'With some of them, of course,' Cianna answered, quickly passing her sword to Aeisla as the men clustered around her.

She took a cock in her hand, tugging at it. Another pressed himself into the crease of her buttocks, erupting the instant he touched her skin, spurting sticky, hot come between her cheeks. The one in her hand came too, all over her hip. She pulled back, trying to exert some control over the situation, but going straight into the hands of two men behind her. One grabbed her breasts, rubbing his cock in the slimy crease between her buttocks. The other curled his fingers around her belly, slipping two up her vagina.

'Stop! Not my tuppenny!' she exclaimed. 'One at a time!'

Her protests were ignored, the men closing in on her, pressing their erections to her flesh. She tried to struggle, but her feet were taken, pulled off the ground to sit her down hard on her wet bottom. Her hair was grabbed, a cock forced into her mouth, even as her legs were spread wide, four men struggling for the privilege of being the first to fuck her. A cock was jabbed towards her eye, which she shut an instant before it touched. He came, delivering a full load of sperm across her face, even as one of the struggling men got his way and her vagina filled with cock.

As he began to fuck her, the man in her mouth exploded, leaving her gagging on sperm. She pulled her head back, coughing, with sperm bubbling out around her lips, several men tussling to be the next in her mouth. One came, right in her face, and another, closing her other eye to leave her blind. The man inside her came, pulled back, another filling her slimy hole immediately. More sperm splashed in her face, her mouth was filled, her hands pulled up to take a cock each. Sperm spattered across her breasts, more in her face. A man slid under her, prodding between her buttocks, finding her sperm slick anus and easily forcing the little hole. Another man came in her mouth as her rectum filled with cock. One cock was pulled out, another stuck in immediately.

She was being jerked from side to side, rubbed on, fondled, pinched, slapped, with wad after wad of sperm erupting over her and into every orifice. Several used her bottom, more her vagina, still more her mouth. Soon every inch of her face was plastered with sperm, her breasts also, with men groping them to smear the slimy mess across the smooth skin. Her belly was covered, her hands slippery, her hair matted. It hung from her ears and chin in streamers, bubbled from her nose, farted rudely from her anus and vagina each time they were vacated, squelched loudly as they were refilled.

It stopped as abruptly as it had stared, leaving Cianna sat in a sticky pool on the ground, unable to see, her mouth hanging slack with a mixture of come and spittle running from her lower lip. Her vagina was sodden, sperm and juice running from the open hole. Her anus was nearly as bad, bubbling out its sticky load between her bottom cheeks, and sore. Her skirt was still up around her waist, but absolutely sodden with sperm, while her chemise had been torn off and trodden into the filthy mess on the floor.

'Well done, good girl,' Sulitea's voice sounded from behind her. 'You too, Babalyn.'

Cianna risked opening one eye a crack. Sulitea stood above her, a speck of come on one foot, otherwise clean. Further back was Aeisla, holding both swords and quite unmarked. Babalyn was a different matter, like her, sat in a pool of sperm and girl juice, her huge breasts plastered with it, her face filthy, her eyes shut beneath thick clots, with a disgusting white forth bubbling from her nose. The men had retreated, standing in a huddle and happily boasting to each over of what they had done, or how much come they had produced.

'So,' Sulitea addressed them calmly, 'you must now keep your bargain.'

'We work,' one of the bolder men said. 'I am a shoveller.'

'I also,' another said.

'I am a dung boiler,' a third added.

More spoke, adding their own tasks to the list, until Sulitea held up her hands.

'One of each of you,' she said. 'You, first. You are a dung boiler, you say. Why do you boil the dung?'

'If I do not, the pushers will beat me,' he answered immediately.

'No,' Sulitea said. 'What happens when you boil the dung?'

The man shrugged.

'For what purpose must the dung be boiled?' she demanded.

'I do not know,' he said.

'Who does?' she asked through clenched teeth.

The men shook their heads, looking at each other, shrugging and speaking in low, quiet voices. Finally one spoke up.

'The pushers know these things,' he said. 'The supervisor also, and his assistants, who are free men.'

'The pushers are slaves?' Sulitea asked.

'Slaves,' the man agreed, 'set above us to make us work well.'

'And they will know?'

There was a chorus of agreement.

'Where do I find these pushers?' Sulitea demanded. 'In the compound?'

'You cannot go to the pushers!' a slave exclaimed. 'They will beat us for what we have done.'

'I won't tell them,' Sulitea responded. 'Now where are they?'

None spoke, except to each other, a general murmur of dissatisfaction.

'Tell me!' Sulitea shouted. 'Tell me, or I will have the big Ice Cannibal split your skulls for what little brain there is within!'

Aeisla swung up her sword. The slaves cowered quickly back.

'The smaller shed, up the slope!' one stammered. 'But you must not say you have been here!'

'I will not, you have my word,' Sulitea answered him. 'Cianna, come. Aeisla, remain here, outside. Retie the door and guard it. Show no mercy to any who come out. Do you here that, worms, the giant cannibal will be outside your door, eager to feast on the first man who attempts to get out!'

The slaves cowered back further and the girls retreated, adjusting their clothing as they went. Outside, a pale glow could be seen above the horizon, showing where the largest of the moons was due to rise. Already the night seemed less dense, and a leat showed as a long line of dull silver, running between the shed they had visited and the next. Cianna went to it, ignoring Sulitea's demands for haste as she and Babalyn helped to wash each other.

Soaking wet, and with the taste of dirty sperm still thick in her mouth, she put her soaking clothes back on. Despite her loyalty, she was feeling distinctly resentful towards Sulitea, who she felt might have taken a share, and to make matters worse, she needed to come.

Leaving Aeisla and Babalyn in the shadows beside the slave shed, Cianna and Sulitea made their way up the gentle slope, running low over the rapidly brightening ground. It proved easy to identify the pusher's building, a structure a third the size of the big slave sheds, with dim light showing in the windows. They moved cautiously forward, to peer within. Four men sat around a table, one in the act of throwing dice from a cup. All were big, and solid, obviously much better fed than the ordinary slaves. Mumbling something under her breath, Sulitea went to the door, pushing it wide. Immediately all four swung round, their mouths dropping open.

'Before you begin,' Sulitea said quickly. 'We are not cannibals. We mean you no harm. We only seek knowledge.'

'How did you get into the compound?' one man, the biggest, demanded.

'Who are you?' Sulitea asked him, ignoring the question.

'Aglat,' he answered crossly. 'I am the chief pusher here. Now who are you? Girls sent down for us? None were due, to my knowledge.'

'Girls are girls,' another said, the shortest and fattest of the four. 'Let's fuck them anyway.'

'Be quiet, Uthos,' Aglat ordered, turning back to Sulitea.

'You are Ice Cannibals,' he went on with certainty. 'Everybody knows how one of you became wrestling champion by tearing the throat from her rival, then killed an Exquisite to feast on his blood…'

'I did not… ' Cianna began in anger, but stopped suddenly.

'Think of us as you wish,' Sulitea said tiredly, 'but be assured that we have no desire to eat you. I am Sulitea, this is Cianna. We want knowledge from you. Are we secure here? What of the supervisors, and other free men?'

'Supervisors!' Aglat exclaimed. 'What a joke! Do you think free men would sleep in the compound? They keep to their villas on the hill. At night this is our place, and so long as things go smoothly the supervisor and his staff allow us to do as we please. Keep above production targets for a month and we are given girls, fail and we are demoted.'

'And the guards?'

'Live outside the wall, where they cannot be overwhelmed. If there is revolt all go to the rope. There has been no revolt in a hundred years. We are secure.'

'Sometimes we spend all night fucking fine fat sluts like you,' Uthos added. 'Who should care?'

'Then it seems you are in a position to bargain,' Sulitea said.

'We are,' Aglat answered. 'What do you offer, and for what in exchange?'

'We wish to know how the nitre is made.'

'For black powder?'

Sulitea nodded.

'You plan a revolt!?'

'No. We have no interest whatever in Makea, save to gain the knowledge we need. Once we have it, we will leave, forever. There will be no consequences.'

'So you say. The penalty for revealing our knowledge to other slaves is death by drowning. Hubaln?'

One of the other men stretched, looking thoughtfully at the girls.

'My opinion,' he said at length, 'is that they have been sent down by Supervisor Jaidhos, to test us. Naturally we would never think of revealing our knowledge.'

'Wise thinking,' Aglat agreed.

'We are not from your supervisor!' Sulitea exclaimed. 'Would he send strange girls in the middle of the night if he wished to test your loyalty, girls asking outright questions? He would do it in some less obvious fashion.'

'Perhaps,' Hubaln replied.

'What of you Greifal?' Aglat asked. 'Uthos?'

'I believe them,' the one addressed as Greifal answered. 'Jaidhos has never done such a thing before, and what would be its purpose when we cannot leave the compound? What are you offering in exchange for the knowledge, girls?'

'Your freedom,' Sulitea answered. 'As we got in, so may we leave.'

Greifal merely laughed, the other also.

'Freedom?' Aglat said. 'To do what? To be hunted down in the hills? To be killed in some unpleasant and inventive manner? Even if I could hide I am marked.'

He cocked up his leg, lifting the hem of his brilliant orange work suit to expose a broad circular tattoo.

'Life would be a constant struggle,' Greifal went on, 'and brief. Here, we have an easier life than many; adequate food, some comfort, girls occasionally. Your offer is worthless. Still, you look like you have fine fat breasts under that chemise, and a well rounded arse too. A fucking might buy a little information.'

'Be cautious,' Hubaln warned.

'Why trouble with their demands anyway?' Uthos put in. 'I say we tie them and fuck them well, whether they want it or not. Then send them off with sore cunts and whipped arses, to Jaidhos or otherwise.'

'They are Ice Cannibals,' Aglat pointed out. 'You heard what happened to the Exquisite Ulourdos? He was found with his throat torn out, his sword still clutched in his dead fingers. I for one prefer them willing.'

'I also,' Greifal agreed. 'Excuse Uthos, girls, he is nothing but a lout. Still, a good fucking seems fair exchange for our knowledge. What do you say?'

'You may fuck Cianna,' Sulitea said. 'That in exchange for your knowledge, my word on it, do I have yours?'

'I wish to fuck you also,' Aglat answered her. 'Indeed, I for one want my cock in both of you.'

There were grunts of agreement, even from the reluctant Hubaln.

'I do not mate with slaves,' Sulitea said haughtily.

'Come,' Aglat said, 'we have a bargain, let the rule be good fellowship. To be so aloof can cause only bad feeling.'

'You might wish to watch us together,' Cianna suggested, 'after which you can take turns with me, or perhaps Sulitea will change her mind.'

'I will not change my mind!' Sulitea said, throwing Cianna an imperious look. 'You are getting above yourself, Cianna! Still, I suppose they might watch me punish you, or sit on your face.'

'There is no cause for argument, girls,' Aglat cut in. 'Play together for us, this is a fine suggestion. Then we will fuck the copper haired one. For this I will tell you what I know.'

'Your word on it?' Sulitea demanded.

'Certainly,' he said, 'so, boys, we are to fuck an Ice Cannibal! Such shame we can only boast among ourselves. Perhaps we should put them in the black earth beds to play.'

There was an immediate chorus of agreement and lewd chuckles.

'Black earth beds?' Cianna asked doubtfully, sure she had caught a knowing look between Aglat and the other men.

'Yes,' he went on, 'you will enjoy it. Come, we will show you.'

He got up, the other behind him, walking to the door. Greifal came last, taking the lamp and ushering Cianna and Sulitea to the door with mock formality. Outside, now in bright moonlight with half the face of White Teimis showing above the jungle, they made their way down a path to one of the wider sheds. Aglat untied the door, opening it to reveal a row of broad pits stretching away into the gloom. Each was full of a black substance, that quivered as the door was pushed too behind them. Sulitea walked to the edge of the nearest, peering doubtfully down.

'In there?' Sulitea asked. 'What is it?'

'Black earth,' Aglat replied. 'It is harmless, I assure you. We have had many girls disport themselves in it.'

Cianna stepped forward, sniffing, but finding her sense of smell already so overwhelmed that she could detect nothing. The black earth had the appearance of a thick mud, and was clearly not simply dung as she had at first feared. Cautiously, she dipped a toe into the substance. A thin crust had formed on the top, which cracked easily, allowing her foot to sink into warm, slimy muck. She giggled, enjoying the feel of it squeezing up between her toes.

'It's nice,' she said, letting her foot sink deeper with a squelching sound.

'Get right in,' Hubaln suggested, 'bottom first, you will find it even nicer.'

Cianna hesitated, then shrugged and let her foot sink deeper, the black ooze rising half way up her calf before she found the bottom. Carefully, she stepped in, then paused to unfasten her skirt and remove her chemise. The men chuckled as she went naked, Uthos squeezing his cock through his trousers. Squatting down, she let her bottom touch the surface of the muck. The crust broke, and as she sat the thick ooze squeezed up between her bottom cheeks and over her sex, a feeling so delicious that she gave a moan of pleasure.

'Good, is it not?' Aglat said.

'Lovely,' Cianna replied, kicking her legs out to let her bottom settle.

Sat splay legged in the bed, the muddy substance reached her waist. It was warm, and felt delicious against her skin. Smiling happily to herself, she took up two big handfuls, plastering the muck onto her breasts, cupping them to let it ooze between her fingers and smearing it over the round white globes. Two more handfuls followed, slapped on as she leant back against the edge, to form fat, dirty crowns to her breasts. Giggling, she watched one pile run slowly off, to fall back into the tank with a wet plop. The other she smeared into her cleavage, pushing the plump globes together to make the muck ooze out between them. She took some, smearing it over her the rest of her chest and up to her neck, then turning to Sulitea.

'Come, Sulitea, Mistress,' she urged. 'You have had me in mud often enough, in Boreal, and more recently, in…'

'Yes,' Sulitea cut her off quickly. 'Very well, I will do it.'

Stepping away from the men, Sulitea carefully unfastened her chemise, spilling out her breasts with her back to them. Her skirt followed, unwrapped and discarded, to leave the full white moon of her bottom on show. Aglat smacked his lips in appreciate, Uthos reaching out to take a pinch of the soft flesh. Sulitea slapped his hand away.

'This was not our agreement,' she stated. 'You may see me nude, you may watch me with Cianna, no more.'

'I swear that the princesses in Kea can be no less haughty,' Greifal laughed. 'In the earth with you then, and lets see how you and your friend disport yourselves.'

Sulitea threw him a dirty look and stepped gingerly into the black earth. Her foot went in slowly, sinking to calf depth, her expression changing from uncertainty to pleasure. She stepped in, squatting down to put her bottom in the muck, as Cianna had done. Her legs came apart as she lowered herself, until she too was sitting splay legged in the black earth, covered to her waist.

'Let me do your titties, Mistress,' Cianna offered, 'and then perhaps we can masturbate together for their pleasure.'

Sulitea nodded, with an embarrassed glance to the four men. Uthos had his hand down his trousers, squeezing a hard penis. The others were less obvious, but all showed conspicuous bulges. Cianna moved into a kneeling position, her bottom pulling stickily from the mess. She crawled to Sulitea, who pushed out her breasts.

'You're pregnant, aren't you?' Greifal remarked.

Sulitea gave a shamefaced nod.

'It is only light,' Aglat said. 'Three months at most.'

'A shame,' Hubaln replied, 'I like a heavily pregnant girl. It fattens their breasts and buttocks, while their cunts are forever juicy.'

'There flesh is looser though,' Hubaln added. 'It may be easier to get up their arseholes, but it is not so tight once inside.'

'That Vendjomois piece they sent us was tight enough,' Aglat objected, 'and she was eight months gone if she was a day.'

'But she was tiny,' Uthos replied, 'with my cock in her, it was amazing her ring didn't split…'

The men turned their attention back to the girls as Cianna scooped up two big handfuls of muck. Plastering both onto Sulitea's breasts, she began to rub it in, smearing the fat globes with black slime, and stroking them once they where properly filthy. Sulitea sighed, her nipples popping up through their covering of dirt, the tips pink where Cianna's fingers had brushed them. The men watched, Uthos with his trousers pushed down at the front, his balls and erect cock sticking up over the edge.

Sulitea's hands went to Cianna's breasts, returning the favour by smoothing the filth over the creamy skin and teasing the nipples to erection with her thumbs. Aglat freed his cock, then Greifal, lastly Hubaln, to leave four big, hard erections poking out at the girls, each above a fat set of balls. Cianna smiled at them, smacking her lips in anticipation.

'You're going to come in and fuck me, aren't you?' she asked. 'Or you could do it between my titties. Look at them, all slimy. Wouldn't that feel nice?'

She held her breasts up, squashing them together to offer a slide for his cock.

'Delightful,' Aglat said, 'but no. I am mindful of your friend's sensibilities. Play together. I suggest you fill your cunts. The feeling is exquisite, so I'm told. Certainly it is good when I put my cock in one.'

Cianna giggled and sat back a little, spreading her thighs as far as they would go. Lifting herself, she brought her sex above the surface, leaving muck hanging from her pubic hair and running slowly down her filthy skin.

'Watch,' she said, pressing her fingers between her thighs to slip three into her vagina. 'Lovely, I'm nice and open. Here goes.'

Reaching down, she scooped up a handful of the muck, taking the thicker stuff from close to the surface. Pressing it between her thighs, she forced some into the mouth of her vagina, sighing as the hole stretched and filled. Sulitea watched, one hand on her breasts, toying with a nipple, the other under the muck, between her own thighs. Cianna gave Sulitea a smile, took another handful and squashed it up into her hole. More followed and more, until her vagina was packed full of it, the mouth an open hole. Turning, she went down onto all fours, to show off the wad of black stuff in the entrance to her body. Sulitea giggled, the four men started to tug harder at their cock.

'Shall I do you?' Cianna offered, turning back to Sulitea. 'Oh, that is nice. A little squeezed out as I turned.'

'Yes, do me,' Sulitea said softly. 'Masturbate me when I'm full.'

Cianna came close, sliding her hand between Sulitea's thighs. Sulitea's sex was open, Cianna's fingers going in with ease, in and out, to smear muck up the hole. Sulitea sighed, clutching onto Cianna's hand to press it more firmly in. Using just her fingers, Cianna began to squeeze the earth up into Sulitea's hole, packing it in little by little. Sulitea was soon breathing deeply, then moaning as her hole stretched out, until it was in the same condition as Cianna's stuffed full, with a plug bulging out at the entrance.

'I can feel it in me,' Sulitea sighed. 'Touch me. Kiss me.'

Moving in close, they began to kiss, light pecks to each other's faces, and to explore, their hands moved gently over slimy midriffs and breasts. Cuddling closer, they pushed their chests together, the four plump pink globes of their breasts squashing against one another in their slippery coating. Cianna giggled at the sensation and shook her chest, brushing her erect nipples against Sulitea's. Sulitea sighed in response and caught her breasts up, rubbing them against Cianna's. Both were looking down, admiring the rounded curves of their breasts and the hard, protruding nipples, all smeared in muck.

White come suddenly spattered across the dirty pink globes. Cianna turned, finding Aglat with his cock in his hand, just in time to catch the second spurt full in her face. Already filthy, she shook off what she could, two heavy blobs falling to her chest, which she smeared over her skin, and Sulitea's, adding sperm to the filthy paste that covered their breasts. Catching up a stray blob from her nose, she wiped it on one of Sulitea's nipples, then bent down, to kiss the sperm from the little tight bud, the muck also, leaving the rose pink flesh clean and wet.

At that Sulitea pulled her in, their thighs locking together, their arms coming around each other's backs. Cianna slid her hands under Sulitea's bottom, feeling the big, slimy cheeks, then probing for the holes. One finger found the mud packed entrance to Sulitea's vagina, and pushed inside, then another, squashing out the mud. Sulitea's kisses became yet more passionate.

Cianna began to tickle Sulitea's anus, wondering if she could squeeze mud up into her Mistress' bottom. Her finger went in, to find the cavity already packed full, making her giggle.

'Not up my bottom,' Sulitea whispered gently. 'I'm a bit urgent.'

Cianna giggled and slid her finger out, but went on tickling the little ring as she began to masturbate Sulitea's tuppenny. Sulitea held on, tight, her bottom pushed out, her neck to one side, allowing Cianna to kiss the sensitive skin. Their breasts were pressed together, their nipples brushing as they moved, skin against skin, revelling in the delicious slimy texture of the mud. Sulitea's clitoris was beneath Cianna's thumb, bumping from side to side, the muck starting to squeeze out as her vagina contracted. Cianna rubbed harder, feeling Sulitea's muscles tense and jump. Sulitea's anus went slack, then tensed, and Cianna stuck a finger well up, unable to resist it. Sulitea cried out in ecstasy, coming as Cianna mashed slime and filth into the cavities of her body, screaming aloud, then quite as their mouths pressed together in one long, blissful kiss. Grinning, Cianna pulled back, her fingers slipping from Sulitea's holes. Looking up, she found the men's eyes fixed on them. Three of their cocks were rock hard, Aglat's half stiff despite the recent orgasm.

'I'm going to fuck her cunt,' Hubaln grated, hastily stepping out of his trousers. 'Arse up, copperhead, over the edge.'

Cianna turned willingly, raising her bottom and pushing back, to stick it out above the edge of the pit, crossing her legs to make it as easy as possible for him to fuck her. He came close, squatting down, his turgid erection in one hand. Cianna could feel the thick, muddy plug in her vagina, then a new sensation, her hole stretching, with the mud squeezing out as his cock was forced into the already bulging cavity. She cried out in pleasure, and reached back between her thighs, finding her sex.

Hubaln drove his cock to the hilt in her hole, Cianna touching the muck as it squeezed out, over her tuppenny and his balls. As he started to fuck her she was already rubbing herself with it, slapping it onto her vagina, rubbing, reaching down to slap more on. His thumb found her anus, forcing the little slimy hole, his fingers clutching between her buttocks, holding her by rectum and bottom as her fucked her. She started to come, rubbing harder, crying out as it hit her, a second time, and a third, still with him pumping hard into her vagina.

It stopped, suddenly, and she knew that there was sperm up her hole as well as the black earth. He pulled out, slowly, but she stayed in position, reaching back to scope as much as she could out of her vagina. It was smeared it over her sex and belly, rubbed in, to her tummy, her pubic mound, her sex, to bring herself to yet another exquisite climax.

Cianna sat her bottom back down in the mud, wiggling it to enjoy the squashy sensation to the full. Opposite her, Sulitea sat splay legged, smiling as she casually smeared muck over her breasts. Hubaln had stood away, his cock and front of his body filthy where his skin had touched Cianna's. Both Uthos and Greifal where clearly ready, erections straining and tense, while Aglat's cock was hard again.

'Buttocks up, Cianna,' Greifal ordered. 'This is going up your arse.'

Cianna lifted her bottom, looking apprehensively at the big cock which was about to be stuffed up it. Reaching back, she found her anus, which was slimy and loose, two fingers going inside without difficulty.

'I'm for the pale haired piece,' Uthos grunted. 'Get it up, girl, like your friend.'

'I don't...' Sulitea said weakly.

'Let him,' Cianna sighed. 'It feels wonderful, when the cock goes in and the mud squashes out. You need it. I know.'

Sulitea opened her mouth to speak, but shut it abruptly. Tucking her feet beneath her, she lifted her bottom, sticking it out over the edge of the pit in the same rude position as Cianna, filthy buttocks thrust out, vagina gaping on its plug of dirt, anus winking lewdly upwards. Uthos grinned at the sight and got down, Sulitea shutting her eyes tight in shame.

The cocks went up, Uthos' into Sulitea's mud packed vagina, Greifal's into Cianna's rectum. The men began to work them, fucking and buggering, rocking the girls' bodies to make their dangling breasts swing and slap on the surface of the muck. Sulitea's poise quickly went, her hand going back to masturbate, urgently, losing control, to slip face down in the filth. She stayed there, not caring, her head to one side, her mouth open and half full of dirt, her eyes shut in ecstasy, jerking to the motion of Uthos' thrusts, then coming with a long, loud cry as he jammed himself into her to the very hilt, spunking deep up her.

Cianna was still on all fours, watching, her mouth open, her breathing deep, to the same rhythm as her buggery. Greifal was well up her bottom hole, his balls pressing to her vacant tuppenny with each push. As Sulitea's head went into the mud Ciana gave a giggle of pleasure, smiling as she watched her Mistress climax, face down in the filth.

Uthos pulled out, leaving Sulitea to slump down in the muck, but only briefly. With a wicked grin on her face, she crawled across to Cianna, who opened her mouth to protest, but too late, as Sulitea's filthy breasts where shoved into her face. She gave in immediately, the men laughing as she began to lick at the dirty globes, sucking dirt from the nipples, kissing at the filthy upper surfaces, rubbing her face in the slimy cleavage. Greifal grunted, jamming himself hard up Cianna's bottom, to knock her forward. Sulitea went down, backwards, holding onto Cianna, who went with her, her anus pulling off the invading cock even as Greifal came. Sperm splashed over her bottom as she went down on top of Sulitea, and they were rolling together, right in the mess, laughing as they smeared it in each others faces and hair. They wrestled, slapping at breasts and bottoms, probing for vaginas and bottom holes, pushing each others' faces into the muck, until both were covered from head to toe and dirty in every orifice.

At length they broke apart, gasping and giggling, high on sex and the pleasure of playing in mud, reserve completely gone. Aglat stood at the edge of the pool, erect cock in his hand. Sulitea crawled over, Cianna too, to stick their bottoms out, ready for penetration, side by side with their arms around each others' shoulders. Kicking off his trousers, Aglat grinned and squatted down.

'I'll fuck you both,' he declared, 'then up your arses, and in your mouth for the finish. How's that?'

'Just my tuppenny, please,' Sulitea answered, 'but I'll suck.'

'You will,' he said, and prodded his erection to Cianna's vagina.

It slid up, deep inside, and Cianna moaned in pleasure as he began to fuck her. Her hand went back, to toy gently with her sex and to feel his balls, in no hurry to come. Sulitea was doing the same, masturbate lazily as she watched Cianna fucked, then with more urgency as Aglat turned his attention to her, pushing two fingers up her vagina.

His cock pulled from Cianna's hole, his fingers replacing it. Moving behind Sulitea, he put his erection up her, pushing hard to make her breasts swing and her bottom wobble. Cianna giggled at the sight, rubbing harder at her tuppenny as she felt the first twinges of approaching climax. The big cock came out of Sulitea's hole, and Cianna was buggered, her slimy anus quickly forced, the full length of his penis slipping up in two smooth pushes.

'Too loose,' he complained. 'Who's been up you, a horse?'

He jammed it in anyway, buggering her with short, hard pushes, only to grunt in frustration and pull out, leaving Cianna's anus gaping wide. He moved to the side, his cock pointing at Sulitea's raised bottom. She was masturbating, eyes closed, unaware of his intentions until his cock found the ring of her anus. Suddenly her eyes went wide, and she gasped as her muscle popped, her mouth coming slowly wide as her rectum filled with a disgusting squelching sound.

Aglat gave a grunt of satisfaction, buggering her as he had Cianna, with short, hard pushes. Sulitea stayed down, making no effort to stop him, her mouth wide, drool running down her chin, still playing with her sex. The rhythm picked up, her breasts swinging, the nipples brushing the surface of the muck. She began to gasp, to pant, patting at her sex, clutching at it.

Cianna swung round, thighs wide, her hand between them, masturbating as she watched Sulitea buggered. Unable to resist, she leant forward, pulling the full white bottom cheeks as wide as they would to, to expose the junction between cock and bottom hole, with Sulitea's straining anus a tight pink ring around Aglat's penis. He was getting faster, Sulitea more urgent, gasping and mumbling in her ecstasy. Cianna pushed her face in, licking at Sulitea's bottom as they masturbated together.

Sulitea came, screaming aloud, her dirty buttocks tightening in Cianna's face. Aglat grunted, jammed himself hard up Sulitea's bottom, to make her scream again, and pulled back, his cock sliding free, filthy with dirt, to jerk up, full into Cianna's open mouth. Sulitea's anus stayed open, the contents squeezing out, all over Aglat's balls as Cianna sucked in desperate eagerness on his penis. He came, full in her mouth. As he did so, so did she, in utter rapture, swallowing down sperm and slime as she snatched and clawed at her sex. Her clitoris was burning, her vagina and anus pulsing and winking behind her, her eyes staring wide as Sulitea emptied herself over Aglat's cock and balls.

Only when her vision went red did she stop, to sit back, gasping, with mess running from her open mouth. The men were silent, staring. Aglat sat back, to let Sulitea finish what she was doing, her dung coiling into a pile beneath her on the black earth. She began to pee, sobbing with shame as it all came out. Her hand slipped and she sat down in it with a loud squelch, but made no effort to rise, only turning an accusing look at Aglat.

'I said not up my bottom!' she told him.

'What matter?' he answered. 'a little more is no great harm.'

'More?' she demanded.

'In the black earth,' he explained. 'Dung is thoroughly rotted, in a great pond, then boiled, to cleanse it. It thus becomes black earth, which is put into beds to dry…'

'It becomes black earth?' Sulitea repeated. 'Black earth?'

'What you are sitting in,' he said.

Sulitea's eyes and mouth went wide, an expression of utter horror as she looked down at the black muck.

'This, 'she said quietly, 'is dung?'

'Boiled down dung,' he answered, 'well rotted too. Black earth.'

Her face set in utter disgust. Slowly, she lifted herself, dirt falling from her breasts and belly, her bottom coming up with a sticky, pulling noise.

'You made us!' she gasped. 'You tricked us! In this!'

'You enjoyed it, hugely,' Greifal pointed out.

'Girls often react this way,' Aglat commented, 'but there is no sense in it. The black earth is healthy, and improves the complexion.'

Sulitea climbed slowly from the pit, to stand dripping on the shed floor. Cianna joined her, unable to find words, either for what she had been made to do or for what she had done herself. The men ignored them, but walked to a line of spigots above a long trough, to wash their genitals and legs. With little choice, Cianna joined them, Sulitea last, both suffering jocular comments and the occasional pinch of their bottoms in silence. Clean, the men watched the girls douche with amusement, after which Sulitea finally found her voice.

'So,' she said coldly, 'you have had your pleasure with us. Now for your half of the bargain. Describe how nitre is obtained.'

'It comes from the black earth, as you may have guessed,' Aglat said.

'The details,' Sulitea said patiently.'

'No,' he answered casually. 'Take them.'

Instantly Uthos' grip fixed in Cianna's hair, twisting hard and hurling her down. Sulitea screamed, then again, an odd, ululating note. Cianna kicked out, hitting Greifal hard, only for Hubaln to catch her other ankle. Uthos came down, a knee on her chest, even as her nails raked his face. Then his full weight was on her, more than she could lift, pressing the breath from her body. Still she fought, kicking frantically, clawing and biting at anything within reach, but achieving little through the tough canvas of their clothes.

At last they had her pinned, Uthos sat across her body, her arms crushed under his knees, her wrists in his hands. Hubaln was on her legs, his massive arms wrapped tight around her knees. To one side Sulitea was also down, held tight by Greifal and Aglat, spitting curses, her face a mask of fury. Uthos blew out his breath, and quickly raised a hand to his face to wipe away the drops of blood welling up from one cheek.

'She cats!' Aglat spat. 'But we have them!'

'You do not,' Sulitea answered him.

The door exploded, torn from its hinges, splinters of wood showering down on them. Hubaln screamed, hurling himself to the side as a vast grey hand snatched out. Uthos was torn away, gibbering in terror. Cianna scrambled to one side, on her belly, beneath the raking claws. Clear, she bounced up, turning to find Sulitea raising one shaking hand to the grotesque face visible beyond the door. Hubaln lay in a black earth bed, his face contorted in fear. Uthos had struck the wall and was unconscious, with blood trickling from his head. Greifal was pressed to the wall, wide eyed, a wet stain spreading across the front of his trousers. Aglat was clutched in the demon's hand, his face a dark ash grey. Sulitea pulled herself up from the floor, shaking, her mouth set tight as she turned to Aglat.

'Treacherous pig!' she spat. 'You have less honour than a goblin! We made a bargain, which I kept. You gave your word!'

'She,' Aglat babbled, glancing at Cianna, 'is worth a thousand standard in Kea. The supervisors would have given us girls, meat in our apatta, wine… What is it? Have it release me, I beg!'

'I should have it eat you!' Sulitea stormed. 'I will, if you do not tell me what I need to know, now!'

'I can not!' Aglat whimpered. 'It is forbidden! I will be drowned in the dung pond!'

'You tell me. We leave,' Sulitea said through clenched teeth. 'You live. That or die now. Choose.'

'It is not simple!' Aglat said weakly. 'It would take hours to explain. Guards will come soon!'

Aeisla appeared in the doorway, both swords held ready, Babalyn behind her.

'Keep watch, Babalyn,' Sulitea ordered. 'Aeisla, in here.'

'There are noises from beyond the wall,' Aeisla answered. 'The guards are roused.'

Sulitea cursed and spat at Aglat.

'Kill him, Aeisla,' she ordered. 'We'll try another.'

'No!' Aglat yelped as Aeisla swung a sword up. 'But it is long, complicated. It will also be beyond your understanding. First black earth must be made, then it must be leached, the saltpetre concentrated a number of times, converted to pure nitre of potash, crystallised and refined. All requires exact knowledge!'

'Guards are at the gates!' Babalyn called from outside. 'Opening them!'

'We'll take this one,' Sulitea said, 'and another, for the proportions. Where do the men from the mixing mill live, Aglat, speak!'

'I don't know!' Aglat babbled. 'We never leave our compound! I know nothing of this!'

'It's true,' Cianna supplied, 'but Supervisor Maerdrhen runs the mixing mill. He will be in his villa.'

'Not now, hewon't,' Sulitea said as a crash rang out from somewhere outside, followed by yells of anger and fear. 'Come.'

They ran, Aglat screaming as he was snatched from his feet. Outside, the night was illuminated in a brilliant silver wash, White Teimis shedding its full glare on the scene. The gates in the compound wall stood wide, guards pouring through them and up the slope. Sulitea spoke a string of words. The demon dropped Aglat and turned on the guards, bounding down at them. Bows came up, a swarm of arrows striking into the demon, to no effect.

'Up,' Sulitea ordered, 'I'll call it back as we reached the wall.'

She turned and ran. Cianna followed, snatching the sword offered by Aeisla. A hideous din rang out behind them, screams and yells, mixed with an inhuman wailing. Ahead was the small gate that led towards the main mill, securely shut. Cianna reached it, throwing herself down, panting. Sulitea called, to no effect, the demon dancing below them in a maddened frenzy, clawing and snatching, its great body bristling with arrows.

'Summon your winged creature, Sulitea,' Aeisla demanded.

'I cannot hold two,' Sulitea answered, 'and I cannot banish if this one will not respond.'

They had been seen, two groups of guards moving towards them, beyond the scope of the demon's fury, Hubaln and Greifal gesturing frantically in their direction. The gate behind them groaned, swinging wide.

'We meet in the Feat Hall then,' Aeisla said, and swung round, slashing into the opening with her sword.

A man screamed. Aeisla hauled the gate wide and threw herself through the opening. Cianna followed, aiming a wild cut at the first man she saw, who staggered back, clutching his shoulder. Others were beyond, a third guard, and mill staff, unarmed. Aeisla stood to her full height, towering over the guard to cut down with all her force. He parried desperately, as Cianna lunged, sinking the point of her sword into his thigh. Dropping his sword, he ran, hobbling off into the night after the retreating mill staff.

They ran, up the slope towards the dark wall of the jungle. Ahead were villas, the windows bright with lights, men standing out on the balconies, shouting questions. Cianna ran on, glancing back only to see that Sulitea and Babalyn were following. Aeisla was ahead, already by Bulzar's villa, from which a blaze of light shone down on them.

'Aeisla, no, the troll!' Cianna screamed.

A figure stepped from the villa, full into Aeisla's path, holding a sword. She cut up once and he fell, but a second man was behind. Cianna slammed into him, recognising him as Raigos an instant before her blade caught him in the stomach. He went down, falling back into villa, across the massive body of Voqual, which lay still, stuck with arrows and with a hole blown in the chest.

She hesitated, her head coming up at a movement, to find Nairgren staring at her in astonishment. In sudden fury she lunged forward, missing him as he leapt back. She followed, stabbing viciously through the bead curtain.

'Cianna!' Aeisla screamed, following. 'Away!'

Cianna took no notice, hacking the curtain aside to spray beads across the floor of Bulzar's main room. Nairgren stood within, his men Telak and Aqual also. To the side was Bulzar, dead, his body roped to the couch.

'It's her! It was true!' Telak exclaimed.

Screaming, Cianna hurled herself at them, her foot landing on beads, to send her sprawling across Bulzar's body. Aqual brought up his sword, laughing, only for the sound to turn to a choking scream as Aeisla's blade embedded itself in his chest. Cianna struck up frantically, parrying Telak's cut, even as Nairgren thrust at her, driving the point of his sword into her shoulder. She screamed, clutching as his sword wrist as Aeisla's punch took him in the face, driving him back. Her sword was snatched from her hand, driven into Telak's body as she rolled to the floor.

Nairgren had risen, facing Aeisla across the couch, both ready. Cianna crawled back, clutching for a weapon. An oil lamp stood to the side. She caught at the handle, hurled it, full at Nairgren, who dodged, the lamp exploding against the wall to spray a sheet of burning oil across the window drape. Aeisla struck, and

Nairgren's head jumped from his shoulders. Cianna stood, clutching at her wound, blood seeping from between her fingers. Aeisla caught her around the middle, pulling her up, as Sulitea and Babalyn appeared behind them in the doorway.

'Get his books,' Cianna gasped. 'Bulzar's, from the workroom.'

Babalyn moved immediately, only for a huge man to dash from the workroom, cannoning into her to send her sprawling.

'That's Maerdrhen!' Cianna exclaimed.

He hit Sulitea, knocking her aside, and dashed into the night. A burning drape collapsed, catching another lamp, which sent a flood of burning oil across the floor. Babalyn scrambled quickly away, Aeisla pulling Cianna through the door.

'The books!' Sulitea protested, but stepped hastily back as the oil caught another drape.

They retreated onto the lawn, moving for the jungle as flames shot up in the villa. Men were coming up the slope, shouting, then yelling in fear and panic as they saw the fire. A girl darted from the burning villa, then another, Bulzar's two Vendjomois, who fled screaming down the slope. Weak and dizzy, Cianna struggled to use her feet, half-carried by Aeisla, through the flickering light, to the first of the trees.

'Stop,' Sulitea said, 'the lank demon, it is dissipated. I can summon.'

'Not now!' Babalyn exclaimed. 'The mill may catch.'

Sulitea ignored her, sinking to her knees, her hands moving, mumbling incomprehensible words. Behind them sparks were already rising from the burning villa, catching on the breeze, directly towards the main mill.

'We must run!' Babalyn urged. 'It will be terrible, you have no idea!'

'Shh!' Aeisla urged, ducking down into the foliage.

Men were visible, plenty, but no longer paying them attention. Orders were being screamed, to form bucket chains, to open sluices, to evacuate the villas. Cianna stayed low, trying to ignore the sick feeling in her stomach and the pain of her wound, her good hand clutched to her necklace as she prayed for strength and courage.

A crack sound above them, fresh screaming, a malign croak as a great blast of air swept down on them, hurling the flames of the villa into sudden, searing fury. Not twenty paces from them, Sulitea's winged horror alighted, turning to stare at them through eyes as red as the fire beyond.

Cianna ran forward, clutching at her arm, leaving Aeisla to help the frightened Babalyn. Sulitea scrambled up, onto the broad, hairy back, Aeisla boosting Cianna behind her, then Babalyn. Sulitea began to whisper to the demon even as Aeisla joined them. It rose, padding forward, trotting, running, the beat of its wings sending a fresh burst of sparks across the landscape, heedless of the Makeans scattering under its great claws. Cianna clung tight, mumbling prayers, then crying out in joy as the motion suddenly became smooth and they shot over the nitre plant wall with no more than her own height to spare.

They rose, swinging around in a great arc, ever higher to the slow, ponderous wingbeats of the demon. Below her, Cianna saw Julac spread out in the silver moonlight, the burning villa like a single glowing eye in a grotesque face. Her teeth gritted in her pain, she shook her fist at the antlike Makeans then, spat. The wind snatched the spittle away, and she followed it with her gaze, to see the great expanse of the jungle spreading out beneath her, with fields to the sides. Kea itself swung into view, the streets outlined in light, the Great Pit where she had fought Moloa clearly visible, with patrons spilling from the doors.

Briefly she wondered if Moloa had been made champion again, and what Jelkrael was doing, and Klia, the spiteful Yuilla even, only to think of the dead Bulzar and turn her attention back to Julac. It was now far below, but the fire was brighter than ever. For a moment the demon's wing cut off her view, before it was visible again. Now there were fresh areas of red, growing, blending, at an impossible pace until all merged to a vast, incandescent ball, bursting into the night sky, a great pillar of flame, searing her eyes until she was forced to bury her face in the leathery skin beneath her. Sound hit them, a great deafening roar, drumming in her ears, on and on, then the shock, lifting the demon high, crushing her to its back, to leave her terrified and shaking, her hands locked in the coarse fur, with a substantial wet patch spreading from around her sex.

Morning found them on an island beach off the coast of Cypraea, seated on the rotting trunk of a once great tree. Cianna's wound had been cleaned and dressed by Babalyn and Sulitea, while Aeisla had hunted crabs in the lagoon. These they had eaten, along with bananas from a substantial bunch cut down by the demon, which rested placidly beside the sea. For a long while Sulitea had said nothing, simply staring out across the water, her chin resting in her hands. Suddenly she spoke.

'I have it,' she declared. 'The perfect plan. It is this. Returning to Makea…'

She broke off in a squeal of surprise as Aeisla grabbed her by the hair. An instant later she was across Aeisla's knee, skirt up, plump, pale bottom stuck high, arm twisted into the small of her back. Immediately, Aeisla began to spank, her teeth set in determination, delivering slap after slap, quickly turning the broad white ball of Sulitea's bottom to a flaming red. The sound of the smacks almost drowned out Sulitea's shocked protests, squeals and gasps, while her desperately kicking legs gave a fine show of soft pink tuppenny and wrinkled anus, making Cianna giggle.

Finally it stopped. Sulitea made no effort to get up, but lay still over Aeisla's lap, gasping for breath, her legs well splayed behind. With an approving click of her tongue, Aeisla reached out for the banana bunch, pulled off the longest and fattest fruit she could find and stuck it firmly up Sulitea's vagina.

'We are not returning to Makea,' Aeisla stated, with a final pat to Sulitea's still quivering bottom.

Epilogue

The demon turned, its wings tilting, twisting in the air. A dull boom hit Cianna's ears, there was a jolt, another, then nothing. Slowly, she released her grip in its hair.

'We are down,' Sulitea declared. 'Perhaps two leagues north of the town. Babalyn?'

Babalyn said nothing, but climbed slowly from the demon's back, the shaking of her body visible even in the moonlight. On the beach, she looked about, her mouth open, and suddenly burst into tears.

'Babalyn?' Cianna asked, jumping down to put an arm around her friend.

'I know the beach,' Babalyn said softly. 'I used to play here as a child. My home is a half-league inland, no more.'

'Your navigation is improving, Sulitea,' Aeisla remarked dryly.

Sulitea didn't respond, but spoke a single word, causing the demon to slowly dissipate. They set off up the beach, following Babalyn through dunes, along a track between fields and at last to within site of a great villa, the walls showing blue even in the moonlight. Babalyn broke into a run, along a section of paved road, through a high arch, to another, with bright lamps illuminating the brilliant pale blue of the turquoise tiles. A woman was seated on the porch, as dark as Babalyn, but older and more fleshy still. She was sipping at a glass, from which she looked up in shock as Babalyn ran at her, then joy. The two embraced, kissing, tears streaming down their faces as the older woman babbled questions and shouted for others to come.

Cianna waited, Sulitea and Aeisla beside her, feeling happy yet slightly embarrassed. Other people emerged from the villa, servants or relatives, and last a tall, straight man, his frizzy hair faded to grey, his expression uncertain, then radiant as he took Babalyn into his arms. At length Babalyn broke away, gesturing to where the three girls stood waiting on the lawn.

'These are my friends,' she said, 'Sulitea and Aeisla, who I met before, in the Ara Khum desert, and Cianna, without whom I would never have returned. They brought me free, out of Makea! Girls, this is Raiklin, my father, and my mother Asaya.'

They were ushered inside, more embarrassed than ever as the questions were turned to them. Food and drink were served, Asaya pressing more and more onto them, Raiklin demanding their story. Babalyn gave it, seated on her father's lap, losing no opportunity to paint Cianna as a heroine, but also including lewd details that would have been left out of any saga. By the end Cianna was scarlet with blushes, but the Aprinians merely smiled.

At the end Raiklin pushed Babalyn off his knee with an affectionate pat and stood, to make a short and formal speech, ending with an offer of any reward they cared to name. As he finished, both Sulitea and Aeisla looked to Cianna.

'Knowledge,' she said. 'How do you make the black powder for your bombards?'

'Much the same way everyone else does, I would suppose,' Raiklin answered, sounding puzzled, 'although perhaps with greater skill. Here, I have an old armament manual somewhere. There is a chapter on gunpowder making. It is yours, freely, but that cannot be all, it is too little by far.'

He reached up to a bookshelf, pulling down a tattered volume, which he threw casually onto the table.

THE END

R420 Km
100 Meb
/220
0 7527 484

363

13093.80

37.

34 31.

1309380

4945.76

154. 35.

2120

806880. 134.48 60
4945.00
309380

Lightning Source UK Ltd.
Milton Keynes UK
UKOW05f0815060913

216588UK00001B/5/P